HER IMPECCABLE SCOUNDREL

WICKED WIDOWS LEAGUE
BOOK FORTY-FOUR

ALINA K. FIELD

HAVENLOCK PRESS

HER IMPECCABLE SCOUNDREL

Anxious to save a cherished inheritance, Blythe Blatchfield, widowed Countess of Chilcombe, knows she must repair her reputation with the Beau Monde in order to face the powerful marquess challenging her dissolute husband's will. She vows to resist handsome rogues like her late husband, and to never again give her trust so blithely. But when the new earl, absent from England for many years, finally appears, new rumors swirl around Blythe. Facing the loss of everything, she finds herself needing the help of an old enemy, the man whose interference years earlier led to her unhappy marriage, the new Earl of Chilcombe.

Called back to England to take up his late cousin's title, diplomat Graeme Blatchfield is eager to see his cousin's widow and learn for himself whether the rumors about the woman he once held a childish infatuation for are true. Having plunged into marriage with the last earl—Graeme's fault for revealing their tryst—she's been tainted by her husband's decadence. Forced by matters of the estate to spend time together, he soon discovers the vulnerable and lonely woman underneath the society mask. Can he get her to forgive him—and more?

PROLOGUE

*B*lythe Blatchfield, Countess of Chilcombe, pulled her cloak closer in the dwindling light, urging her mount into a trot, and followed the fresh tracks of Sir Morris Pierpont's phaeton. In two miles or so, the lane would join the old Roman road leading to Andover. and from there, to London. A mile or so beyond that junction, a traveler would reach the old Black Sheep Inn. She was relying on Sir Morris stopping, if not for the good ale brewed there, then to rest his horse, or perhaps even a visit with the barmaid known to favor the deep-pocketed gentlemen traveling the route.

What she would do when she found the fellow...

She reined up, anguish flooding her. She took in deep breaths of the cold clear air until her panic subsided and reason returned.

What will I say to Sir Morris?

Earlier her husband's valet, Newton, had sent a message

to her at Bluebelle Lodge, summoning her in all haste to nearby Risley Manor.

She'd delayed. If Archibald Blatchford, Earl of Chilcombe, had pushed the limits of his favored poison too far—if he was dying—she had no wish to rush to his bedside and endure the silent censure of the attending physician. As if she had any control over her husband's addictions.

Archie, however, still lived. Bleary-eyed and barely coherent, he'd let Newton explain about a previously unknown property dispute involving Bluebelle Lodge and the manner of resolution—a new will.

Bluebelle Lodge, her refuge, the precious legacy her late guardian had fought hard to include in the marriage settlement—Archie meant to just *will* it away, leaving her, and the dear ones she cared for there, utterly homeless.

Newton had been one of the witnesses and he'd paid close attention to the contents. Indeed, the new will omitted the generous legacy that had been promised to the faithful valet. Instead, Archie had given Newton money that very morning.

The other witness to Archie's signature had been Sir Morris, and it was he who was carrying a second signed copy of the new will to Archie's London solicitor. The other signed copy had been locked away in Risley Manor's muniment room, safe for now, until she could find a way to retrieve it.

Her immediate concern was the duplicate Sir Morris carried. He must let her see it, perhaps even copy it for the solicitor she would need to engage.

The snow that had threatened earlier began to fall fast and furious. With a touch of her heel, the horse trotted on and passed through the gates and onto the dips and turns of the lane leading to the road. Around the next tight turn, she pulled her mount up and her gaze swept over the scene.

A wheel spun horizontally in the rising wind, while its match lay broken on the ground beneath it. The tall vehicle had teetered and overturned. Two horses stood in their traces, seemingly unhurt.

She moved her mount closer. A body came into view, and her breath tightened as she recognized the large frame and prematurely balding head of Sir Morris.

Dismounting, she went to him. The open eyes were unseeing, and she sent up a silent prayer. One arm twisted unnaturally and his head lay in the basin of a shallow rock pooling with blood. Quickly shedding a glove, she called his name and checked for a pulse, finding none.

She tried again, casting her gaze over the terrain. A basket had spilled its contents—a flask, a bundle of food. And there... an open valise.

She donned her glove and went to the valise. Among the shirts, linens, and small clothes was a document folder. She opened it and, raising her cloak as a shield against the descending flurries, flipped through the contents. Letters in a feminine hand she returned, but the next one she unfolded, glancing at the signature.

Lord Vernon Falfield. Heart pounding, she skimmed the brief missive and tucked it into her bodice.

No will yet. She combed through the items of clothing more carefully. An oil-cloth-wrapped cylindrical bundle had been wedged at the bottom. She slipped off the string and unrolled it, fingers tingling inside her gloves.

Breathless, she skimmed the heading on the parchment: *The Last Will and Testament of Archibald Blatchfield, Earl of Chilcombe.*

No time to read it now. Quickly rolling it, she stowed it

under her cloak and glanced around. The fields on either side were Chilcombe land, which she knew like the back of her hand. Traveling cross-country, she could reach Risley Manor more quickly and send help for the horses.

Or... This road was well-traveled. Perhaps someone else would come along before then.

She found a stout log, mounted her horse, and made her way through the deepening snow, trying to sort through her jumbled thoughts.

The will... She'd never surrender it until she'd at least had a chance to read it. If what Newton had told her about the contents... It was certainly not valid given Archie's dazed state. She would challenge it.

Reaching the edge of the field, she entered the woodland. Distant shouts reached her from the direction of the road and she wheeled around. A splash of red revealed a coach and she breathed a sigh of relief. Sir Morris had been found.

She turned her mount then paused. The snow had settled peacefully over her tracks; no one had seen her come this way. No one, not even Newton, knew she'd chased after Sir Morris. That had been a split-second impulse, turning her horse to follow him instead of returning to Bluebelle Lodge.

If she could retrieve the other copy... Perhaps no challenge to the will was necessary. One of the witnesses was dead, and the other, Newton, stood to lose in this new version. He, the butler and housekeeper, would all lose the generous bequests mentioned in the will Archie had made when he and Blythe married.

She pulled her cloak closer and headed to Bluebelle Lodge.

CHAPTER ONE

"*I*'m afraid there's a challenge to the will, my lord."

Graeme Blatchfield, new Earl of Chilcombe, suppressed a shudder. He wasn't yet used to this elevated rank, and the news the solicitor's clerk imparted was more than an unhappy wrinkle in his plans.

The young clerk, Mr. Emory, couldn't be much more than twenty. He had the pale skin, gaunt look, and ink-stained fingers of a conscientious fellow who spent too much time at his desk, and he was visibly nervous about bringing a client bad news.

Summoned by duty, Graeme had just arrived in England. HMS Phoebe had rescued him from an anticipated long delay in Cape Town and cruised into Portsmouth without fanfare, delivering him months earlier than expected. At the port's busy Keppel's Head Hotel, he'd had his first hot bath, hearty meal, and comfortable bed in many weeks.

Mail had awaited him. The College of Arms's letter confirmed his title; the King's writ summoned him to take his seat in the Lords; and the Foreign Office's directive required an in-person report on his last assignment.

Aside from the official demands, there was a letter from the earl's steward reporting that his homes and estates were in better order.

Better than what? That information went unmentioned.

The letter from the Chilcombe solicitor, Mr. Fleming, had been cryptic as well. Though his late cousin, Archie, had slipped this mortal coil over a year ago, his will had unexpectedly *not* been settled.

Restless after so many months on ship, Graeme borrowed a horse in Portsmouth and rode most of the way behind the chaise hauling his trunk, traveling as far as Kingston Upon Thames. Stiff and sore from a day spent on horseback, he'd decided, in his first exercise of aristocratic privilege, to summon Mr. Fleming to his private sitting room at the inn.

Mr. Fleming hadn't appeared, being away in Suffolk on some important business. Emory had come in his place.

So much for the new Lord Chilcombe's noble power in summoning the solicitor.

"It may be some time before it can be resolved," the young man said.

Graeme tethered his temper. The long journey had given him months to stew and speculate, and to remind himself that the career he wanted was not in Parliament. His plan to arrange for management of the Chilcombe estate and be off to a new diplomatic assignment might have hit a sizeable obstacle.

"Go on, Emory," he said.

"It is rather complex, I'm afraid. It has to do with a new

will containing changes, the principal of which pertains to a cottage and property called Bluebelle Lodge. The late earl's will, executed at the time of his marriage... well, it was a complicated arrangement hammered out as part of the marriage settlements with the previous owner of Bluebelle Lodge, Mr. Davies, who was also Lady Chilcombe's guardian. The gist of it was that the property was to go to the countess in lieu of any of the normal support she would receive by means of dower or jointure."

Lady Chilcombe. *Blythe*. He felt a rush of longing and quickly suppressed it.

There'd been a letter waiting in Portsmouth from her as well, brief and more formal than a diplomat's missive. He'd been wondering whether she'd taken up residence in a dower house, if there was one at Risley Manor.

"Someone is contesting her claim to the property?" he asked.

"It's more complicated than that. There apparently was a dispute about boundary lines. Mr. Davies' widow predeceased Lord Chilcombe, leaving the property to the Chilcombe estate. It has been alleged that Bluebelle Lodge was not the previous owner's or his wife's to bequeath. Nor, subsequently, Lord Chilcombe's."

Graeme remembered Davies, a genial older man, and his affectionate wife, who'd once been Blythe's governess. The childless couple had welcomed Blythe into their home when her parents both took ill and died, leaving her orphaned.

"What a bloody mess," he said. "Go on."

Emory blinked and sat up straighter.

"As a means to easily settle the matter of the disputed property—the earl being quite ill at the time—a new will was purportedly executed, leaving the property to the claimant instead of Lady Chilcombe."

"And so, Lady Chilcombe is left with... what?"

A long pause ensued. "It seems that she will receive the small dowry she brought to the marriage—five hundred pounds—as well as her wardrobe and the jewels that are not part of the estate." His voice sounded tight and he cleared his throat. "As I mentioned, in the marriage settlement, she waived her right to dower or jointure. This fact is acknowledged in the putative new will in which the late earl left her..." Mr. Fleming paused, his color rising. "One pound."

One pound.

Blythe had been disinherited.

Why?

Memories of the bright, cheerful, beautiful girl she'd once been flooded him. He held them back along with the anger that rose in his throat.

"I should like to see this new will," he said.

"As would Mr. Fleming, my lord. He has only seen what is claimed to be a fair copy of it. He did not draft it. He had no knowledge of a boundary dispute, else he would have directed a review of the devolution of title among the documents stored at Risley Manor and Bluebelle Lodge. Mr. Fleming has been the Chilcombe solicitor for the last twelve years and is very careful about due diligence."

"I see," Graeme said. And he did. He'd known his cousin Archie was a villain; perhaps he was also an idiot.

Or the property claimant had blackmailed him.

"Mr. Fleming will certainly show you both the copy of the putative will and the original will, executed at the time of the earl's marriage, as well as the marriage settlement, but they are held at Mr. Fleming's chambers."

"How long do we expect the matter to drag on?"

"As to that, I cannot say, my lord. The Pregorative Court

of Canterbury was reluctant to proceed with this thorny matter until after your arrival."

Thorny matter indeed. A will executed shortly before the earl's death, a will that violated the terms of the marriage agreement—what had Blythe done to deserve that?

"The countess is challenging this new will?" he asked.

"Actually, it is the old will that is being challenged, as no one has seen more than a copy of the new one the earl is alleged to have executed."

"Ah, yes, you did mention that."

"Risley Manor has been searched for a copy, to no avail."

Which begged the question, was there a new will? Perhaps he'd pursue that question with an inquiry agent.

The whole matter reeked of fraud. He couldn't imagine why the court had not dismissed the challenge. Unless...

"Speak plainly, man. Challenged by whom?" he asked.

"The Marquess of Diddenton."

Diddenton. Graeme dredged up a memory of a boozy dinner on board a naval ship in the San Francisco harbor where Diddenton's name had come up. He was a powerful peer with connections to the British East India Company and the Canton opium houses, as well as highly placed friends in the Foreign Office. He was thus, perhaps, also a man with the power to help—or harm—a man's diplomatic career.

Emory cleared his throat. "My lord, may I move on to a discussion of the entailed property?"

After Emory left, Graeme found his way to the busy taproom, the clerk's news settling like a dark cloud around him.

If the few rumors he'd heard through the years were true, Archie had lived a sordid life. The solicitor's clerk had confirmed that he'd died a pathetic death as well as leaving a bloody mess with that business of a new will.

The last time Graeme saw his cousin, Archie had been deep in his cups, celebrating his accomplishment of siring a baby boy with the countess. Graeme's father, older brother, and an older male cousin, each in line to the title before Graeme, had been alive then too.

The title might be useful but he'd never wanted it. He'd never envied Archie anything except—for a brief foolish moment—Blythe.

He paused at the bar and ordered a pint and then made his way to a table, thinking. What he was sorely lacking was gossip. The sort that filled in the cracks, the empty pauses, and the unmentioned scandal.

As to scandal... He'd ruthlessly forced Blythe from his thoughts years ago. And yet... the news of his cousin's death, hand-carried to him in the Columbia District of Canada, had stirred memories and piqued his curiosity. Blythe was free now. What sort of woman had she become? And how soon could he see her?

A pert barmaid brought him a brimming mug and he quaffed a hearty gulp.

"Ho, there's a man I recognize."

The voice came from a tangle of gentlemen who'd just entered. One of them disengaged and approached his table.

"Blatchfield, is that truly you? Are you going to cut me now that you're an earl?"

"Morley?" Graeme stood and extended a hand. Manus Morley had been a schoolmate, one Graeme had rescued from trouble more than once. They'd run into each other in Paris several years earlier and Graeme, there serving on Wellington's staff, had introduced his old schoolmate to Paris's fashionable haunts.

"You're a welcome sight." He clapped the younger man on the back, pulled out a chair, and signaled to the servant. A baron's younger son, Morley had the handsome looks and cheerful manners that gave him entrée to society. He was just the man Graeme needed to talk to: a wag, good at gleaning gossip and willing to share it.

Morley put up his hands. "'Fraid I can't join you tonight. Just came over on the packet. I ran into those fellows and shared a coach. Heading up to town with them. But damn if I'm not happy to see you."

"I've just arrived myself. Making my way to Chilcombe House tomorrow." Graeme leaned in and smiled. Morley was a good enough friend that there was no need to beat around the bush. "Is there anything I should know before I arrive there?"

"Well." Morley's eyes glittered and he laughed. "I may be behind on the news, but I *did hear* that Lady Chilcombe has come out of mourning with fanfare." He cocked his head, eyes filled with mischief. "She christened her return to society with a grand ball at Chilcombe House."

"She's at Chilcombe House?"

Morley nodded.

A fluttering of awareness quickened his heart, and his fingers thrummed the table. He'd see her as soon as tomorrow afternoon.

Blythe as a merry-making widow. For the short time he was here, he'd have to enter society. If she was well established in the ton, perhaps she could ease his path there.

Perhaps she could ease more than his path with the ton.

The longing he felt… it was only to satisfy his curiosity before sending her off to… to somewhere.

"She's only just recently returned to town," Morley said. "Before that… well, she was away for some months, but no

11

one quite knows where." At Graeme's frown, he held up his hands defensively. "Not speaking ill of her, but—"

The barmaid's appearance interrupted Morley's next thought. Still standing, he accepted the tankard.

"But... you're brimful of, er, intelligence?" Graeme raised his drink, saluting his friend. Good intelligence gathering allowed a man to gossip, and gossip often held nuggets of truth. Sometimes boulders.

"Not quite brimful..." Morley glanced around and lowered his voice. "It pays to keep my ear to the ground. I've had to make my own way after Father died, you know, and I've been dabbling as an inquiry agent. I'll see if I can learn anything else. Look for me at White's tomorrow afternoon. Or better yet—I'll call on you and escort you to the club myself."

Morley glanced back at his friends, and Graeme had a sudden thought. He'd never spent much time in London but he'd heard that gossip there spread quickly.

"Do me a favor, Morley," he said. "Don't tell anyone I'm back."

Morley blinked, his lips quirking. "Ah. A surprise arrival. I'll tell these fellows you're a client."

Graeme raised an eyebrow. "We'll talk tomorrow then."

CHAPTER TWO

*B*lythe Blatchfield, widowed Countess of Chilcombe, ought to be grateful. Days earlier, just as dawn broke over London, she'd sent the last guest home from the mad crush of a ball she'd held here. Her drawing room had been filled with callers ever since.

The ball had been her official come out after her year of mourning, an event she'd paid for herself out of the pin money she'd squirreled away for years. She'd planned a smallish affair for guests like her friend Lady Loughton, whose daughter was having her first season. The other invitees had included members of the ton who hadn't cut her entirely, as well those who hadn't yet had the opportunity to do so.

The gathering had mushroomed beyond her wildest imaginings.

To her surprise, notes of acceptance had poured in, as well as requests for invitations. The ton was eager to see the scandalous countess who'd disappeared into the countryside with her husband and his disreputable friends.

Despite her murky past, despite the watered down

ratafia and skimpy supper on offer, her carefully planned reappearance in society was a raging success. Those with a nose for more scandal were rewarded by the scene of a duke insulting Lady Loughton's daughter.

Many of the best of London attended. She was gratified, even as she hoped they wouldn't lay the blame for the young duke's misbehavior on the hostess. She needed to curry the favor of the beau monde if she was to confront a scheming marquess. She needed to find her place in society, and the higher the place, the better.

If only her morning callers represented the best of the ton. Unfortunately, the most dedicated ones were inveterate gossips like Mrs. Netley and her daughter, as well as a scattering of brash young bucks.

It wasn't merely tittle-tattle about the misbehaving duke they wanted. Her late husband's sordid life and death, and the old rumors about the Chilcombes' marital arrangements, still had gossips probing. The lusty gentlemen enjoyed gossip too but were mainly here to test the new widow's virtue.

The news of Diddenton's claims of a new will disinheriting her added to the titillation, despite the marquess's struggle to produce a credible document. A document she prayed he would never find.

The impasse would end, somehow, when Graeme Blatchford arrived in England. The court would either tell the marquess to find another widow to impoverish, or Blythe would be cast out of her home. If that happened, her fight would be with the new Earl of Chilcombe to honor the terms of his late cousin's settlement agreement. And fight, she would.

A buckskin clad leg brushed her skirts, making her skin crawl. The loathsome man who'd seated himself next to her,

Lord Vernon Falfield, was her late husband's bosom friend and the fourth son of the scheming marquess. He'd been a participant in the goings-on at Risley Manor. He was also very likely the source of the gossip about her at White's, Boodle's, and Brooks's.

After Archie's death, she'd banned him from Risley Manor and Bluebelle Lodge, and even escaped for a time to Lady Wyndham's Matron Manor, a haven for widowed ladies like herself. Upon her return to town, her servants had held him at bay, except on her at-home days.

Today, he'd wedged himself and his Pomona green waistcoat onto the settee next to her.

"The latest *on dit*," Lord Vernon said, "is that the Swilling Duke has fled town."

Laughter ensued, along with speculation about the duke's destination. The silly young duke, who'd expelled his dinner on Lady Loughton's daughter's ball gown and passed out—dubbed the Swilling Duke by the wits—was only displaying publicly the least offensive behavior she'd seen in Archie and his friends privately.

She turned her gaze to the mantel clock, wondering how soon she could send all of them away and pay a promised call on Lady Loughton.

"Speaking of traveling peers," Mrs. Netley trilled over the hubbub in the room, "when will the new Earl of Chilcombe arrive?"

Blythe steadied herself. She fielded this question at least once at every social event she attended, and yet every time, her insides quaked from the uncertainty. She aimed to be gone from Chilcombe House before the new earl swanned into London looking down his nose at her.

"Has he been found?" one pink of the town asked.

"Lord Chilcombe's date of arrival is uncertain," she said,

"but I'm informed that we might expect it to be in a few months." July, if the winds are favorable, the Foreign Office said.

"At which point you will be cast out?" Lord Vernon asked with a sly, sympathetic pout.

Mrs. Netley visibly perked.

Blythe uncurled her hands and drew in a breath, refusing to be baited. Chilcombe House had to be maintained anyway, and she would stay until she needed to move into lodgings an easy drive to Doctor's Commons.

If only her own dear little son had lived, her one worry might be an unfriendly daughter-in-law years from now precipitously tossing her out of Chilcombe House.

"Dear Lord Vernon," Blythe said blandly, "I am not living in the plot of one of Mrs. Radcliffe's novels."

The others laughed, as she meant them to do.

"I've heard that there's to be a hot air balloon ascension next month in Sussex," she said, "and if any one of you is *au courant* on all matters scientific, you must tell us everything you know about it."

Delighted, one rattlepate clapped his hands and launched into a report, while Mrs. Netley settled back in disappointment, and Blythe eased in another breath to slow her racing heart.

Smiling and nodding at what must be all the right parts in the monologue about Mr. Graham's balloon and the aeronaut accompanying him, she heard barely a word.

She was *not anymore* living the plot of one of Mrs. Radcliffe's novels. Archie's death had given her a reprieve from the gothic, sordid existence that he'd thought to impose, and that she'd refused to embrace. She hadn't so much won the battle as simply outfoxed and outlasted him.

It had been an exhausting trial, one she wouldn't

willingly renew with any man. She might have to fight for Bluebelle Lodge and its lands, but Graeme Blatchford wouldn't cast her out of Chilcombe House because she wouldn't give him the chance.

Though the despicable brat surely would attempt it.

She'd been a good steward, even before Archie died. She'd seen to the much-needed repairs on Chilcombe House, begun before Archie's death. She'd stretched the budget allowed by the court to sweep out the stench and sordidness of the late Earl of Chilcombe and his friends, both here and at Risley Manor, the Chilcombes' main seat. She hoped that by the time Graeme set foot in England, the old will would be proved, and she'd be residing permanently at Bluebelle Lodge.

Mrs. Netley was voicing her disgust at female aeronauts when the drawing room door opened and the Chilcombe butler, Adwick, white-faced under all his dignified aplomb, caught her eye. Before he could speak, another man stepped around him and surveyed the room.

A stranger to her, he was a man of perhaps thirty, starkly handsome with light brown hair. Not as handsome as Archie had been, not as tall nor golden-haired like her Adonis of a husband. Still, wide-shouldered and square-jawed under the start of an afternoon beard, he stirred a warmth in her that she hadn't felt in years.

Along with the awareness rippling through her came a touch of apprehension. Despite the need for a shave and coats dusty from travel, he carried himself like a man in command, entitled and privileged, and signaling... disdain, perhaps.

His unsmiling gaze made a circuit of the room, noting Mrs. Netley and her daughter, moving over the dandies, fops, and pinks of the town, then flitting over her to Lord Vernon.

And then quickly returning to her. His study of her sent his lips into a thin line and then his eyes widened.

Her heart raced and stuttered, while around her the air shimmered and the floor threatened to open and take both herself and the lovely Queen Anne settee down into... into...

No. *No, no, no.* She would not faint. Would not. *Would not.*

Adwick cleared his throat and announced the arrival of the Earl of Chilcombe.

CHAPTER THREE

*B*lythe's spies and correspondents in the various seaports and government offices had failed her.

Pulling herself together, she stood. "What an unexpected surprise," she said truthfully, and added, "And most welcome."

His frown said he didn't believe her. As well he shouldn't.

"Lady Chilcombe," he said, bowing.

Before he'd left England, the serious boy had become a young man with a reputation for impeccable manners. Those manners she knew hid a contrary nature and an utter lack of charm and humor. A strange mix of traits for a diplomat.

He'd grown since then; filled out, matured, toughened. He was a stark contrast to his cousin, Archie.

It seemed she must drastically move up her date of departure from Chilcombe House.

And go where? Her friend, Lady Loughton, had a houseful of family descending on Loughton House and no room for a homeless countess.

She would ask there for shelter anyway.

Or she could gather her things and retreat to the country, except that she needed to be in town, active in the social swirl, close to her solicitor, close to the court handling the disputed will.

Shaking off her dithering, she went to greet the new earl, mustering her composure, groping for words, her senses muddled. They'd been friends once, many years earlier, and she wasn't immune to a handsome, active, masculine man's scents—cologne, horses, and fresh air.

Up close, the glint in his hazel eyes signaled... a challenge? That this was his home, not hers?

Or could it be humor.

"You have only just crossed the threshold?" she asked, her voice trembling. Despite the chaos of life with Archie, she'd never grown comfortable with sudden disruption, with careful plans gone awry, with watchfulness and danger.

Remembering the crowd waiting with bated breath to see what came next, she steadied herself. She had to win over society. Any hint of weakness might be her downfall with the ton, and eventually, with the court deciding the matter of Archie's will.

The new earl reached for her hand, said "Excuse us," to the crowd of visitors, and led her out. Adwick followed them, pulling the drawing room door closed.

Too startled to speak, she freed herself from the large, warm, masculine hand and composed herself yet again.

"I gather I have arrived earlier than expected," he said. "You look well, cousin."

Cousin? She supposed they were that now, but by marriage only. Warmth rose in her cheeks to match the heat she saw in his eyes.

Oh, this would not do.

"You will want to refresh yourself," she said, mustering a bored tone. "Adwick, please show the earl to his chambers. And then, my lord, I will see this crowd out and meet with you at your earliest convenience."

He studied her, his expression unreadable, said thank you, and left.

Blythe pressed a hand to her heart and slipped into the drawing room.

In the seconds it took to return to her guests, she'd prepared a task list in her head: tell her maid Radley to begin packing; send a servant to Mivart's Hotel on Brook Street; and send a note to her estate agent telling him there was no longer any time to quibble over leases.

Getting rid of this lot in her drawing room—the new earl's drawing room—would be easy. Their call on the scandalous countess had harvested quite a juicy morsel of gossip. By dinnertime, all of London would know that the impeccable Earl of Chilcombe had arrived to claim his home and found the old earl's countess residing there.

By breakfast, they'd learn that Lady Chilcombe had departed said home. There would be much gossip about her departure, but staying under the same roof with the new earl alone would stir far more.

* * *

THE BUTLER, A RAMROD STRAIGHT, AUSTERELY HANDSOME man with gray hair, led Graeme up a flight of stairs and down a hallway covered in carpeting.

The air of understated elegance matched that of the lady below.

Blythe.

The rich blue of her gown had turned her eyes, her changeable eyes, from gray to blue. She was more beautiful than ever she'd been as a girl. He'd wanted to take her in, all of her.

There'd be time for that. She'd been defensive, as well she might be given the possibility of that new will.

It was instinctive to take her side, and perhaps incautious until he knew more.

The butler stopped and opened an ornate painted door, and he stepped into a generously proportioned sitting room. Through an inside door, he caught the eye of a liveried male servant, who put aside a stack of shirts and hurried out to present himself.

"This is Clive, my lord," Adwick said. "One of our footmen. I've assigned him to assist you until your, er, valet arrives. He is unpacking your trunk."

"Thank you," Graeme said. "That's helpful. At present, I have no valet. Perhaps Clive could fulfill that duty in the interim."

The butler blinked and then went on. "Your rooms have a bathing chamber. If you wish, Clive will draw your bath and assist you with shaving."

A bath. The third in four days and much needed. A bath would rid him of the smell of horse and ease a few persistent aches in his posterior.

"I do wish. Thank you, Adwick."

"I'll send up a tray while you wait." Adwick excused himself and left.

"A bathing chamber," Graeme mused, looking around at the mahogany furnishings.

"The chamber is straight through here, my lord." Clive motioned toward the room where he'd been working. "The water is heating."

He'd seen some elaborate bathing suites in his travels but had seldom had a chance to avail himself of them, especially during his last assignment.

"By all means, lead on." He entered another elegantly furnished room, the bedchamber. The carpets and curtains looked new. The furniture, if not new, had been reupholstered and the wood polished to a reflective gleam.

"I didn't realize the accommodations of Chilcombe House would be so modern," he said.

"Her ladyship had the bathing chamber put in when the structural repairs were starting, before the old earl's death, and then she refurbished this suite for good measure."

"Refurbished? What? Everything is new?"

Clive paused, expressionless. His tone had been approving; now he looked as though he thought he might have said too much.

"It's nicely done," Graeme said. "Do go on."

"Yes, well, my lord, her ladyship took great care with the repairs and the decorating. Everything is new—that is, the carpets and curtains and upholstery. The furniture is original." He paused for a breath. "Except for the bed. This one is new. She ordered the old one to be carried out and burned."

"Did she indeed," Graeme said.

Clive sent him a look, nodded, then dropped his gaze.

There'd been admiration for the countess in that description of the refurbishing and more than a note of approval about the bed.

"By your leave, my lord, I'll go and check that the water is hot."

* * *

AT THE WRITING TABLE IN HER BEDCHAMBER, BLYTHE SEALED the letter to Mr. Stockwell, the land steward at Risley Manor, and rang for a servant.

Adwick appeared carrying a salver piled with letters. "The footman has returned with notes from Mivart's and the estate agent," he said. "And some other mail has arrived for you."

"That is quite a lot of letters."

"Most of these are for his lordship. Two are for you," he added, handing them over.

"Indeed." Blythe choked back a laugh. Word had traveled fast. Invitations were pouring in from the curious and the mamas with marriageable daughters. Or perhaps the responsible papas. They would want to make sure the new earl was not as disreputable as the old one.

She accepted her correspondence and glanced quickly at the note from Mivart's—yes, they could accommodate her ladyship. The estate agent's note was equally short. He would see her the following morning.

She recognized the careful penmanship of one of her two letters and cracked the seal on it, smiling. Coralie wanted to know if Blythe would be at Bluebelle Lodge in June for her fourteenth birthday, which Mr. and Mrs. Stockwell promised would be a grand celebration. The tenants' children would come, if no one else would, and Mr. Stockwell would play his fiddle, and they'd have games and dancing. Nicholas was over his latest cold and reading all the books he could get his hands on.

Blythe sighed. Despite being shunned by the better society of Hampshire, Coralie made the best of life. An earl's vivacious daughter ought to have at least the company of the local gentry's children. Blythe would find a way to visit in June, even if she had to take the public coach and walk the seven miles from Whitchurch to Bluebelle Lodge.

Nicholas's future was another concern. Small and prone to chest colds, she'd like to bring him to London to see a proper physician. If his health improved, then what? The grandson of a marquess, especially a child as hungry to learn as Nicholas, ought to have a proper education. Not that she'd want the marquess in question to have anything to do with the boy.

She would find a way. If she could keep Bluebelle Lodge.

The next part of the letter brought a frown. A gate had been torn from its hinges and several escaped sheep hadn't been found.

Mr. Stockwell senior, the steward at Risley Manor, and his son Samuel Stockwell, who managed Bluebelle Lodge, had reported similar incidents over the last year. They'd speculated the problems were caused by travelers or vagabond ex-soldiers. No one wanted to accuse a marquess or his son.

The loopy handwriting of the second letter was unfamiliar. Blythe broke the seal and skimmed to the signature.

Her pulse pounded, excitement mixing with apprehension and growing to outrage... And more than a little fear.

MY DEAR CONTESSA,

I hear you are looking for me and I know what you want. I'll give it to you for five hundred pounds. I know someone who'll pay more but I'm giving you a bargain seeing as how you took care of Maddy and her boy. Have it ready and I'll send word next week where to bring the money. Coins only no bank draft. A generous time for you to pawn what you need to.

I'm not well, thanks to the earl and I need that money.

L. C.

Lunetta Casale

HER EFFORTS TO FIND THE WOMAN HAD BORNE FRUIT after all.

She had no doubt that Lunetta Casale—a ridiculous stage name—was ailing. This woman, whom Archie brought to Risley Manor as a nurse, might have been made ill by Archie somehow.

A shudder went through her. After their separation, Archie had dallied in very low circles those last few years; he'd taken the cure more than once.

After the local quack and Mr. Jarrow, the magistrate and coroner, ruled that his death had been from illness, Lunetta had disappeared.

And then Blythe had held her breath, wondering if the new will would surface. It hadn't been in the muniment room when she'd searched before Archie died, nor in Archie's desk after his death. The steward, Mr. Stockwell, hadn't found it. The men sent by Jarrow had not uncovered it either. None of the servants confessed to having ever seen it.

Before he was felled by an apoplexy, Mr. Jarrow had never asked Blythe about the will either. She'd carried on as if the new will had never existed.

Jarrow's likely suspect was Newton, Archie's valet, who'd had no love for his fellow servants, nor for Blythe. Newton had taken the two hundred pounds Archie gave him the morning he witnessed the will and left Risley Manor the next day for parts unknown. He hadn't been found.

The magistrate had not even bothered to look for Lunetta.

Blythe locked the threatening letter in a drawer of her writing desk.

She heard the great entry door below her chamber open and close, and a man's deep baritone and footsteps on the stairs. She shuddered, waiting long moments for someone to knock on her door and tell her Lord Vernon was calling again.

She went to the window and looked out. Grosvenor Square bustled as usual but there were no carriages stopped in front and no horses being held by urchins. Whoever was visiting had walked here.

When the bedchamber door opened, it was her maid, Radley, who entered carrying in clean laundry.

"Is there a caller?" Blythe asked.

"Yes. A gentleman for Lord Chilcombe. Must be a close friend as he had Adwick escort him up to his bedchamber."

"Ah, well, we have time then before I meet with the earl. How quickly can you pack our trunks? We're moving to Mivart's Hotel."

GRAEME SENT MORLEY ON HIS WAY AND THEN TURNED BACK to the mirror to tie his own neckcloth.

Morley had kept to his promise to call and escort him to White's. In truth, the gossip Morely had learned had been troubling and better imparted in the privacy of Chilcombe House.

Archie's life and death had been the subject of

speculation at Bow Street; Morley learned this because he was a good friend of one of the magistrates serving there and was wangling for a position himself while he carried out investigations for hire.

As for Blythe... there were those who suspected that Archie had shared her with his gentlemen friends. There were others who thought it had not been lung fever that Archie had succumbed to; that in fact Blythe had delivered a fatal dose of opium.

The land dispute matter... little had leaked out about that. But Diddenton was a crafty dog, rich beyond belief from the opium he sold in China... as well as in the Fens and the East End.

Morley had more to tell him, but Graeme sent his friend on his way to White's, promising to meet him there later after he'd had a chance to review the pile of post he'd told Adwick to leave in the study.

He'd talk to Blythe as well, though what he would say... It was too soon to question her. He'd seen that defensiveness flare in her eyes.

He found Adwick waiting outside his door. The butler cleared his throat. "Her ladyship asked me to assemble the staff so that you can meet them. They're in the hall."

A handful of servants awaited him, and it struck him that, other than Clive, they were, all of them—even the two chambermaids and the kitchen maid—on the far side of forty years old or perhaps even older.

Adwick introduced them and apologized that the housekeeper wasn't present. The earl's arrival was unexpected, and she'd been given leave to visit her dying sister.

Blythe was also missing.

"I should like a tour of the house one day," Graeme said, "but for now though, show me the way to the study, please."

A SHORT WHILE LATER, GRAEME STOOD AT THE STUDY window looking out on a riot of color in the well-ordered garden and then returned to the massive desk.

Neat stacks of correspondence and logbooks sat as if the earl's secretary had just put them in order. Did the earl have an absent secretary?

A note on the top of the new stack proved to be an invitation to a ball, addressed to him, as were the others underneath. None of the names of the senders were familiar.

From another corner, he picked up an opened letter seeking an investment in a rail line. Notes had been scribbled for a proposed reply: *ask about right-of-way leases, lines connecting, support in Parliament, names of committed backers.* All erudite questions.

In his letter, the solicitor had claimed the estate was in order. What Graeme had seen so far of Chilcombe House confirmed that. All seemed to be well-maintained, the staff well-ordered.

And Blythe had had Archie's bed carried out and burned. After the gossip conveyed by Morley, he felt strangely relieved about that.

He stepped over to a table and picked up a well-thumbed journal. *Fleming's British Farmers' Chronicle.* Underneath that was *Evans and Ruffy's Farmers' Journal.*

He knew something about agricultural trade, but about day-to-day practices he was woefully ignorant for a man who'd just inherited acres and acres of good English soil.

A wisp of floral fragrance announced a silent arrival; not even the door hinges had creaked.

Blythe sailed in, only her skirts whispering, followed by Adwick carrying another laden tray. Morley had helped himself, but Graeme had barely touched the one delivered to his bedchamber, except for the dint he'd made in the decanter of good brandy. The butler settled the new tray on a nearby table, bowed, and departed.

Graeme's gaze landed on Blythe and his breath caught again. He'd barely had a chance to thoroughly take in her appearance. Now he took a good look. Despite the dissipated life she'd allegedly shared with his cousin, she looked as fresh as the girl he'd once pined for, her skin fair under a faint spray of freckles, her brown hair free of gray. Her figure, under the lower waistlines and puffier sleeves of the new fashions wasn't quite as lush as he remembered from that fateful night...

Tilting her head, as if reading his thoughts, her face a mask of placidity, she greeted him and stepped closer. Shallow worry lines had settled between her eyebrows, but otherwise, she'd aged little.

She was still beautiful, and despite himself, he felt drawn to her. Thirty-four to his thirty years of age was not an impossible age difference for a lover.

He shoved the tempting thought down, for now. In the years since he'd last seen her, he'd learned to look beyond the physical, and most importantly, to be discreet. Until he saw which way the political winds blew, dallying with Blythe wouldn't help his ambitions.

She folded her hands at her waist and still said nothing.

He'd also learned to hold his tongue and let others fill up the silence.

She gestured toward the desk. "The latest business

reports from the solicitor as well as the ledgers for Chilcombe House are there. Those for Risley Manor are in Hampshire, but you'll find reports from your land steward, Mr. Stockwell. I've sent off a letter to him, and I know that he will be happy to report here to spare you traveling there. If you will inform me what time you want dinner served, and where, I shall make all the arrangements."

Her formal manner contrasted with all the femininity before him. She sounded like one of the subalterns assigned as his secretary at one of his postings.

Or like his own younger self, reporting to Wellington in Paris.

"Whatever time and place you've set for dinner will be fine with me." He pointed toward the tray. "Won't you join me now?"

She pursed her mouth, blinked, and said, "Certainly," and set about pouring tea into the cup—the single cup provided —murmuring questions about sugar and milk.

A single cup. There was a message in that arrangement.

He smiled and said, "You must have that one, my dear."

Gratified by the way she bristled at the added endearment, he pulled the bell himself, and sent the servant to bring a second cup.

When it arrived, she placidly filled it. "Cook has sent up a simple nuncheon on that covered dish. Adwick will convey your instructions to the kitchen if you'd prefer something different."

This... this air of formality was not what he'd expected. He remembered Blythe as friendly and jolly, the sort of girl who'd make an affectionate wife, and the rumors portrayed her as vulgarly accommodating with Archie's friends. This Blythe appeared polite and distant, but he recognized the animosity simmering under the façade of courtesy in what was now his home.

His home, and hers. What was he to do with her? What would she allow him to do with her?

For now, he would probe her a little and see what he could find under the composed surface.

"You were surprised to see me." He studied her over the rim of his cup.

She lifted her eyes, the first true meeting of their gazes since the drawing room. Vulnerability flashed and was quickly shuttered. Her back stiffened, her chin rose infinitesimally.

"Certainly," she said, "had I known you were arriving today, I would not have been entertaining callers in your drawing room."

"A drawing room filled with gentlemen, I noticed."

"Did you not see Mrs. Netley and her daughter?"

Perhaps he had, but he only remembered the coxcomb in a green waistcoat and collars so high they touched his ears, seated so close to Blythe that his leg touched hers.

"Ah, well, she was indeed there," she said, her tone mild, "and I give you fair warning. She is the greatest gossip of the ton, second only to Lord Vernon, the man who was seated next to me."

"Lord Vernon," he mused. Morley had mentioned Lord Vernon.

"Lord Vernon Falfield. He was a friend of the late earl. A frequent visitor to Risley Manor. No doubt he will call on you."

"I trust you will entertain him for me?"

Again, she lifted her gaze from the teacup and said nothing.

Morley's gossip about Lord Vernon had included

rumors about Archie and Blythe's entertainments. It was hard to believe this composed lady could have been the tart depicted in the old caricatures Morley described.

Though rumors, he reminded himself, often held a grain of truth.

The silence grew uncomfortable. "I suppose the social niceties require me to convey my condolences to you on the death of your husband."

"Yes, well. And you have lost your cousin. Though the inheritance is a boon to you." She frowned into her cup. "And, I hope, you will be a boon to the people who are depending on you. Archie was not much engaged in..." The worry lines deepened. "In estate matters."

Would she tell him now what Archie *was* interested in?

"He was fortunate to have competent administrators," she said. "Mr. Fleming and the land steward are both men of sterling character."

Were they indeed? Or were they two more of Lady Chilcombe's lovers?

A churlish thought. He shook it off.

"I hope that is true as I don't intend to stay in England any longer than I must. But tell me, how do you know they are men of sterling character?"

Her chin came up. "Results, my lord. And regular audits of the books by, er, a third party." She stood. "Look at the time. I must go."

The clock was on a sideboard behind her and she hadn't swiveled her head an inch.

He followed her to the door and touched her elbow. A shiver went through her, and he felt the trembling move up his own arm. "Where are you off to?"

"I beg your pardon?" She glanced pointedly at his hand, a

wash of color creeping up her neck. "I have business to attend to."

The tight blue muslin of her lower sleeve encased a firm shapely arm. His hand itched to explore more. It was no wonder she had attracted bloody lovers.

"Business more important than my arrival?" he asked, releasing her. "Are you off to order a new bonnet before I have a look at the accounts?"

Her bosom rose and fell as she contemplated the question.

"You will of course want the solicitor to explain the financial arrangements. I shall not be a bother to you, my lord. Financially or otherwise."

"Otherwise? You won't try to pester me with social engagements?"

He thought of the pile of invitations. Her input there might be needed. Not that he would follow her advice until he knew just how scandalous her friends were. After all, he had a diplomatic post to pursue.

"Or, my lady, do you mean a bother to my *reputation?*"

"Your reputation?" Her eyebrows lifted. "You were quite a proper young man when you left England, and I had thought your character fixed. But if you've acquired skeletons, my lord, I'm not likely to discover them. If I did, I'd keep them hidden from the wags and gossips. I have years of practice."

She left, pulling the door closed behind her.

CHAPTER FOUR

*T*here'd been a world of bitterness in that last statement. Graeme stared at the closed door a moment, remembering a vision from the past: Blythe in the arms of his cousin, Archie, her bodice pulled down, her breasts exposed to Archie's fevered groping.

All the old emotions stirred—anger, jealousy, and above all, the desire that had consumed him, despite the fact that he'd been a young lad and she'd been almost five years his senior. He'd opened his mouth and brought attention to the couple, attention that had forced a marriage, when all he'd wanted was to stop Archie. It had been his fault she'd been made to marry.

Calf love, it had been, an infatuation that could never bear fruit—then.

What he'd learned that day had made him cautious with women and careful about expectations. He'd had lovers but never fallen in love. He'd never expected to marry.

An earl without male relatives would *have* to marry and produce an heir.

What he needed was a simple transaction: a sensible

young woman of good reputation who would bear sons, manage the house while he was away for months, perhaps years, and who wouldn't stand in the way of his career.

He went back to the tray and lifted the cover and set it down again, his appetite gone. The journals and papers on the desk beckoned him to work, but what he wanted was another proper drink.

What he needed was a clear head.

He rang for a fresh pot of tea and went to the desk.

A HALF HOUR LATER HE THREW DOWN THE LOGBOOK HE WAS reviewing and rubbed his eyes.

The columns of numbers marched profitably down each page, but one number revealed payments on a sizeable loan from an unfamiliar bank.

If the estate was doing well, why the loan? There was the work on the townhouse of course, or... had his cousin been a gambler? Morley hadn't mentioned it. Perhaps Archie's expenses were related to the ladybirds he'd welcomed into his home. Clothing one countess was expensive, but two or more of the ladies in a harem?

What was the truth about Archie and Blythe? He glanced at the clock. Morley was waiting for him at White's.

In the hall he found the butler directing two footmen with a large trunk.

"What is this?" Graeme asked.

"The trunk is mine, my lord." Dressed for outdoors, Blythe descended the stairs, an older, plainly attired woman following her with a valise. She hadn't been part of the line of servants earlier so she must be the lady's maid, and had been busy upstairs packing this trunk.

Blythe hadn't said she was traveling.

"Where are you going?" he asked.

She pulled on a glove. "Adwick, thank you, that will be all. Radley, will you check whether I left behind the book I was reading?" All four servants dispersed, and she faced him, tying the bow on her massive bonnet. "The new earl has arrived. The old earl's countess is departing. My duties here are done. I've found other accommodations."

Outside the open door, a shabby carriage stopped. A servant in Chilcombe livery ran up to it.

The carriage was a hired hack. She wasn't traveling as far as Risley Manor in that.

"Are you off to a coaching inn to hire a chaise? Doesn't Chilcombe have a traveling chaise or carriage to take you to Risley?"

"How I travel is not your concern, my lord."

"You're... what? Off to stay with a friend?"

"Bearing in mind the impact of my presence on your reputation, I thought it best that we do not dwell under the same roof."

A cold chill passed over him. The rumors must be true. "Who is he?"

Her mouth firmed. "The fact that you have the discourtesy to ask that question proves the need for me to leave." The tension in her was palpable. "I have found temporary lodgings. I have taken the liberty of asking one of your servants to see that my maid and I are safely settled, after which, he will return to Chilcombe House."

"Who is providing these temporary lodgings?"

She leveled the same quelling gaze he'd once seen Wellington direct at an unwelcome mushroom who'd needlessly sought his attention.

Perhaps the exuberant young girl had become a formidable woman.

He might be unwelcome but he wasn't a mushroom. He was the earl. Surely, he had some say about the dowager countess's conduct.

All the more reason to have her gone, yet the thought of her leaving, to go off to a lover—

"*I* am providing the accommodation, sir," she said finally. "I have arranged quite respectable lodgings elsewhere. This is your home now, not mine, Lord Chilcombe."

"No," he said, anger rising. "I see your gambit, Blythe. You want me to appear to society to be a scoundrel, casting you out of your home." If he had any hopes for a plum assignment, he'd best protect his reputation as a gentleman.

He walked to the door, beckoned the servant outside, and told him to send the hack on its way.

Blythe grasped at composure and pushed down the urge to shout.

She'd had one year and one month without an Earl of Chilcombe meddling in her life. "It is *not* your decision to make."

"I arrive in town and displace a countess from her home? What will *that* do to my reputation? What sort of gentleman do you think I am? If anyone is to leave it will be me."

"*If* anyone is to leave?" she said, her voice rising as she lost her internal battle. "I'm not thinking of *your* reputation, I'm thinking of mine. Except for cheating at cards, you gentlemen may do whatever you please, never mind the cost to your wives and children."

She squeezed her eyes, suppressing a burst of angry tears, gathered herself, and found him staring at her like she was the lowliest sort of insect.

The insolent prig.

Easing in a breath, she went on. "Had I known your arrival would be so soon, I would have already been gone."

"Is there no dower house? Until the business of the will is settled... for heaven's sake, Blythe, if you must leave, why not return to Risley Manor?"

Archie had made great use of the Risley Manor dower house before moving his beastly activities to the north wing of the manor. If *she* were the earl, both dwellings would be torn down.

"This is your home now. I will not spend a single night under the roof of an unmarried man. I bid you adieu, Lord Chilcombe."

"No." He repeated, his jaw locked. "You will, of course, stay here."

Speechless with anger, she struggled for words.

"What's needed," he said, "is a chaperone. I'll take rooms at an inn until you can search out some older relation."

Her only older relation was Great-Aunt Winifred, and the old besom had cut ties after she'd paid a call at Risley Manor, and Archie had invited his *nurse* to join them for tea.

"It will have to be one of *your* relations," she said. "I have none handy."

"What of Cousin Freddy's widow? She must be forty if she's a day."

"If you'll recall, that particular wife died quite some time ago. The current widow is not yet two and twenty."

Though, come to think of it, Melusine Blatchford's presence would be perfect revenge on this managing earl.

"It may be indelicate to mention," she said, pausing to adjust her bonnet, "but Freddy's widow would *very* much like to have a title. *Countess* would work quite well. She's young enough to bear many children, though she's only managed to produce daughters so far. Invite her here, if you dare. Perhaps her mother could come along and chaperone your courtship of her."

Graeme blinked and pressed his lips together.

"I say!" a man bellowed from the doorway. " Ain't this Lady Chilcombe's house? Why is this cheeky chap sending my hack away with my trunk still atop it? Put the case there, if you please."

A scrawny fellow in regimentals directed the earl's footman to place a scratched, battered trunk on the tile next to Blythe's more elegant luggage.

Tall, sandy-haired, and lean—far too thin, actually—the visitor turned a bright grin on her and opened his arms. "What kind of welcome is this, Blythy?"

Will. Will was here. She hadn't seen him in years.

Moisture welled in her eyes and throat, and she heard Graeme's indrawn breath. Nudging the pompous prig out of the way, she walked into the welcoming arms, feeling... safe, protected, for the first time in ages.

"Will," she said pulling back to examine him. He seemed to have grown taller since his last leave and was far too careworn for his age, but mischief gleamed in his eyes, like it had in the old days when the brat had pulled pranks on her. "Has the army not been feeding you?"

"*Arrgh.* Aye, feeding me bullets and plague, and a few poisoned spears on the side. I just landed at Deal two days ago, and lucky I was to find transport. Who's this fellow?" he added in a stage whisper.

Heavens. Will and Graeme might have arrived on the same ship. She was glad that they hadn't.

"I may ask the same about you." Graeme's smooth tone would cut butter but the stony look in his eyes told her what he was thinking.

She swallowed a defiant chuckle. "My lord," she said, "may I introduce Captain Willis Lynford? Will, this is Graeme Blatchford, the Earl of Chilcombe, who like you, has only just arrived in town."

"The new earl? I thought you wrote that he'd be arriving in... Beg pardon. Er, pleased to meet you. I suppose I'd best look for a bed elsewhere." Will's eyes narrowed. "I say, are you living here, Blythe?"

"No," she said, and at the same time Graeme said, "Yes."

She locked eyes with him, furious at the cool, knowing look he sent back. "I'm leaving," she said.

"She's staying, Captain Lynford."

Will took a step forward. "I say, sir. Just what are your intentions toward my sister?"

Blythe sighed. She'd kept her letters to Will cheerful, omitting her marital trials. It seemed the rumors had reached him anyway.

"Your sister?" Graeme looked skeptical, and so he might. Where her half-sibling was tall and fair, like his father, she was of average height and dark, like hers.

And then the earl's eyes lit. "Ah, I remember. You had a half-brother who went off as a coronet." He extended his hand. "Welcome, Captain Lynford. Your sister and I were just discussing the need for a chaperone. Of course you'll stay here with us."

Trapped, she was. Will needed a place to stay and rooms for both of them at the hotel would sorely tax her funds.

Will's was another face she hadn't seen in years, but at least his was a friendly one, and she so very much needed a friend. Plus, she could see him properly fed. She needn't do more than suffer meals with the odious new earl while fattening up her brother.

He'd be a terrible chaperone though, off visiting

alehouses and clubs and probably making the rounds of the London brothels.

Perhaps she *would* take herself off to Mivart's. Or… she'd sent a note to Lady Loughton requesting a ride to the Harrington rout that evening. She might as well call and inform her in person of the change in plans.

"Will, you'll want to settle in, but later this evening the Harringtons are hosting a rout. Will you escort me?"

Her brother's eyes twinkled. "Putting me to work already?"

"If you've made other plans—"

"I will escort you," Graeme said. "I had an invitation to the rout in my stack of mail."

Will turned a solemn look on the new earl. "Of course I'll accompany my sister."

She sent Will off with Adwick and beckoned Radley. "The rain has stopped. We may as well walk."

"Wait and I'll get my hat," Graeme said. "Where are you going? I'll accompany you and then continue on to White's."

"I'm calling on Lady Loughton. That is the opposite direction."

"Nevertheless. It's been ages since I've been in town, and I've been cooped up on a ship for months. It will be good to stretch my legs and get my bearings."

* * *

"Do let them come in," a woman called.

The butler who answered the door at Loughton House dipped his head and ushered first Blythe, and then Graeme, in.

A tall, dark-haired young woman descended the stairs and greeted Blythe with a kiss on the cheek. Blythe introduced Lady Mary Elizabeth Loughton, wife of the current Baron Loughton, who as it happened was not at home.

Graeme tried to excuse himself, but Lady Loughton insisted they both join her in the library.

"Please make yourself comfortable," Lady Loughton said, pointing to an arrangement of chairs and sofas. "We are all at sixes and sevens here, but I'll go and fetch my mother-in-law. I know she'll want to meet you, Lord Chilcombe."

Graeme eyed the shelves of books and the papers piled on a large desk in the corner.

"I wonder whether Lord Loughton would appreciate us in his domain," he said.

"It's as much Mel's domain as his," Blythe said.

"Mel?"

"Mary Elizabeth. Mel to her friends."

"And you are a good friend?"

"Yes. Mel is a banker, you know. A principle shareholder at Sawley's Bank."

"Ah." The mysterious loan in the logbooks was from Sawley's bank.

Before he could ask more questions, Lady Loughton returned with two other ladies. The dowager Lady Neda Loughton was a petite blond with sparkling blue eyes, who didn't appear to be much older than forty. The other lady was a comfortably plump woman of perhaps sixty; Lady Hermione Gravelston, the younger Lady Loughton's older cousin.

A tea tray arrived next, and tea was served while he answered all the polite inquiries about his travels. The ladies were no doubt sizing him up, while he did the same, relieved to find that Blythe's friends were decent, sensible ladies.

"Have you heard anything new from the court?" the younger Lady Loughton asked.

"I haven't," Blythe said, looking at him, a question in her eyes. "But Lord Chilcombe has only just arrived."

"I'm sorry," Lady Loughton said. "I don't mean to pry."

"Do forgive us, Lord Chilcombe. We've all been so worried for Blythe's sake," the older Lady Loughton said. "Perhaps it's a good thing that you haven't heard any news."

Lady Gravelston huffed. "Or it might be a bad thing if that villain is scurrying about trying to conjure up a witness to the new will," she said and then winced. "And I also must beg your pardon, Blythe, my lord."

"In that vein, no news is good news, I suppose," Graeme said. "However, Lady Chilcombe has received some happy news. Her brother has arrived at Chilcombe House this afternoon on leave from the army."

Having successfully distracted them from a discussion of the Chilcombe will, he settled back as the ladies expressed their happiness and wishes to meet Captain Lynford. Blythe inquired about the Loughton family members who'd be arriving soon, and he, having finished his tea and done enough of the pretty, took his leave and promised to see them at the evening's rout.

* * *

BLYTHE WATCHED GRAEME LEAVE AND BREATHED A SIGH OF relief.

"Well," Mel said. "I suppose I oughtn't to have brought up the subject of the will. He's rather formal, your new earl."

Blythe grimaced. "My immediate dilemma is staying under the same roof with him. I was set to remove myself to Mivart's Hotel, over his objections, when my brother arrived. Chilcombe has it in his head that my brother will serve as a proper chaperone. But you know how young men are. I of all people must be careful of my reputation. It would be better for me to leave the two together to their bachelor ways."

The two Ladies Loughton exchanged a glance, but it was Lady Gravelston who spoke.

"There's not a bed free at Loughton House. Why, I'm meant to share a bed with Nancy, and the mood she's in after her dealings with the duke..." Her cheeks grew pinker and she smiled. "Not that I blame the dear girl. I wonder... might you have room for me, Lady Chilcombe? I'll still be close to my dear Mel and Neda, and I can keep the gossips at bay. And I assure you, I'm not a gossip myself."

"Not much of one," Mel said with a smile.

The older lady shrugged. "Unless I hear news that is useful for you. What is he really like, your new earl?"

"He was a friend when we were children but I haven't seen him for years. He was always a well-behaved boy—a few years younger than me, and later, a very proper young man. Not much given to hijinks. He doesn't seem to have changed."

"Even in diverting us, he was well-mannered." Neda always looked for the good in people. "That must serve him well in his occupation."

Lady Gravelston sent a mischievous look over her teacup. "Do you not find him rather handsome?"

All eyes trained on Blythe and she felt warmth rising in her cheeks. "I suppose," she said, noncommittally. "But handsome is as handsome does, and I've yet to know him well enough to judge."

"I beg your pardon for joking with you so newly

widowed," Lady Gravelston said. "The trials of widowhood, isn't that right, Neda? I have lost a beloved husband as well."

Blythe sighed. Archie had been a beloved husband for not much more than a month, after which she'd made discoveries that brought her to her senses.

"My dear," Neda said, "this is a terrible strain you're under. I would insist you stay here with us, but Hermione is right, we are packed to the rafters. Your servants now are loyal, and the earl will come to appreciate your help making his way in society. Your brother has been away from England for too long to be much assistance. You need a female ally in that house, and Hermione, if she is willing, is perfect for the role."

"Will I have to share a bed?" Lady Gravelston asked with a cheeky grin. "If not, than I am more than willing."

* * *

GRAEME FOUND MANUS MORLEY READING THE DAY'S newssheets at a table, while gray-haired members napped in nearby club chairs.

Morley signaled a waiter and ordered him a drink, then lifted his glass in a toast. "To the new Earl of Chilcombe," he said. "How did you find the rest of the house and your account books?"

"The rest of the house is exceptionally well-kept also," Graeme said. As were the books but he didn't wish to discuss them.

"Is it now?" Morley leaned back and crossed one leg over the other, but his casualness didn't fool Graeme.

"You must come around for dinner one night. I'll send a note."

"That would be capital. Chilcombe House had a scaffold

up most of last year. But wait until you see Risley Manor. Parts of it are crumbling. They had a leak in the roof that all but brought down the ceiling over the earl."

His senses alerted again. "You've been to Risley Manor?" Morley's descriptions of the goings on at Risley Manor had all been expressed as things he was told about.

Morley sighed and leaned closer, speaking softly. "I did say I had more to tell you."

An elderly gentleman nearby stirred, and Morley lowered his voice to a low murmur. "I was there a couple of years before your cousin died. I was on my way to a friend's in Wiltshire when I ran into Lord Vernon on the road. He insisted I tag along with him and pay a call." Color touched his cheeks and he glanced away.

"And? Are the gossips right about..." About Blythe. He didn't have to go on. Morley knew what he meant—he'd raised the subject earlier in his room.

"The earl was there, but the countess wasn't at home."

"Away, or just not *at home* to the two of you?"

"Not there, I suspect. I never saw her."

"But the other ladies?"

Morley frowned. "Chilcombe had rooms in one of the wings. Had a very fetching nurse fussing over him and two pretty maids winking at Lord Vernon and me."

"Did you stay for the orgy?"

Morley didn't so much as bat an eye. "I did not. My wild, wicked days are behind me. Plus... the earl's appearance put me off the notion entirely. Rail thin and pale as a ghost. Had the tremors until his nurse dosed him."

Archie had been addicted to opium. That much of the gossip Morley shared must be true.

"I paid my respects and plowed on. Found a second-rate

inn in the next town but the food was good. Thought it best to take my dinner there too."

"Thank you, Morley. If you're holding back anything else—"

"Yes, well... When I left Risley Manor, I asked the groom who brought my phaeton round where I might find her ladyship." He frowned. "I've always liked to, er, know things, you know? Told the groom my sister was a good friend of her ladyship and she'd asked me to check on her. Fellow was a little simple and he didn't disappoint. Wouldn't say where she was, but he said she always seemed to know when his lordship and his friends were coming and she never was around when they arrived. I asked about her in the taproom at the inn where I dined. One traveler tittered over his ale, but I swear, the locals—rum crowd of farmers and yokels, not your high-class sort—shot him daggers and all of them clammed up."

A flash of color caught Graeme's eye. The peacock who'd been seated next to Blythe, Lord Vernon Falfield, was coming their way. He looked like a pinch-faced Lord Byron with amber snake-eyes.

Graeme exchanged a look with Morley. "You didn't tell me about your travels after we met in Paris," he said. "Did you go on to Greece before the revolution there started?"

"Never made it," Morley said. "Florence, though. Had a grand time there."

"Might I join you?" Lord Vernon bowed and pulled over a chair. "Welcome to White's. Lord Chilcombe, I saw your arrival at Lady Chilcombe's. Lord Vernon Falfield. Morley is always running off to France. His stories of his travels will put you to sleep."

"Is that so? He's just been telling me about visiting my cousin at Risley Manor."

"Didn't stay for the fun, did you, Morley? I say, Chilcombe, you have big boots to fill. Archie was a game fellow, that's for sure."

"Was he? I can't say I knew him well. Our families weren't close."

"Particular friend of mine." He grinned. "The countess too. Now there's a lovely lady. She won't be troubling you for support much longer."

"You mean she'll remarry?" he asked. "Or are you implying something else?"

Lord Vernon laughed. "Don't get your temper up, old fellow. I'm not impugning the lady." He beckoned a waiter. "Another round for you two?"

Graeme glanced at his watch. "Not for me. I'll bid you both good day."

"I say, don't leave yet," Lord Vernon said. "I was hoping to find you here. My father, Diddenton, wants you to pay a call on him tomorrow."

"I'm not free tomorrow," Graeme said. "It will have to be another day."

"Make it so," Lord Vernon said, softening the remark with an oily smile. "Diddenton don't like to wait on earls." He laughed again, a false, horsey sound. "Pompous old prig, he is."

One pompous prig to another; the marquess would have to wait on *this* earl.

"Don't forget that promised dinner invitation," Morley said.

"And one for me as well?" Lord Vernon flashed a cheeky grin.

Graeme shrugged and left, making his way to Chilcombe House, wondering what Lord Vernon was implying about Blythe, wondering how he should deal with the lout. It wasn't just her reputation at stake, but his as well.

He could handle a pistol and sword and he was good with his fists. But he was even better with his brain.

Blythe was a widow, and widows were free to take lovers. Despite his first impulse to think the worst of her, his instincts were telling him that Blythe wasn't seeking an affair. Perhaps she hadn't even been a participant in Archie's depravity.

Diddenton was claiming Chilcombe property and pushing forward a will that disinherited Blythe.

He needed to find out more. Someone at the Foreign Office might know what this was all about.

He'd call on Diddenton after he'd armed himself with more information.

And there was an additional option—he could hire his nosy friend Manus Morley to supplement the solicitor's inquiries. That property dispute ought to be thoroughly investigated.

CHAPTER FIVE

*W*hen Graeme came down for dinner, he found Lady Hermione Gravelston waiting in the drawing room. Rising to greet him, she dipped her head and smiled.

"I fear you've acquired a houseguest in the last hour," she said. "I hope you don't mind. Blythe invited me."

It seemed Blythe had found a more suitable chaperone than her brother.

"You're most welcome," he said, and went to fetch her a glass of sherry. "You're a cousin to the younger Lady Loughton, is that right?"

"Yes, and Mel is very dear to me. She invited me to join her and Lord Loughton for the Season, but as they've had an unexpected arrival of other family members, well, Blythe kindly offered me shelter here." She leaned in and said with a smile, "I assure you, I'm quite respectable."

"I never doubted it. Is Lady Chilcombe joining us?"

"I'm here now." With a swish of skirts and a waft of that enticing perfume, Blythe crossed the room, graceful and confident.

"Will is taking a tray in his room," she said. "I stopped to look in on him and woke him up. He'll come with us tonight to the rout."

"Poor dear," Lady Gravelston said. "Travel has worn him out. Where was he serving?"

"In Africa. I suspect it was dreadful duty."

"And what of you, my lord?" the lady asked. "I'm told you were resolving a dispute in Western Canada. How did you find your return journey?"

Over dinner, Lady Hermione peppered him with questions, drawing out stories of his various duty posts. He might have gone into the army like Blythe's brother, Will, but his aptitude for languages had captured the attention of Sir William Taylor of the Foreign Office. In various postings, he'd had a hands-on schooling in both good and bad diplomacy—schooling that he hoped to put in use in service to the Crown as soon as he could resolve the problems he'd encountered here.

* * *

THE CRUSH OF BODIES WAS—AS WAS USUAL AT THESE EVENTS —suffocating.

Even more so since Blythe and Hermione had arrived at the Harrington townhouse with two handsome, eligible bachelors in tow. Mamas with marriageable daughters gathered round, even the ones who had previously been less than welcoming to Blythe.

Will had his share of interested young ladies, but it was Graeme they hovered around. And he surprised Blythe with the charming way he made small talk with shy misses whilst almost imperceptibly deflecting the simpering leeches.

While the wave of females carried him away, she

mingled and chatted, grateful for her widowed female friends. Neda was often nearby, and Hermione stayed close, her genial good humor a bulwark against the gentlemen cruising by, nibbling at Blythe, seeking to try their luck.

Drink in hand, Will had acquired his own circle of ladies, some of whom she knew to be married.

She would have to tell him which husbands were more likely to duel. Her brother had inherited money but no land. He wasn't penniless—he had enough income for uniforms and mess fees—yet he wasn't a prize for an unmarried girl. For the married ladies though…

She turned her head to look for Will and saw Graeme speaking with Mrs. Netley and her daughter, his face politely bland.

He'd been forewarned. While she watched, he looked her way, and their eyes met. His lips quirked and his eyes crinkled, as if he wanted to smile.

Warmth rushed through her, not the swelter from the mass of bodies, but a heat from inside, inappropriate and most certainly unwanted. The only *feeling* she was after was peace, the sort of blissful peace she'd feel when she could call Bluebell Lodge her own.

She glanced past him and saw another man coming to greet him—a friend of his, by the looks of it.

"Introducing the earl to the ton, are you?"

The sly voice spoke too close to her ear.

"It seems he needs little help from us, Lord Vernon," Hermione said.

Lord Vernon turned a haughty gaze on Blythe's companion. "You have the advantage of me, madam."

The self-centered fool hadn't noticed Hermione. Of course he hadn't.

"Lady Hermione Gravelston." Hermione tapped him

with her closed fan. "And we have met before, Lord Vernon. Not that I suppose you should remember *me*."

He grinned. "So charming a lady. Of course I remember you."

She scoffed. "There's no need to lie. Your father is Diddenton. I'm from Hampshire as well."

"Ah." He turned his attention to Blythe. "My dear, Blythe. How do you do tonight? I'm told your brother has descended upon you as well as Chilcombe. A veritable bachelor establishment."

"No, indeed," Hermione said. "We have equal numbers, don't we, Lady Chilcombe?"

"Lady Hermione has joined us too," Blythe said. "She is a dear friend who just arrived in town. We intend to enjoy the Season together."

He bowed. "I shall be happy to serve as your escort."

Hermione laughed. "You will have to join the queue behind Chilcombe and Captain Lynford. They've both promised to attend on us."

Blythe's lips quivered. That had been a blatant lie.

"I protest. You must help me move to first place in the queue," Lord Vernon said, "and help me win this lady's favor. I've waited a whole year while she grieved Archie's death, and now she is free, I'm crushed that she shuns me."

"Shuns you? You paid a call on me only this morning."

"In a crowd of callers and only during morning hours. There was a time, Lady Gravelston, when I was welcome at Chilcombe House at any hour."

Blythe's throat choked with anger. She looked away and saw that Graeme was watching her while he bent his ear to his gentleman friend. Then he excused himself and walked her way.

"The late Lord Chilcombe was your bosom friend then?" Hermione asked.

"The closest of friends."

"I see. Yes, I'm sure there were certain callers my late husband would have welcomed at any hour. It is very hard to lose a good friend, but a wise gentleman understands that some things must change in relation to a friend's widow."

GRAEME ARRIVED IN TIME TO HEAR LADY HERMIONE'S motherly set down.

He'd seen the anger in Blythe's face and instinctively come to intervene. She, however, had composed herself. It was the other fellow whose face had reddened now.

"Are you enjoying yourself, my lord?" Blythe asked, her tone polite. "May I make known to you this friend of my late husband?"

He shook his head. "We are already acquainted."

Blythe quickly excused herself to go speak with a friend of her own. She glided away, Lady Hermione at her elbow.

Gentlemen craned their necks watching her, and he could see why. She carried herself proudly, defiantly almost, and still one could detect a vulnerability and innocence that may or may not refute the scandal spread about her. An intoxicating mix for some men.

Men like Lord Vernon. And if he was honest, himself too.

He caught the villain watching her, his look both predatory and possessive.

Besides wanting to swive Blythe, what was the fellow up to? He was Diddenton's son, and Diddenton had unearthed a draft of a new will, one very favorable to the Falfield family.

"It's sweltering in here," he said. "I'm heading for those open balcony doors."

Though it wasn't raining, the brisk night air was dense with dampness. He was a bit surprised to find that Lord Vernon had followed him.

"Cheroot?" Lord Vernon pulled a silver case from his pocket.

He waved it away. "Thank you, no, but don't let me stop you."

Lord Vernon lit the tobacco from a nearby torch and blew a big cloud of smoke. "Unfortunate thing, that new will," he said.

So, they were to have *that* conversation. Graeme rested a hand on the balustrade and waited. He sensed that the fellow wanted to pick him over for information. He didn't intend to give any, but he'd learn something from the dastard's line of questioning.

That was the other thing he sensed: Lord Vernon was up to no good and not a man to be trusted. "How is that?" he asked.

Lord Vernon raised his brows in feigned surprise. "You haven't heard? Why I suppose not if you've just arrived in town, though I'm surprised your solicitor didn't inform you."

"Why don't you tell me about it."

Lord Vernon's oily chuckle crawled over his skin before the man quickly sobered. "I suppose it's no laughing matter, not where Lady Chilcombe is concerned. Left out of the will, she was."

"Left out?" He watched the fellow carefully. "And just how would you know that?"

"Don't you know? My father is the one who challenged the old will and submitted the fair copy of the correct one.

He and Archie discussed it and agreed on it as a resolution to that property dispute."

"Hmm. How did Diddenton obtain a copy of the new will?"

Lord Vernon blinked and pressed his lips together. He hadn't prepared an answer for that question.

"How do I know? I suppose Archie's man sent the copy along to Diddenton."

"His man being…?"

The not so wily fellow blinked again then shrugged. "A messenger? A groom? Who knows?" He frowned. "Sir Morris Pierpont was meant to be carrying the signed copy to London."

Graeme raised an eyebrow. Lord Vernon was leaving out bits and pieces here. Why did Diddenton need a copy of the will? Why was Sir Morris rushing to London with a signed copy of the will? Despite his addictions, Archie was neither dead nor dying at the time the new will was supposedly signed.

Which prompted another thought—was Archie's death a month later truly due to natural causes?

"He was supposed to deliver it to Archie's solicitor, settling the business of Bluebell Lodge. Fleming was squawking about title searches and new surveys."

Well, there was one answer.

Lord Vernon puffed on his cheroot and shook his head. "Morris turned over his phaeton and cracked his head just outside of Risley Manor. No will in his bag. Diddenton was fit to be tied."

In the room behind them, a young gentleman and lady appeared at the door, looked out, and moved on. "Who witnessed the signing of the will?" Graeme asked.

Lord Vernon huffed. "Morris was meant to do it, along

with whomever else they could find, the steward or Archie's valet. The steward was not around that day. Morris is dead, and the valet took off a day later for parts unknown."

"Maybe the countess persuaded the late earl to change his mind about the new will."

"Blythe wasn't there at the signing."

Graeme's temper spiked at the lout's familiar use of Blythe's name. Had they been intimate? She'd given Lord Vernon the cold shoulder tonight but perhaps there'd been a lover's quarrel.

The thought of her with this fellow made his hands curl into fists.

"Archie's nurse passed through the room and said she saw Morris and the valet bent over a document on the table. Heard Morris promise to deliver it when he left after lunch."

"Archie had a nurse?"

Lord Vernon sent him a sly smile. "He called her that. She tended to his, er, medicine and, er, other needs."

In other words, Archie's mistress had lived there in the family home, dosing him with opium and servicing his carnal needs. Damnation. Why had Blythe tolerated it? he wondered... Had she found a way to retrieve that new will? Would she tell him, the new earl, if she had, or would she lie?

"Devil of a thing." Lord Vernon stubbed out his cheroot, leaving a dark circle on the stone balustrade then tossed the butt into a bush. "Suppose I ought to tell you. Archie felt bad about leaving Blythe nothing."

"Then why didn't he leave her another property or an income?"

Lord Vernon shrugged. "He asked me to take care of her. Good friends for years, you know. I promised him I'd marry her."

Heat rose in him, blood pounding into his ears. The urge to throw this dastard over the balustrade to join his cheroot butt was overwhelming.

"And what does Lady Chilcombe say to that?"

"She'll go along with it. It's the best possible choice for her, isn't it? She's been desperately trying to repair her reputation—hid away for months at some countess's estate that only allows widows in, and now this reappearance. Shunned all of us who were Archie's friends even before he kicked up his toes. But I'm afraid there's still gossip. It'll be the best thing for her, and I'll get her out of your hair."

And if the old will holds, she'll bring that property into your marriage. Either way, the Marquess of Diddenton would get that property he wanted so desperately.

"Lady Chilcombe is not *in my hair*, as you say. She is my cousin by marriage, and the Chilcombe estate will support her as long as is necessary."

Graeme recognized another figure in the doorway.

Lord Vernon's eyes narrowed and he opened his mouth, but Graeme spoke first.

"I should not like to hear that you're one of those spreading gossip. I'm sure her brother will feel the same way."

"I say." Will Lynford appeared at his elbow. "Been looking for you, Chilcombe. What's this about gossip and my sister?"

Lord Vernon shot Graeme an angry look and dipped his head to Blythe's brother. "Lord Vernon Falfield at your service."

Blythe's much taller brother stared down at Lord Vernon. "I'm Captain Lynford. Thought I'd left the fighting behind."

Falfield held up his hands, palms out. "No gossiping on my part, Lynford. I have the highest regard for Blythe."

Will's jaw moved. "You mean *Lady Chilcombe*."

"Yes, Lady Chilcombe. I say, Chilcombe, you ought to bring this fellow along to White's tomorrow. Lynford, I'll introduce you to some of the fellows there. But now I must bid you adieu and go and mingle."

Falfield scuttled away, and Will turned an angry gaze on Graeme.

"Who is he?"

"A close friend of the late Lord Chilcombe. He says he means to marry your sister."

"Over my dead body. I don't know much yet about what she's gone through these last fifteen years but... Blythe was made to marry one donkey's arse; I'll not have her forced to marry another. Anyway, I'm pretty sure Blythe don't want him." He bit his lip. "She sent me to ask if she and Lady Hermione can take the carriage home and send it back for you."

"That won't be necessary," Graeme said. He'd had enough for one evening. "I'm coming too."

* * *

Sir William Taylor's clerk greeted Graeme with a nod and then ushered him to an interior door, opening it without knocking.

"He's here, sir."

Graeme had sent a note arranging this time and was gratified that he wouldn't have to wait. A good sign probably. He meant to answer any questions about the report he had sent, and more importantly, let the Foreign Office know of his interest in another assignment.

He passed through into the room lined with dark wooden shelves and paneling.

Sir William was not alone. A man in perhaps his sixties sat in a well-padded armchair angled to view both the man behind the desk and anyone entering. Graeme had a quick impression of fine tailoring over a fit frame, white curly hair, sunken cheeks, and amber eyes, under the austere mien of a man looking down from a high place in the world.

A peer of the realm but which one?

Sir William rose and greeted Graeme; the other man did not. His superior quickly made introductions.

Lord Vernon had been wrong about his father. The Marquess of Diddenton had apparently decided to wait on the Earl of Chilcombe after all, albeit in the lair of a government official.

"I've had a chance to read your report. I've a few questions which I'll deal with later," said Sir William, glossing over the apparently less important business of the Crown. "Diddenton asked for some of your time this morning."

Then Sir William left, closing the door behind where Graeme was standing.

A second chair had been placed in front of the desk. No invitation was forthcoming to utilize it.

The rudeness pricked Graeme's temper. Pompous old prig, his son had called him, and he was reminded of one old sheik he'd encountered—stiff, haughty, and disdainful. And as dangerous as a viper.

He was an earl now, with a license to play that same game. He seated himself and nodded to the older man.

Diddenton raised an eyebrow. "You'll know why I'm here, Chilcombe."

Graeme settled back into his chair and picked an

invisible spot of lint off his sleeve. "It would be helpful for you to tell me."

The older man's mouth primmed and his gaze sharpened. "I hope that you do not plan to be coy with me. My son has informed you about the problems with your predecessor's will."

He couldn't very well say no. "It's true that he has spoken to me."

"Then you will know the court has delayed proving the will because the signed copy could not be found, nor did they wish to proceed on the matter until you returned."

"I understood that the delay resulted because *you* were contesting the late earl's will."

"The earl made a new will before he died. There were two signed copies of that new will. I want at least one of them found."

"Yes, I understand that would be to your advantage." Graeme let the comment hang in the air before going on. "How do you know there were two signed copies of this new will?" he finally asked.

The color rising in Diddenton's cheeks flamed higher and a finger twitched on the arm of the chair. "Your superior here is a close friend of mine. He has told me of your ambitions, and I am not without influence. It would be to your advantage to take this matter seriously."

The words had dripped with disdain. What sort of person would *discover* a last minute will so punishing to a widow and so favorable to himself?

The sort that would send his son scurrying and sniffing around Blythe and himself. But he wasn't Diddenton's son and he didn't have to kowtow to him. He'd been schooled by some of the greatest snobs in international diplomacy. "And what is it you suggest I do?" he prodded.

"Find it." This time, two fingers had twitched. "I know it was signed. There were servants who saw that it was signed. The one copy never reached the solicitor in London. The late Lord Chilcombe claimed the other was placed in the muniment room for safekeeping. It's not there. Both copies might be somewhere at Risley Manor. Or someone took them."

"The steward—"

"Bah. Claims to know nothing of it. He wasn't there at the signing. He didn't return to Risley Manor until just before the earl's death."

Would Blythe have taken one or both copies? It would be understandable. Unethical, illegal, as well. A crime, but an understandable one.

"Speak with Jarrow, the magistrate. He searched the house for me."

"For *you*?"

Diddenton's eyes gleamed at his reaction. He stood. Reflexively, Graeme did as well and regretted it almost immediately. Diddenton didn't deserve such courtesy.

"There's a plum assignment at the Persian court." Diddenton walked to the door. "It won't be available for long."

Graeme watched as the door closed on the man, shaking his head. He'd wanted a juicy assignment, one in a hotbed that challenged his skills. He didn't have to leave England at all.

Diddenton wanted that land badly. Why?

If the will couldn't be found, Diddenton would sue Graeme for the property, but that meant the marquess would have to produce more documents related to the land dispute, documents that perhaps didn't at present exist.

If the new will *was* found, Blythe would sue the new Earl

of Chilcombe to honor the contract made by his predecessor.

He settled back into his chair and waited for Sir William's return, contemplating his next steps. After this meeting ended, he would call on the Chilcombe solicitor. It was time to have a look at those records. And then he'd run Morley down at White's.

It was a fact that Diddenton traded in opium, and Archie had been addicted to the vile substance. Would Diddenton have gone as far as murder to push the matter along?

CHAPTER SIX

"What's this all about, Blythe? It's not as if Chilcombe plans to evict you."

Seated beside Will the next day in the Chilcombe town carriage, Blythe patted her brother's hand.

He'd been strangely silent on the drive home from the previous evening's rout, as had Graeme, both men allowing Hermione to chatter on about the evening.

Will had obliged Blythe by accompanying her today when she'd met with the estate agent and visited two properties.

The first one, a smallish townhouse on a fashionable Mayfair square, had been out of her reach. The other, in Soho, was affordable but on the edge of a deteriorating neighborhood. She ought to settle for that second one, but she found herself dithering and wondering how long Graeme would tolerate her presence.

"Dear Will, you were away when I married and probably so young you wouldn't have concerned yourself with contracts and such. Do you remember that after Mama and your father's deaths, when you went into the army, I went to live with my old governess and her husband, my guardian, Mr. Davies, at Bluebelle Lodge?"

"I do."

The childless couple had been very dear to her. Both had died within the last two years.

She told him about the marriage settlement, about waiving her right to dower. After compromising her reputation, Archie had balked at marrying her because of her pittance of a dowry. Mr. Davies had negotiated an agreement that bequeathed Bluebelle Lodge to Chilcombe after his and his wife's deaths, and Archie's will, executed at the time of their marriage, gave her the estate free and clear upon his death.

"The Marquess of Diddenton has come forth claiming there's a new will that changes matters."

Will frowned. "Is there?"

"He says so. He's proffered a copy of what he says is Archie's new will, granting Bluebell Lodge to Diddenton and leaving me one pound." Her chest trembled and she fought the panicky anger that always loomed just thinking about it. "He hasn't yet uncovered a signed copy, but he's managed to hold up the settlement of the estate."

Will's mouth firmed and his face flamed. "If Archie wasn't already dead, I'd run him through myself. And if this new Chilcombe thinks to put you out with nothing—"

"He hasn't threatened that. Not so far. But if Diddenton somehow conjures a signed copy of the will he's claiming is valid—well, I suppose I will have to take Graeme Blatchford to court. The Earl of Chilcombe will have to honor the marriage contract his predecessor signed."

"He could buy back Bluebell Lodge. Why on earth would he give it to Diddenton anyway?"

She told him about the property dispute. "Diddenton wants it for a lime pit."

"Sounds like a very convenient property claim." His frown deepened. "What the devil happened, Blythe? When I mentioned your name last night, some of the fellows went silent. Others were swallowing grins. It was all I could do to not grab one fellow by his neckcloth."

She glanced out of the window and squeezed his hand. "You're a man now, Will, but you're still my little brother, and some things I won't discuss with you. I'll tell you this much though. The last few years of his life, Archie was addicted to opium and other... other certain activities. He... entertained often. Friends with similar tastes. I spent a great deal of my time at Bluebell Lodge. Eventually, all of my time."

"Did he—did *they*, these friends—molest you?"

She let out a breath. "No."

There it was. Not quite a lie. They'd not had much luck with laying hands on her, but the damage to her reputation had denied her the society of most of her neighbors.

The worst had been losing both her son and the unborn babe she'd miscarried.

"Opium. Bloody hell... beg pardon, Blythe. Had Archie been injured? I knew fellows who couldn't shake the stuff after they recovered from wounds."

She shook her head. "After our son died..." She drew in a breath. That pain still festered, along with the resentment she'd carried for far too long.

They'd had a fierce row, and she had removed herself from the north wing where the earl and countess had shared a dilapidated floor. The wing had been built—grandly but poorly—early in the last century by an aspirational Lord Chilcombe. She'd moved herself to the older but more solidly built south wing.

"After our son died, Archie took himself off to London, took on a titled mistress, and dabbled a bit in the delights of the opium dens."

Then he'd returned to Risley Manor, demanding another attempt at an heir.

"I lost another child."

She'd wished for death herself then.

"While I was recovering, I removed myself to Bluebelle Lodge, and he returned to his earlier interests in London."

Where he'd abandoned the aristocratic widows and adulterous wives and pursued not just the opium but other sorts of delights in the more specialized brothels that offered women more adventurous than Blythe. She couldn't tell her little brother about that.

"We… we weren't much together after that. He was in London where his needs were more readily met, and then he decided to…"

He'd appeared with his doxy at Risley Manor, where it was easier for him and his friends to carry on outside the scrutiny of polite society.

"He found a way to accommodate his needs at Risley Manor. His gentlemen friends used to come down for hunting parties and such. I stayed at Bluebell Lodge."

"I see." He glanced out the window, but she could tell he wasn't looking at the passing scene.

"Just how badly did these gentlemen friends importune you, Blythe?"

A tremble went through her and she fought for an even tone. "Any importuning was in their imaginations." Oh, they'd tried. "The servants were loyal to me."

She'd worked hard to win that loyalty. She'd forged a

bond with Mr. Stockwell, the steward, a man as morally strict as the grandparents who'd raised Archie, a man with a much stronger sense than Archie of what a landholder owed to his servants and to the people who worked his land. The steward might have robbed Archie blind, so malleable was her foolish husband. He'd seen what Archie was, and it had taken much persistence on her part to have Stockwell accept that she was more honorable than her husband.

Together, she and Stockwell had made a plan. They'd sent the youngest servants, both males and females, off to other positions with good references, and then hired the oldest servants of good character they could find to replace them. They'd seen to it the staff were well paid for their loyalty to Blythe.

Her own maid, Louisa Miller, had needed to leave as well. She married Stockwell's son and moved to Bluebell Lodge, where she served as housekeeper while her husband managed the farm. Miller's aunt, Mrs. Radley, stepped in as Blythe's lady's maid. Radley had a tolerable sense of fashion, enough for Blythe's needs. Most importantly, she was older and a soldier's widow, one who'd followed the drum and would never be cowed by men behaving badly.

"You're not without a defender now, Blythe." Will's mouth tightened.

Alarmed, she grabbed his chin and turned his face toward her. They'd rounded a corner into Grosvenor Square and would arrive home in mere moments. "You are not to engage in any foolish duels. Do not even think of it."

"You're my sister," he said. "If I can't fight for your honor, tell me what I *can* do to help."

She squeezed her eyes shut on incipient tears. Crying

wouldn't do—it would only incite him to make a foolish challenge.

As the carriage pulled up in front of Chilcombe House, she arranged her careful mask of indifference. "Don't concern yourself a bit. I have all under control. Your mere presence is balm to my soul. Not that I expect you to be tied to my apron strings, no." She smiled and then an idea occurred to her. The search for Lunetta Casale had proven unfruitful, not the least because Bobby, the boy she'd employed, had difficulty accessing the places where the woman might be.

"I expect you to go out and carouse with your friends, Will. No duels, of course. There is one person of interest you might keep an eye out for."

The carriage door swung open. "I must go and change. Come and see me later," she said, "before you go out again. I'll give you the details then."

UPSTAIRS IN HER BEDCHAMBER, SHE FOUND RADLEY SEATED near the fire, mending the lace trim of an unfamiliar purple gown.

"Shall we be moving house today, my lady?" Radley asked by way of greeting.

"Not yet. That gown isn't one of mine, I think."

"You think right. It's Lady Hermione's. I saw the rip and offered my help. She hasn't brought along a lady's maid."

Blythe stripped off her spencer and settled onto the opposite chair. "Very generous of you. Is she back yet from visiting Lady Loughton?"

"Not that I've heard. I'll just be a moment and then help you out of that dress. While you were gone, you had callers. Adwick turned them away. The earl returned not fifteen minutes before you, looking as grim as Wellington after he lost Burgos, the footman said. Went straight to his study."

She almost smiled at Radley's editorial addition— Wellington at Burgos. The footman had not been in the army and was not the sort to follow military news in that close detail. "Did you learn where he went this morning?" She had seen Graeme briefly in the breakfast room. He'd gone out before she'd even had a chance to fill her plate.

"The Foreign Office, the stable lad said."

"I suppose he had to report in."

"Where are we going today?" Radley asked.

"We'll visit the lending library."

Radley raised an eyebrow. The library shelves at Chilcombe House were jammed with books. Archie had not been the sort to stock the shelves with new publications, and neither the maintenance disbursements while the will was pending, nor her personal savings, allowed for the extravagance of purchasing novels. "I've yet to find a copy of Mary Shelley's latest story," she said.

Radley's eyes lit. "You must loan it to me after you've finished, my lady."

A jiggling of the door latch brought a maid with a tray.

"Tea and some lemon cakes, my lady." The maid settled the tray on the small table between the chairs, while Radley clipped a thread and set aside her work.

"How thoughtful, Sarah," Blythe said. "I'm parched. I wonder... would you knock on my brother's door and ask if him if he'd like to join me?"

"Captain Lynford is in the study with his lordship," the maid said.

A niggle of apprehension went through her. "Oh?" What was Will up to?

. . .

BLYTHE HURRIED INTO A NEW GOWN AND MADE HER WAY TO the study. Graeme was there alone, standing near the window and frowning into a snifter of brandy.

He looked up and the frown on his face softened almost imperceptibly.

Framed in the light, his hair flashed hints of gold. She could see traces of the boy he'd once been, a handsome boy, yet he'd grown into an even more attractive man, gentlemanly and more capable of charm than she'd initially thought.

They'd had that first skirmish over her desire to move to Mivart's, but since then he'd been nothing but kind to her.

Kind without raising the suspicion he wanted more.

"Your brother has been in to give me a tongue-lashing. I have no intentions of casting you out, if you're wondering."

She let out a breath. "I'd hoped to catch him before he troubled you with... with my business."

"It seems your business is my business, Blythe."

Blythe. There it was—the use of her Christian name. She'd best leave her guard up.

"No." She shook her head. "I hope all went well with your morning meeting."

"The superior I was reporting to had a visitor. Lord Diddenton."

Diddenton. A slow burn started in the pit of her stomach.

As a new bride, she had met the marquess years ago at one or two society events. Since her return to town, she'd not been included in the social events attended by the lofty members of his circle.

What had Diddenton said? What accusations had he made?

What did he know that Blythe didn't know?

She felt certain that Diddenton hadn't found the other

signed copy of the will, else he'd have proceeded swiftly to evict all the residents of Bluebelle Lodge.

Could she trust Graeme enough to give her a true answer about what had transpired? Or ought she to shrug off the matter until the court ruled on the will? Or perhaps, push Graeme to convince the court there was no new will?

No... not yet. She didn't know Graeme well enough yet to make that last argument.

"I fear I must visit Risley Manor sooner than expected," he said. "I'm leaving early tomorrow. You need not come with me."

Heart pounding, she turned away and asked "Why?"

"Why am I going, or why do you not need to come along?"

Groping her way around a chair and seating herself, it was a moment before she looked up at him and saw the eagerness in his eyes. Her heart stuttered.

"Both, I suppose."

It seemed a matter of self-defense for her to go along and see what he would find. He'd been with Diddenton. Perhaps they'd arranged for Graeme to "discover" the missing will.

"I visited the solicitor, Fleming after the meeting with Diddenton and viewed the pertinent documents regarding the will and the property matter. I'd like to speak with the Risley Manor steward and visit Bluebelle Lodge."

That was a gauntlet thrown down. She needed to be there when he went to Bluebelle Lodge.

He stepped closer, took the chair near hers, and leaned in. "If you did wish to accompany me, you may stay at Bluebelle Lodge. That way, Lady Gravelstone need not come along. Though I shall not cast her out either. Nor your brother. I'll wager Lynford would like some free time in town to sow some wild oats."

She nodded, hiding her relief. Will could seek out Archie's old nurse. Lady Hermione could entertain some of her friends here and be pampered by the Chilcombe servants.

It would be good to check on the safety of everyone at Bluebelle Lodge. Would Graeme be shocked by the presence of the children? A problem to be dealt with later. "Very well," she said. "I'll have my maid begin packing."

At the door she turned back to him. They'd planned to attend another society event that night, a ball in St. James Square. "Shall I send our regrets for tonight?"

"I think we ought to go. I'm curious as to who will attend. Let Will and Lady Gravelston know about our journey tomorrow—but not a word to anyone else."

She suppressed a shudder and nodded. With his spies lurking around Bluebelle Lodge, Diddenton would know soon enough.

* * *

GRAEME GRIPPED HIS GLASS WATCHING HER AS SHE LEFT, ALL the old desires flaming back to life.

Captain Lynford had barged through the door, defending his sister, ready to fight. They'd been out looking at lodgings, and she'd explained why to her brother. Perhaps she'd told Lynford more than Graeme had been able to glean from Fleming's partner. Fleming was still out of town, but at least he had been able to see the marriage contract, the purported new will submitted by Diddenton, and the original will—which surely was the valid will.

He hadn't promised she'd have a home just to mollify her

brother. Nor because it was the right thing to do, the honorable thing. Whatever she'd done, or, more likely, whatever had been done to her...

He wanted her near him. He wanted to get past this formality, the prickliness, the walls she'd put up. He wanted to know her.

And then what, Graeme?

He'd learned to shake off impossible feelings years ago, and he did so again now. Whatever happened, he'd see her settled in some property or other.

Whether it would be Bluebelle Lodge was uncertain. He remembered the place; remembered calling there with a friend for a lark.

No—not a lark. He'd wanted to see *her*. Even then...

There'd been other visits after that. Calf love had struck him with full force. That was all it had been, he a lad just starting to grow whiskers, she a young woman ready to make her come out. Though, as he recalled, her guardian hadn't had money to provide her with a season in London. She was destined to make her curtsy among country society, and he'd dreamed that she'd still be unmarried by the time he was grown.

Around that time, Archie reached his majority, and the maternal grandfather who'd kept a tight leash on him died. He'd been an absent earl since his childhood, but once his grandfather died, he'd hied himself off to Risley Manor, the ancestral home of the Lords Chilcombe, where he'd hosted a grand ball.

And there Archie had met Blythe and seduced her.

Graeme shut his eyes and remembered. She'd been lovely then, but this older, wiser Blythe was lovelier still.

* * *

"AND A GOOD THING IT IS THAT WE HEEDED YOUR COMMAND, my lord, and stopped for the night," Hermione said cheerfully. "I wonder if the road won't wash out with this rain."

Outside, the storm had grown into a gale. Blythe lifted a spoonful of the inn's excellent trifle, while Graeme looked up from his dish. "I do not command ladies," he said. "I merely offer strong suggestions that take into account your welfare and that of the servants and horses."

"And your own," Blythe said. "We *did* have room for you in the chaise where you would have been dry."

"If not warm," Hermione said. "Oh, I'm not complaining. I am glad to make this journey with both of you. You ought to have joined us inside, my lord. Radley's stories were quite riveting."

While Blythe had quietly endured the rattling journey, Hermione and Radley chatted nonstop. Hermione shared stories of her happy marriage, and Radley told tales of her time following the drum. Graeme had ridden along outside, one manly buckskin clad leg distracting her far too often. When the rain began pelting him in earnest, he'd decreed they must stop at this out of the way inn. At least the innkeeper's wife ran a good kitchen.

"We might have asked you about your travels as well, my lord," Hermione added.

Especially this bit of traveling. She had walked away from yesterday's discussion with him and realized later he'd never answered her question: why was he really going?

Her intuition—or perhaps after years of living with Archie, her well-honed protective instincts—told her she ought not trust him. It was to his benefit to resolve the matter of Archie's will and do it quickly so he could get on with his career.

The worry rose again—he might arrange to *find* the will.

On hearing the news of their travel, both Will and Hermione had apparently made the same leap of intuition and insisted that Blythe must stay at Risley Manor and not Bluebelle Lodge. How else was she to learn what was going on?

She was almost certain Mr. Stockwell would tell her; at least she hoped he would.

It was a risk though. Stockwell might see that Graeme Blatchford was a completely different and more reliable article than the late earl. He might decide he didn't need to trouble the late earl's widow with the running of Risley Manor; that in truth, it would be an entirely improper course of action now.

And if another search was conducted... She'd checked every nook and cranny of Archie's suite, of the whole north wing, and even gone through the muniment room. She was almost certain the second copy of the will was not there.

What if it were, though? Or... the nagging worry that ate at her: what if Graeme, in collusion with Diddenton, found a *forged* copy?

Hermione had insisted she come along as a chaperone. Will wanted to come as her male protector. She'd eventually persuaded him that he'd help her best by seeking out Lunetta. With Hermione as chaperone, she'd be safe at Risley Manor.

"We might as well rest for the night," Graeme said. "That way I can deliver you to Bluebelle Lodge while there is still light for the coachman to make his way to Risley Manor."

Perhaps this was the time to bring up her change in plans.

"Since Lady Hermione has been gracious enough to accompany me, I have decided to forgo those plans and stay at Risley. I'll take the rooms I was using in the south wing, and you may stay in the earl's chamber in the north wing."

"I was given to understand that the north wing is in disrepair. Crumbling is the word that was used."

Alarm made her shoulders tense. Graeme had been gathering gossip. He would only know about the condition of Archie's rooms at Risley if he'd been speaking with her late husband's old cronies.

"Lord Vernon speaks," she said and then bit her lip.

Men gossiped, of course they did. They also made things up to show their prowess, things that might ruin a defenseless woman's reputation.

Archie had shredded her reputation long ago, long before she'd left him, but she had a defender now in Will. Though the last thing she wanted him to do was challenge one of Archie's wicked friends.

She swallowed a sigh. Graeme would believe what Archie's friends said, or he wouldn't, and it shouldn't matter to her what he thought of her as long as he acted properly.

She must keep telling herself that.

An inn servant came and cleared the table, and she pushed back her chair, preparing to stand. Graeme reached for her hand.

"Stay for a bit, please. Lady Gravelston, might I have a few moments to speak with Blythe alone? I'll have the waiter escort you upstairs."

Hermione's eyes twinkled. "I can safely climb the stairs on my own, my lord. I bid you both a goodnight."

Graeme walked Hermione to the door, saw her into the servant's care, and returned bearing a bottle of port and two glasses.

CHAPTER SEVEN

"*I* have many questions." He poured a measure of wine into each glass. "And I fear only you have the answers. I should very much like to have a conversation without your brother around glaring daggers at me."

Though he didn't smile, the humor in his voice instinctively warmed her, and that sensation instantly tickled her suspicions. Wheedling men had plagued her for too many years.

"Surely the steward, Mr. Stockwell, can tell you everything you wish to know. You're planning to meet with him, are you not?"

"I am. However, neither Stockwell nor the other man I plan to see was married to my cousin Archie."

She swirled the wine in the glass he'd handed her, trying to read the future in the sparks from the candlelight. "Who is the other man you're visiting?"

"As to that, perhaps you can shed some light. Lord Diddenton thought it a good idea for me to visit with Mr. Jarrow."

Her cheeks heated before succumbing to a cold chill. She

took a sip of the warming drink and reached for composure, training her features to indifference, hiding the fear and alarm that stiffened her.

"The magistrate." She cleared her throat. "I see. I wondered about the sudden need to visit Risley Manor."

Her hand trembled as she raised the glass again. She set it down without drinking and looked up at him. He was watching, waiting, trying to discompose her. He must not see that he was succeeding.

"Mr. Herbert Jarrow had an apoplexy a few months ago," she said. "He is bedridden. His son, Mr. Edward Jarrow, has returned home and was appointed as his replacement."

Perhaps Graeme had not thought to look into the full name of the local magistrate, though he surely would know the name of the Lord Lieutenant for Hampshire, Lord Wellington.

"Lord Diddenton didn't tell me that. Do you know why he thought I should speak with him?"

She pressed her lips together against a rising panic and fought for self-control.

Graeme frowned, looking not angry but concerned. Unwelcome tears pricked the back of her eyes and she blinked them away. This would not do. She was stronger than this.

Graeme leaned in. "Diddenton told me he had Jarrow search Risley Manor for a copy of the missing will."

"The will he *believes* is missing."

"Yes. Could there be any other reason for a search?"

As Blythe's heart quickened, a loud clacking began in her head.

When Archie died, there had been whispers about poison. Mr. Herbert Jarrow, who was both magistrate and coroner, had raised his eyebrows at Blythe. The doctor's eyes had widened and then narrowed speculatively, before he'd shaken his head and ruled that death had been due to a lung fever of several weeks' duration.

Mr. Jarrow had decided that no inquest was needed. A toady of the worst sort, he claimed he didn't wish to bring disrepute to the Chilcombe name.

But she'd seen the doubt in his eyes.

Murder was one crime she hadn't committed, would never have committed. She wouldn't raise the topic—she couldn't bear to see suspicion stir in Graeme.

Holding her glass with two hands to control her trembling, she placed it carefully on the table and stood. "You will have to ask Jarrow or your *friend*, Lord Diddenton, if there was another reason for a search."

Graeme shot to his feet and snatched her hand. "No, you don't, my lady. Don't run away before we speak."

THE CHILLY HAND HE HELD TREMBLED. HE'D SEEN THE PLAY of emotions, the shining eyes, the desire to dodge questions, the indignation.

The fear.

"You don't need to be wary of me, Blythe. I won't hurt you."

She huffed out a breath and tried to tug her hand away.

He clamped his other hand over hers. "You're chilled."

It being only April and a damned wet and cold one at that, the fire screen had not gone up and a few coals burned in the grate. "Come, let us move closer to the fire."

She shook her head. "No, I'll be warm enough when I draw my shawl closer. After you release my hand."

The shawl had slipped over one shoulder and dangled below the puffed-out mutton sleeve of one arm.

"Allow me." Graeme released her and draped the covering, resisting the temptation to stroke the white column of skin above the modest neckline of her carriage gown. He turned her chair to face his before seating her and then taking his own seat.

"Shall I pour you more wine?" he asked.

"I have plenty still."

He refilled his own glass. "You told me the Risley steward is competent and a man of good character. I hope that's true. I know so little about farming I'll need to rely on him. I don't know what this business with Jarrow is, and perhaps Jarrow the younger doesn't know either. What I want you to tell me... I want to know what, aside from this business of the will, was going on at Risley Manor. What was my cousin doing?"

Awkwardly stated but open-ended enough as an opening salvo.

Blythe's gaze skittered over the contents of the table and around the room, everywhere but at him. Whatever memories he'd stirred had not been peaceful ones.

He wouldn't get the truth from her, at least not all of it. Not yet.

He was willing to wait.

Blythe sighed and looked up at him. "We were estranged. I lived at Bluebelle Lodge and visited the manor when... rarely. Archie employed women—nurses, he called them. He entertained gentlemen visitors quite frequently. He was an opium user, and that, eventually, became most important in his life."

All of which accorded with what Morley had told him.

What had happened to the glowing young love he'd seen in Archie and Blythe at the wedding he'd reluctantly, resentfully attended? There were so many missing pieces to the puzzle.

"Mr. Stockwell held estate matters together. We did have one quite bad harvest when the crops were blighted. Archie bestirred himself to obtain a loan. We were able to refinance that loan last year with more favorable terms from Sawley's Bank."

We, she said. Not *they*, the steward and the solicitor.

"That would be the bank belonging to your friend, Lady Loughton?"

"I assure you it was business, not charity. We, er, Stockwell presented a sound plan for repayment. I'm sure he'll be able to explain matters to your satisfaction."

"I look forward to understanding the business of the estate. Tell me about Bluebelle Lodge."

"Bluebelle Lodge," she said, "is mine. Left by Mr. Davies, my guardian, and his wife, with the agreement that it would come to me upon Archie's death. If you remember, when my parents died, I went to live with Mr. Davies and his wife, my former governess. You remember, don't you, visiting me? And when Archie and I… when the marriage contract was being rushed through because of our scandalous…" she waved a hand, "interlude in the garden, the arrangement was made that Bluebelle Lodge would be mine. It was Mr. Davies' idea. I suppose he suspected the sort of husband Archie would turn out to be."

That little speech was a minefield of topics they would have to discuss sooner or later—the scandal he'd caused by seeing them and creating a stir; the rushed wedding; the suspicions about Archie which everyone except Blythe seemed to have seen before the nuptials.

"I was happy at Bluebelle Lodge. And I assure you, my

lord, I won't let you or anyone else surrender it to Diddenton without a fight."

"I know," he said nodding, but she was warmed up now and didn't seem to hear him.

"I'm anxious to see the state of things. I haven't been home in a while."

She took a healthy swig of her wine while he pondered that. According to Morley, Blythe hadn't been in London until the start of the Season. She herself said she hadn't been residing at Risley Manor. What had Lord Vernon said? Something about her going to stay at some widowed lady's home?

"You didn't remain at Bluebelle Lodge during your mourning?"

"I went... I went to the home of a friend. Lest you accuse me of residing with a lover, there is a league of widowed ladies who keep a secluded home in the country for other widows who need... a place to stay. People like me."

"Like you? But you had a home, three homes, plus a few outlying properties belonging to Chilcombe."

Her mouth firmed. "Indeed. At the end, I didn't love Archie, but I mourned the pathetic waste of a man's life, the man he might have been, and I was furious, in a rage almost. There was... is, a persistent suitor who torments me. I found I needed to go somewhere and hide from him, and from my own desire to do him an injury."

"Lord Vernon."

"I am not a murderer."

She tugged her shawl tightly and stormed out before he even had a chance to push back his chair and stand.

She wasn't a murderer.

Someone, somewhere, had accused her of murder. Archie's?

Or perhaps the suspected murder victim was the other fellow on the road, the one who'd cracked his head on a boulder. The one carrying the will to London.

What she must have gone through in her marriage. He wouldn't believe for a moment that she had done anything nefarious, certainly not murder. But he wasn't certain he could blame her if she had.

* * *

BLYTHE PUSHED BACK THE COVERS AND PADDED TO THE window, grabbing a lap blanket against the chill.

It had rained all through the last day's journey and the night. Though the day was gray, she guessed it was long past dawn.

Wrung out by traveling and nerves, she'd slept longer than she meant to.

In the breakfast room, a footman, one of the old retainers who'd held on through the madness, informed her that the earl had breakfasted quite early and gone to visit Mr. Stockwell. The sideboard had been cleared and he hurried to fetch her fresh toast and tea.

"Ah, good morning." The cheerful greeting came from Hermione. "I broke my fast earlier but I'll have another cup of tea. Did you hear that downpour last night?"

While Hermione waxed on about the weather and the roads, Blythe buttered her toast.

"Lord Chilcombe was leaving when I came down for breakfast. I told him he ought to rest his mount and let the roads dry, but he insisted he would go." She smiled over the rim of her cup. "I do like a man of action."

Despite herself, Blythe felt a blush rising. If she wasn't mistaken, Hermione was matchmaking.

She ignored the remark. "He was off to find the land steward at his cottage. He told me yesterday he meant to visit the local magistrate as well. So perhaps he's out touring the estate, or off to visit Mr. Jarrow."

"Might he have gone to your Bluebelle Lodge?" Hermione asked.

She considered the question. Mr. Stockwell the younger would have all in good order, but she'd like to be there herself to explain the presence of the two children, rather than leaving it to the Stockwells and the nursemaid, Hetty.

"I suppose anything is possible," she said. "In which case, I must hie myself there this morning to make sure all is well when the lord of the manor pays a call. If you can tolerate the muddy roads, I would welcome your company."

Hermione smiled. "I wouldn't miss it, my dear."

* * *

WITH DIRECTIONS FROM THE HEAD GROOM AND HIS OWN patchy memory of the area, Graeme stopped briefly at Stockwell's cottage, where he found that the steward had gone out to visit one of the tenants but would return midday. The housekeeper promised to pass on the message to Stockwell that Graeme would meet with him that afternoon.

Then he found his way easily enough to Stonebridge Manor, the Jarrows' estate a short distance from Risley Manor. He met Mr. Edward Jarrow on the lane returning from a morning ride.

He followed Jarrow to the stables, where both men left their mounts, and they entered the house through a side door. Jarrow led him up to the library.

"I am glad to meet you, my lord," Jarrow said, when both men were seated.

Edward Jarrow was a man of about his own age, or perhaps a little older. Of medium height and average appearance, he had a friendly demeanor and a look of keen intelligence.

"I'm told you replaced your father as magistrate after he fell ill."

Was he acquainted with the Lord Lieutenant of Hampshire, Wellington, who would have been the man who selected him?

Jarrow waved a hand. "Yes. Coroner as well. When I left the army, my brother was still here. I went north to help a friend who'd inherited an estate. Together we put things there in order."

And now he was in Hampshire to put things in order here? The stables at Stonebridge Manor and this tidy room appeared up to snuff.

"Did you serve under Wellington?"

"In the Peninsula, and of course, at Waterloo. Not that I was on his staff, but I had occasion to meet him."

"I served for a time on his staff in Paris after the peace."

"You shall see him on a different footing when you take your seat in the Lords. Or have you done so already?"

"I just returned to England a few days ago."

"From America, I read in the newssheets."

"The far western shores of Canada. Did you fight there?"

"No, alas, or I might have been tempted to stay. Second son, you know? As it is, my brother's wife inherited a large estate in Virginia, so he went to make his fortune there."

"You have a fine property here."

"Yes. I have improvements in mind, but I've had to go slowly. My father and brother bumped heads quite a lot over the management, and I'm sure Father and I would have disagreed as well. Father's unfortunate illness has resolved that issue, and as there's no entail, the property will be mine after he passes." He smiled ruefully. "That is perhaps too much information upon first meeting, my lord, though it is common enough knowledge among our neighbors and will answer your questions before you can find a diplomatic way to formulate them."

Graeme couldn't help laughing. He liked Jarrow's straightforwardness. The tale *had* piqued his curiosity.

"Thank you, Jarrow. I confess, I know a bit about agricultural trade, but I have much to learn about estate management. I may need to call on your expertise. I've yet to meet with my land steward."

"Stockwell is a good man. His son has done a fine job of managing Bluebelle Lodge as well."

That was welcome news about Stockwell, confirming what Blythe had told him, and quite unexpected news about the son.

Before Graeme could comment, a tea tray arrived with an assortment of cakes and biscuits and Jarrow had the footman serve them.

Jarrow's servants, the ones he'd seen so far, were a good thirty years younger than those serving at Risley Manor.

"How do you find Risley Manor?" Jarrow asked when the footman had departed.

"Old." He shook his head and laughed ruefully. "I was just thinking to myself that neither Risley Manor nor Chilcombe House has more than one or two servants under the age of fifty."

One could imagine why that could be true of the females, but the male servants also?

Jarrow frowned and studied the biscuits, suddenly quiet.

"Did you know the late Lord Chilcombe?" Graeme asked, hoping to draw out information.

"I was at school and then went off to the army before he took up residence at Risley Manor. I met him and Lady Chilcombe once at a local celebration after Toulouse when I was home on leave."

"Ten years ago."

"Yes. How is Lady Chilcombe?" Jarrow asked, a spark of curiosity in his eyes. "I'd heard she'd left the area after the earl's death to stay with friends."

"Yes, for a time. But she's been residing in London most recently. She accompanied me to Risley Manor along with an older friend of hers, Lady Hermione Gravelstone, a relation of Lord Loughton."

Jarrow fixed him with a serious look. "So, you've called upon the local magistrate even before meeting with Stockwell."

Graeme placed his saucer and cup on the table. "Yes. You can imagine this is not just a social call, Jarrow. This matter of the supposedly lost will disinheriting Lady Chilcombe is of great concern. The matter of who holds title to Bluebelle Lodge as well. Lord Diddenton sought me out and suggested I speak to you."

Jarrow sat taller and steepled his fingers. "To speak to me, or to my father?"

"He seems the sort of man who would know that your father is ill, and that you've replaced him. He told me he had you search Risley Manor for the will."

"That was certainly my father he was speaking of. It was just before he fell ill. In any case, there is no way you may communicate with Father. He has not been able to speak since his stroke."

"Did he leave notes about the matter? Is there a coroner's report?"

"No inquest was held. Lord Chilcombe was ill with a lung fever in the days before he died. The physician's reported cause of death was accepted." Jarrow pressed his lips together as if deciding whether to share something unsavory. "There were, however, notes. Speculation that the earl may have been poisoned, and who might have done it."

"Poisoned by whom?"

"Father's list included the name of the earl's, er, personal nurse, as well as the names of those involved with preparing and serving his food. Others were his valet, though the man had unexpectedly left his service a month earlier, too long a time for a poisoning, Father thought. His friend, Lord Vernon Falfield, had visited just before his demise. And... the list included Lady Chilcombe."

His fingers tightened around his cup. "What do you think, Jarrow? Your honest opinion."

Jarrow gave him a long look. "Every human life has value, and murder is a fearsome crime. Yet the punishment is fearsome as well. Ultimately, Father decided to not drag the name of the neighborhood's titled family through the mud of an inquest."

"But I ask again, what do *you* think?"

Jarrow frowned. "The late earl is said to have led a dissipated life, and he was, by all accounts, at the end quite ill with fever. What poison would cause that? Or, if he died from an excess of laudanum, who's to say he hadn't dosed himself accidentally?" He shook his head. "The most likely suspect with opportunity would be the nurse. But did she have a motive? She was not remembered in the earl's will, neither the one signed at the time of the earl's marriage, nor the new one Diddenton claims exists, and the earl's death ended her position. She left the day after for London."

"Before being questioned?"

"Father spoke to her about the earl's death. Not about the alleged new will though."

"Diddenton told me there were servants who knew the new will had been signed. The nurse ought to be interviewed about it. Do you have her address in London?"

"No. To that end, I've made written inquiries with the usual agencies. With Father's illness and estate matters, I've had to delay a trip to London to search for her. Lunetta Casale. I imagine she wasn't someone the earl would have found at a regular hiring agency."

In other words, he would have to visit the brothels. Morley could take on that task. He would write to him immediately.

"If her testimony supports Diddenton's claim," Graeme said, "Diddenton will be searching for her as well."

"I've wondered about that. I've wondered whether Diddenton's son, Lord Vernon, might know her whereabouts. By all accounts, he was a regular visitor to Risley Manor."

"Did your father talk to him?"

"Only briefly when he paid a call. The marquess purchased Wickworth Hall some years ago and the son was staying there."

"Wickworth Hall?" He vaguely remembered the property from his childhood visits. "Near Bluebelle Lodge?"

"Yes. The estates march alongside each other. You didn't know?"

Graeme shook his head. "Convenient for him."

Jarrow eyed him a moment and then went on, "Father spoke to the staff at Risley Manor and searched the house for poisons. None were found. Three of the old servants—including the disappearing valet—had small bequests in the will. The old will, that is. The new one leaves them nothing. But there was no reason to believe the housekeeper, butler, or missing valet poisoned him."

"And Lady Chilcombe?"

"Father spoke to her that day. She came over from Bluebelle Lodge before the earl passed away but she was never alone with him. In the end, he could not find evidence to accuse her." He leaned forward. "Certainly, Lady Chilcombe had motive under the terms of the will signed at the time of her marriage. But this business of a new will... Diddenton has written speculating that Lady Chilcombe stole both signed copies of the new will, and might have had something to do with Sir Morris Pierpont's death as well as her husband's, so that she could thwart the new will's provision to cede Bluebelle Lodge to Diddenton."

"Preposterous." Graeme rose and stalked to the mantel, staring into the empty hearth, but seeing the fear in Blythe's eyes. *I am not a murderer.*

"That is my sentiment as well, Chilcombe." Jarrow stood and handed him a brandy.

"I'm glad to hear it," Graeme said. "How did Pierpont die?"

"He overturned his phaeton in bad weather after leaving Risley Manor and smashed his head on a rock. Supposedly, he was carrying the new will, but it was never found among his belongings. Lady Chilcombe had visited her husband just as Sir Morris was leaving and then she returned to Bluebelle Lodge where she was residing."

"Lady Chilcombe is no murderer."

"Diddenton is pressing me. I should like to speak to her. Not to accuse her but to better grasp the circumstances."

Graeme bit back an oath. Hadn't she been through enough?

Still… she was trying to find her way back into society, and she would have to sway opinion to her side in the matter of the will so she could hold on to her inheritance. Would cooperation be the right path?

"I understand that she has only a brother to support her, and he's away in the army."

"As it happens, Lady Chilcombe's brother has just arrived home on leave. He is staying at Chilcombe House."

"Then perhaps he may be present when I—"

"*I* will support Lady Chilcombe during any inquiry."

Jarrow gave him a long look and nodded.

Let him think what he wanted. Blythe was his to look after. "I'm not convinced that my cousin was in a state of mind to give due thought to the property matter, or in fact, to understand the contents of a new will. I shall need to see evidence before part of the estate is handed over willy-nilly in breach of Lady Chilcombe's marriage contract."

Jarrow raised his glass. "Bravo. I shall help you in any way possible to discover the truth."

"Edward." A portly matron filled the doorway and advanced into the room. "You have a visitor, I see."

Graeme bowed while Jarrow introduced his mother. The glint in her squinty gaze and her obsequious smile told Graeme she already knew who he was.

CHAPTER EIGHT

"Come in, come in, Georgiana." Mrs. Jarrow beckoned to a young woman with a striking resemblance to Mr. Jarrow.

He introduced his sister.

While Graeme expressed the usual platitudes at making the young lady's acquaintance, her mother glowed and insisted he stay and hear Georgiana play the pianoforte.

Lady Hermione's playful matchmaking was much less offensive. Perhaps that was because Blythe was meant to be his match.

Meant to be his match. It could be the perfect solution to their problems, if he could convince her.

For now, he allowed himself to be escorted to the parlor and preempted his hostess's questioning by asking her about the surrounding neighbors and parish. While she reported, he nodded and made polite responses, and her daughter sat quietly watching the exchange with the same keen look of intelligence displayed by her brother. The musical performance had been forgotten.

Mrs. Jarrow finally paused and took a breath. "Have you only just arrived at Risley Manor?"

"Indeed," he said. "Late yesterday afternoon."

"And you have called on us immediately. We are honored, are we not, Georgiana?"

"Yes, Mama," she said, dutifully, sharing a hint of a smile with her brother.

Perhaps it was obvious to Miss Jarrow that he'd been paying a call on her brother and not her mother.

Ah well, if he meant to settle in even for a short while at Risley Manor, he'd best find his way through the maze of matchmaking mamas.

Though when he thought of his need for a wife, it was Blythe, *only* Blythe, who came to mind.

"You must come for dinner," Mrs. Jarrow said. "We have an excellent cook. Tonight... oh, not tonight. Tonight is the village assembly. Heavens, you must attend, Lord Chilcombe. It will be quite a jolly occasion—dignified though, of course—and a chance for you to meet all your neighbors."

An assembly that very night. Would Blythe want to attend? She'd refused to dance at the ball they'd attended. He'd have another chance with her here, to hold her in his arms in a waltz, perhaps.

As he pondered how to respond to the invitation, his hostess went on.

"Forgive me for chattering away, my lord," Mrs. Jarrow said, "I haven't given you a moment to speak. You've arrived so suddenly we know very little about you. Is there a Lady Chilcombe who will be, er, joining you soon, or perhaps, who is already in residence at Risley Manor?"

Jarrow sighed. "Chilcombe, my mother is asking whether you are married."

"I have no wife," Graeme said. "However, there *is* a Lady Chilcombe in residence at Risley Manor. My late cousin's widow has kindly accompanied me to acquaint me with the staff and the estate. Her widowed friend, Lady Hermione Gravelston, has come also."

Mrs. Jarrow's brows knitted together. "Georgiana," she said. "Fetch my shawl from my room, please."

Miss Jarrow showed no inclination to leave until her mother rather sharply prompted her again. She slid an apologetic look toward Graeme and departed.

Mrs. Jarrow had more to say, and it would be something unpleasant if she didn't want her daughter to hear.

He didn't want to hear it either. "I beg your pardon," he said smoothly. "But I must away. Regarding that other matter, Jarrow—"

"My lord," Mrs. Jarrow put up a hand to stop him. "Before you leave, it behooves me to say, well, you and Lady Chilcombe residing together at Risley Manor. Well, Lady Chilcombe is not... is not *received* by any of the better families in the area, and I... I wonder if any lady friend of *hers* serving as chaperone is quite the thing."

"Mother..." Jarrow said in a warning tone.

"You have been out of the country for many years, I'm told, so perhaps you are not aware of the... the... gossip about..."

Under her son's fierce glare, she pressed her lips together.

"What a shame," Graeme said. "I had thought to host a party, perhaps a picnic or reception or other sort of fête to meet neighbors. You are telling me no one will accept Chilcombe hospitality because her ladyship is in residence? Well, I will certainly have the invitations sent anyway and we will see what we see."

He stood and dipped his head. "Mrs. Jarrow. Jarrow. Good day to you."

"I'll walk with you to the stables," Jarrow said.

Boots crunching on the gravel, Jarrow kept pace with Graeme.

"My apologies for my mother's frankness," Jarrow said, as they neared the stables. "In truth, she is only saying openly what people will whisper behind backs." He stopped and grimaced. "The *better* families, that is."

"The other-than-better families are not cutting Lady Chilcombe?" Graeme asked, struggling to master his sarcasm.

Jarrow glanced at him. "There are cats in that crowd as well. However, in certain *lesser* families, Lady Chilcombe is pitied, and in one or two others, she's seen as heroic."

"How so?"

"It is not my story to tell. But if you invite the Jarrows to a party, my sister and I shall attend, and beware; I know my mother, and wild horses wouldn't keep her away."

"She and the other ladies from better families."

"They'll want to have a look at the scandalous Lady Chilcombe and her lady friend who might be not quite the thing. Forgive me, Lord Chilcombe. I'm appalled at my mother's gossiping. Unless it would be very hard on the ladies, it might be a good thing for your party to attend the assembly tonight and confront the dragons head on. I will promise a dance to each lady, if you will lead Georgiana out once."

Graeme paused outside the stable and studied the other man.

Jarrow held up both hands and laughed. "Not matchmaking. Georgiana's interests lie elsewhere. It will not hurt her to be seen dancing with an earl there."

"If I were a wagering man, I'd bet that neither lady in my party will dance at all. But in any case, I will ask your sister to dance. If I attend."

"The assembly rooms are at the White Horse Inn. Your grooms will know how to find it." Jarrow extended his hand and Graeme shook it. "I'll send over my father's report and notes for you to review. Let me know when I may call on Lady Chilcombe."

A horse clattered into the stable yard.

"Rupert," Jarrow said. "What's afoot?"

"I'm looking for Lord Chilcombe."

"I'm Chilcombe," Graeme said, unease rising. The lad couldn't be more than ten, and his trousers and boots were coated in mud.

Rupert tugged his forelock and reported. Mr. Stockwell would not be able to see him today. A drain at Bluebelle Lodge had caved in and flooded the new corn. He was helping young Mr. Stockwell see to it.

"You've just come from there?" Graeme asked.

"Yes, milord. Going right back."

"Was it the newly dug drain near Wickworth Hall?" Jarrow asked, looking grim.

"Yessir." Rupert nodded. "Just like the last one."

There'd been other incidents?

"Wait a moment, lad," Graeme said. "I'm coming with you."

"I'm coming as well," Jarrow said. "Have you eaten, lad?"

"No, sir."

"Go along to the kitchen." Jarrow spotted a maid across the yard leaving the kitchen garden. "Jilly, tell Cook to feed this lad and make up sandwiches. Go along, Rupert. Eat and bring food for the others. I'll show his lordship the way."

Grooms ran to saddle their mounts.

"Did the downpour last night cause this?" Graeme asked.

"I saw that drain. It shouldn't have."

"Right, then." Graeme mounted and followed Jarrow out of the stable yard.

* * *

BLYTHE AND LOUISA STOCKWELL EACH HEFTED A HEAVY basket, while behind them, Joseph, their man of all work, trudged along carrying three shovels and grumbling.

Rupert, one of the young grooms, had brought word that the lower fields had been flooded. It had taken longer than Blythe wished to settle the children with Hermione and the nursemaid, find shovels, and organize food.

They came through a thicket and saw the field.

Tears sprang to her eyes. A sloping field of young budding plants rolled down and disappeared into a shallow lake.

Joseph swore quietly and Louisa gasped. Blythe choked down the moisture flooding her throat.

In the distance, they saw the men wielding shovels. The weather had turned and the day was unseasonably warm, the sun high in the sky. Some of them had shed not only their coats but their shirts as well.

"They're sure to be hungry," Louisa said, her quiet voice restoring equanimity to the moment, as usual.

"Yes," Blythe said, and led the way through the higher ground, dodging the young plants so as not to squash hope for at least a small harvest.

With their attention focused on the task at hand, the men did not see them coming. But the tableau spread before them became clearer as they approached.

Four horses grazed languidly. There were seven—no

eight? men—with shovels, digging. Five of them had stripped down to their trousers.

Blythe halted. Louisa paused beside her and put a hand up to shield her eyes.

"I see I won't have to wash mud out of my man's shirt," she said. "And is that Mr. Jarrow? What would his mother say if she saw him like this?"

Blythe heard the humor in her voice, but her heart pounded wildly and she couldn't look away.

"That's Mr. Sanders from Holly Farm and his son," Louisa said. "But who is that tall fellow? He has almost as fine a back as my Samuel."

Yes. It was a fine back; much finer than Archie's had been. She'd never imagined anything so muscular under the linen and wool of his shirt and coats.

And he was digging, wielding a shovel with men who worked the land—his land.

Stockwell would certainly, after so many years working for Archie, find this a novelty. For her part, she could stand here a while and watch the play of the muscles across his back.

He turned and a ripple of lust went through her. His chest was just as enticing, with its sprinkling of brown hair narrowing down to his waistband.

Graeme thrust the shovel into the wet ground, wiped his hands on his trousers, and went for his shirt.

Blythe hastily turned to Louisa.

"That's Graeme Blatchford," she said.

Louisa's eyes widened. "Lord Chilcombe? What is he like *now?*"

"You remember him?"

Louisa had been a young maid at Bluebelle Lodge before

Blythe met Archie. Perhaps she'd seen Graeme when he called there, and later, at Blythe's wedding.

"Of course. He's the one who raised the alarm on your, er, indiscretion, and caused all the fuss."

Shame rose in her. Despite the years that had passed, she still remembered the night Graeme had stumbled upon her and Archie in the dark garden.

That was a long time ago.

"He is honorable," Blythe said, "I think." Her instincts told her that. Could she trust that to be true? Or—she glanced at him again as he poked his muscled arms into his sleeves—was this sudden instinct to trust merely the result of the lust she was feeling? "That is, we shall see, but he has been decent, so far."

"Well, he's grown up quite nicely," Louisa said thoughtfully and then she laughed. "You mustn't tell Samuel I'm gawking at other men."

Graeme strode to meet them, tucking in his shirt tail, the shirt opening flapping as he walked. Mud coated his boots and the bottom of his trousers and smeared his cheek. The elder Stockwell hurried over with him.

Blythe made introductions and set about pouring drinks.

"We must speak with you, Blythe," Graeme said, accepting one of the tin cups and draining it.

"I'll have the other men break and eat," Mr. Stockwell said. "And then I'll rejoin you. If you wish, my lord."

"I do wish," Graeme said. "And bring Jarrow along as well."

"Thank you," Graeme said, turning back to the women. "It was kind of you to bring food and drink out instead of sending a servant."

"And it's kind of you to wield a shovel today."

"Kind?" His smile was rueful. "Yes, well, in my first morning at Risley Manor I've met the magistrate, my steward and yours, and had my first experience of farming. Also, my first glimpse of what looks to be trouble."

"Trouble?"

He nodded. "And I suppose I should apologize for my undress."

That rush of heat swept through Blythe again.

He looked... *bronzed* was the word that came to mind. His hair was lighter, his skin, already tanned from so many months at sea, glowed. His eyes sparkled from the exercise, and the bit of exposed skin revealed a strong neck corded with muscles. Amazingly, he still smelled of starch and shaving cologne.

He looked supremely masculine.

Feelings rumbled in her, feelings she hadn't experienced since her very brief courtship. Feelings driven out by her loathsome husband and his friends.

"Are you quite all right, Blythe?" he asked.

"No," she said. "That is, I mean, what has happened here?"

"The men here believe this is no accident."

"I've received news of a few problems at Bluebelle Lodge," she said. "Mr. Stockwell didn't think I should concern myself much about them. Not with the other troubles on my plate."

The Stockwells and Jarrow joined them. The berm they'd labored to build in late winter had been damaged. Intentionally, it appeared.

Her hands curled into fists. That could only be Diddenton's doing. Oh, he wouldn't have dirtied his own hands directly, but he'd have ordered the damage to be done, all with the intent of driving out the occupants of Bluebelle Lodge.

The presence of the magistrate caused her to temper her speech. "Would the marquess stoop so low?" she asked.

Stockwell glanced at Jarrow, frowning. He shared her concerns, but he wouldn't speak openly either, not to accuse such a high-ranking peer.

BLYTHE HAD SPOKEN CAREFULLY, BUT GRAEME SAW THE anger in her face.

"Given his interest in the property, we have to consider the possibility," he said.

Blythe nodded. "That brook is flowing from Diddenton land."

Graeme looked toward the higher fallow ground.

"That's Wickworth Hall land. His main estate is miles away," Samuel Stockwell said. "His steward comes by at times. I've chased his surveyors off the property more than once."

Graeme rubbed at the mud on his cheek. "Will anyone from Diddenton's estate be attending tonight's assembly?"

"Though it's one of the largest gatherings in the area, the family has never appeared," Jarrow said. "We'd best finish up here. What do you think, Stockwell, another hour's worth of work?"

"My lord, Mr. Jarrow," the elder Stockwell said, "we thank you for your help. Joseph can take your place."

"No, I'll stay and see this through," Graeme said. "I have much to learn. Joseph and Rupert can escort Lady Chilcombe to Risley Manor."

"Lady Hermione is at Bluebelle Lodge," Blythe said. "We

came in the gig and can find our own way back to Risley Manor."

"Lady Hermione cannot come for help, should one of the marquess's surveyors appear on the lane."

Defiance flashed in her eyes, the way it had when he stopped her from leaving Chilcombe House.

He led Blythe away from the others. "Please, my dear. We must be cautious as we determine what's afoot."

She studied him for a long moment and finally said, "And how do *we* do that?"

"I've hired an investigator to look into Diddenton's claim. I plan to write and have him begin searching for the nurse Jarrow told me about. And there's an assembly tonight at the White Horse Inn. I plan to attend. Perhaps someone knows something about what happened here today. And if we learn nothing tonight, it may be I can make the acquaintance of neighbors who'll be willing to talk to me privately later. The worst that can happen is that they'll shun me, and I expect they'll be too curious to do that. Will you and Lady Hermione accompany me?"

She'd stiffened as he spoke, and he saw it again—that look of fear, quickly masked.

The urge to take her in his arms and comfort her was overpowering but he wouldn't touch her. For one thing he was too muddy, for the other... there were too many people around. He wouldn't give the gossips fodder.

"You've gone pale but you must not be afraid. You faced the ton by yourself, Blythe, can you not face your neighbors? You'll have two friends by your side."

She lifted her chin and, lips trembling, nodded.

He went back to his work, watching her gather the baskets, her housekeeper and her two escorts, her face grim.

What did she know of the nastiness of Mrs. Jarrow and

her cronies? Had they cut her before? What the hell had Archie put her through?

Because he could no longer believe the stories of Blythe's perfidy were true. She was most certainly innocent.

If the *better families* attending tonight's assembly thought to cut either Blythe or Lady Hermione in Graeme's presence, they would be in for a surprise.

CHAPTER NINE

"Chin up," Hermione whispered as they stepped into the assembly room.

A reminder to breathe might have been more suitable. Blythe needed the encouragement, here even more so than during her forays in London society. The good people of Risley and the surrounding environs had made their feelings toward the inhabitants of Risley Manor very clear, including the one inhabitant who resided most of the time at Bluebelle Lodge. Perhaps especially her, since... What was it she'd heard whispered? *She was no better than she ought to be.*

A vigorous country dance was underway, so their appearance was not immediately noted.

"What a lovely setting," Hermione said loudly. "Much like the assembly rooms where I live. And the spring flowers—someone in Risley has a very nice garden."

"I see Jarrow is dancing," Graeme said from Hermione's other side, so affably Blythe wanted to reach around Hermione and poke him.

That afternoon, he'd thought she'd gone pale because of

this event. It was true, she supposed, that attending the assembly was part of the reason. To be cut by the likes of Mrs. Jarrow was one thing, but for her to do it in front of Graeme and Hermione would amplify the humiliation.

The other, truly more worrisome reason why she'd gone pale had to do with him hiring an investigator to search for Lunetta Casale. If Graeme's man found her before Blythe's brother did... If the horrible woman had the will...

Heads began turning their way, ladies in their country finery and men in their evening frock coats. Her own gown was the one she'd had made by Madame La Fanelle for her ball, a pale blue silk with capped sleeves and decorative tucking, and a lace trim along the hem, with a hair piece to match with an ostrich feather. Radley had unexpectedly packed it, and Hermione's best gown as well.

They wouldn't shame Graeme with their dress. He, on the other hand, had not had time to visit a tailor. Perhaps no one in this crowd of gentlemen would notice that his coats weren't the first stare of fashion.

He'd returned to Risley Manor later than expected and was so encrusted with grime he'd needed to soak for a while before dressing. They'd not had a chance to speak about what he'd gleaned from Mr. Jarrow.

He'd learned about Lunetta, but what about Sir Morris Pierpont's death?

She had committed no murder—not Pierpont's or Archie's—and yet guilt ate a hole in her nerves.

"And there is Jarrow's sister," Graeme said. "Dancing also. I've promised a dance with her."

Blythe's back stiffened with a sudden spurt of... jealousy? *Good heavens.* What was wrong with her? Of course, Graeme was an enticing morsel for the single ladies here. Providing their papas could find that his character was better than his predecessor's, they would be queueing up for the countess sweepstakes. A few of them wouldn't care about character, they'd simply look at him and see a handsome, virile man in his prime. That would certainly be the case with the widows and unhappily married matrons.

She didn't care. Of course she didn't. As long as she had what was promised to her in the marriage contract signed by the Earl of Chilcombe.

And as long as she was never accused of murder.

She pulled her thoughts together, reminding herself that they were here to introduce the new Earl and to learn whatever they could about the activities of the nefarious Diddenton.

As well as to survive an evening with a community of people who hated her.

"Do you know any of the older ladies in that group by the second pillar?" Hermione asked. "They have turned their attention our way."

"The large woman in the gray dress is Mrs. Jarrow," Graeme said. "I met her this morning."

"She looks displeased," Hermione mused. "Are you acquainted with her, Blythe?"

Mrs. Jarrow had induced the forever absent vicar to have the weak-kneed curate he employed ban her and the children from attendance at Sunday services. Archie had laughed off the insult toward her.

"It has been years since we've crossed swords," Blythe said.

"I am intrigued," Hermione said. "My lord, may we walk that way? Perhaps I'll allow the introduction and I may cross swords with her as well. Blythe?"

She swallowed a sigh. "Why not." Let the new Earl of Chilombe see what she was up against. He could show her what he was made of. She suspected the impeccable fellow would eventually yield to society's judgments.

As they approached the cluster of matrons, the dance ended, and the dispersing couples scattered about the large room, blocking their path.

"Lord Chilcombe."

Blythe recognized Mr. Jarrow from their afternoon encounter when she'd seen him without his shirt, coats, and neckcloth. He looked considerably more polished now, though not quite as handsome as Graeme. He surely must be turning the heads of the young ladies gathered here tonight. Was there a younger Mrs. Jarrow? Graeme hadn't mentioned one.

A young lady came to stand next to him, a curious smile on her face.

"Miss Jarrow," Graeme said, and made introductions.

The girl curtsied prettily, and Mr. Jarrow bowed, an amused look on his face.

"I recalled after seeing you this afternoon, Mr. Jarrow, that we met many years ago, before I married, and just before you left to join the army," Blythe said. "I had recently come to live at Bluebelle Lodge."

"Ah," he said. "That was a busy time, and I'm flattered that you remember seeing me. I suspect you saw rather too much of me this afternoon, Lady Chilcombe. My apologies."

In anyone else, that would seem like gratuitous flirtation, but Mr. Jarrow's open, friendly manners made it seem more like a brotherly sort of apology. He was nothing like his father.

"I thank you for your help today, sir," she said. "It was very kind of you to labor so."

"Stockwell is hopeful the crop may be saved," Mr. Jarrow said. "That is all the thanks I need."

She took a long look at him. Not only was he nothing like his father, but he might also be a man of integrity and... substance. A friend, perhaps, of a sort, to the residents of Bluebelle Lodge.

An ally against the marquess? Who could tell, and it was better not to trust too soon.

"You have arrived late but we are glad you have come," Miss Jarrow said. "We also were late, delayed waiting for Edward." She leaned closer and whispered, "Thank heavens he is wearing gloves."

Her brother grinned, not at all discomfited by the teasing, and Blythe's nerves eased further.

Out of the corner of her eye, though, she saw Mrs. Jarrow trying to elbow her way through the crowd gathered around them.

Others must have recognized Lady Chilcombe and made the leap to identify Graeme. He was quite the attraction.

The master of ceremonies announced a country dance to be followed by a waltz before the musicians broke for the supper on offer.

"Lady Chilcombe, may I have the honor?" Mr. Jarrow asked.

Though her heart sought out Graeme, she refrained from looking at him. He'd said he planned to dance with Miss Jarrow, and perhaps Mr. Jarrow would be the only gentleman here brave enough to dance with the scandalous countess. What harm could come from a country dance with the new local magistrate?

She looked to Hermione, who gave her blessing to being left alone, then bowed her head and said yes. Miss Jarrow very prettily accepted Graeme's request to dance.

"Your waltz, however, Lady Chilcombe, is mine," Graeme said, with that self-assured smile that had her heating inside from annoyance and... oh, she must admit it... desire.

Before they could step out, the crowd parted to allow in a gentleman, and Mr. Jarrow made introductions. The local curate, Mr. Tidwell, was a different one from the man who'd snubbed her and her charges.

"Go and dance, my dears," Hermione said. "Perhaps Mr. Tidwell will introduce me to Mrs. Jarrow." She leaned close and whispered. "Or I will introduce myself, bold chit that I am."

Blythe laughed, and following Jarrow into the line, ruthlessly turned her mind to the dance at hand, ignoring the curious stares and whispers behind fans.

The same thing had happened in London and she had danced there, yes she had. Then, as now, the steps had come back to her, though she was so nervous she found she had to pay careful attention.

With the twin distractions of Mrs. Jarrow barreling down on Hermione, and Graeme flirting with Miss Jarrow, it wasn't as easy here in Risley.

In the times they drew together in the country dance, Mr. Jarrow made polite conversation. Though they started with the weather and crops, he proceeded on to ask about her year of mourning, where she had stayed, and how she'd found London.

She answered his courteous interrogation as truthfully as possible without giving any real information. By the time the dance ended, her nerves were crackling and she was happy to be handed over to Graeme.

Across the dance floor, Hermione chatted, to all appearances amiably, with the curate and Mrs. Jarrow. Her face revealed nothing while Mrs. Jarrow's bore a grim mask of disapproval. The curate was mopping his brow.

The Jarrows were an influential family in the parish with a family tie to the absent vicar who held the living.

Graeme took her hand and followed her line of sight. Hermione smiled their way and made a shooing noise as the quartet shuffled music and other couples paired up. Graeme faced her and continued to hold her hand.

"I never thought to ask it before," he said. "Who is the patron for this parish?"

"You are," Blythe said. "The Earl of Chilcombe."

"And the vicar? Does he live in the parish?"

"He has several parishes. In the past, he would visit perhaps once a year. He's had the living forever, or at least since the previous earl, Archie's grandfather, appointed him. Your grandfather as well, I suppose."

"No doubt the vicar is some elderly second or third son of one of Grandfather's peers."

Graeme's and Archie's grandfather had lived just long enough to see Archie's birth and Archie's father's death. Archie, an earl by the age of ten, had been snatched up by his maternal grandparents and given such a strict Christian upbringing that, when he was free, he undertook to make up for lost time.

"The curate seems a decent sort," Graeme said, interrupting her thoughts.

"He's new. I don't know him."

The discussion ought to calm her nerves, but the memory of being shunned, and of Archie's refusal to correct the vicar on her behalf, stirred an unsettling anger.

There was also the nearness of Graeme and his hand placed warmly at her waist. It was all she could do to not tremble or trip over her feet.

* * *

GRAEME SAW THE WAY BLYTHE FLINCHED THE MOMENT HE SET his hand to her waist and he wondered if his touch was welcome. And if it was, how far she would let him go?

Unworthy thoughts. He tried to push them aside and asked her if she was well.

She glanced up quickly, and he saw the same heat in her eyes that was tormenting him. Without thinking, he swept her into a turn and drew her a bit closer. Only an inch or two closer, but he heard her slight gasp and watched as she struggled to school her face into a bored look.

He knew that was what she was doing because he was trying to do the same thing himself. Their pairing here was the object of many gazes.

He turned them again and saw Lady Hermione conversing with Jarrow, a serious look on both their faces. He had a brief glimpse of Mrs. Jarrow, who'd stepped a few paces away from Lady Hermione. Lips moving, she leaned conspiratorially close to the white-haired matrons gathered near her. The curate had disappeared.

His hand on Blythe's waist tightened.

"Too close, sir," she hissed, a note of panic in her voice.

"Are we?" He looked down into her upturned face. Her hair had been coiled onto the back of her head, a dark fringe of it framing her face and calling attention to winged eyebrows and eyes the color of a stormy sea. "I should like to hold you even closer, Blythe."

Twin flames of color rose in her cheeks. At the next step, her foot came down on his toes.

"Ouch," he said. "Apologies. I think I deserved that."

"Step back," she said with a frigid smile.

He obliged her and they danced on a while in silence, but though she looked away, he couldn't.

He wanted her, and the White Horse Assembly room

was a damned inconvenient place for him to express the desire that had been plaguing him since his return, a desire he ought to try to ignore.

For what did he know of her? It should be a countess holding sway over the social order of her neighbors, not some magistrate's cow of a wife. Something had happened to ruin Blythe.

Something that might be repaired? Would a good marriage do the trick?

Not to him. Not if he wanted a *plum post* as Diddenton had called it.

The thought of her married to anyone else had jealousy rearing inside him.

What other sort of power could an earl wield to help her? Taking her as his mistress wouldn't help his ambitions and would destroy any she might have. And it would be wrong.

He put another few inches between them and glanced toward Lady Hermione and Jarrow.

The elder Mr. Stockwell had joined Jarrow and Lady Hermione and appeared to be having words with a third man.

Blythe noticed the gathering and stiffened in his arms but her face gave nothing away.

"Do you know the fellow?" he asked.

"Not by name." She turned her gaze up to him, a tense smile fixed on her face. "Years ago, he accompanied Lord Vernon on a visit to Archie."

"One of Diddenton's men then."

"His steward, Mr. Stockwell said. He happened to ride over at the same time as Lord Vernon and paid a call on Stockwell."

As the dance came to an end, he gave her waist and hand

a squeeze and bowed. "I shall go meet this fellow and have a manly discussion about farming. But first, let us go and meet the dragons."

* * *

BLYTHE TOOK GRAEME'S ARM AND STRAIGHTENED HER SPINE. Mrs. Jarrow's circle of ladies included Mrs. Addison, Mrs. Swarby, and Miss Smith, a spinster sister of Mrs. Swarby. They were the formidable local ladies.

It was amazing that she could find such as these more intimidating than the highest sticklers of the ton. But then, the rules of the upper class were less restrictive, at least where a noble husband's behavior was concerned.

She would brave this. She could put her nose in the air even higher than this lot.

"Mrs. Jarrow," Graeme said with a bow. "How lovely to see you. Stockwell, I'm happy you are able to attend. Mrs. Jarrow, you remember Lady Chilcombe?"

"Good evening, Mrs. Jarrow," Blythe said.

The besom pressed her lips together.

Graeme frowned and raised one eyebrow. "Will you not introduce your friends?" he asked. "That is, introduce them to *me*. I'm sure Lady Chilcombe is already acquainted."

A long pause ensued. He squeezed her hand which still lay atop his arm. She withdrew it and tipped her head to the older ladies. "Indeed, I know all the ladies, Lord Chilcombe. How could I forget such pillars? Mrs. Addison, Mrs. Swarby and her sister, Miss Smith. Ladies, this is Lord Chilcombe, newly arrived from his services to the Crown in foreign parts. He is eager to acquaint himself with his new neighbors." She dipped her head again, this time to Graeme.

"Do excuse me, my lord, while I see how Lady Hermione is faring."

"Pleased to meet you, my lord." Blythe heard Miss Smith's voice break the tense silence.

Lady Hermione caught her eye and sent her a smile that oozed sympathy. Mr. Jarrow, too, studied her face as he greeted her. Mr. Stockwell turned a frown at her, but she could tell he was distracted by the man at his elbow who he introduced as Mr. Crichton, Lord Diddenton's steward.

Attendees were mingling, many going off to a side room for the dinner donated by the good people of the area. Mr. Crichton glanced that way.

"Mr. Crichton, Lord Chilcombe will be anxious to meet you, I'm sure," she said. She glanced back and saw Graeme, a bored look on his face, listening politely as Mrs. Jarrow's mouth and chin and finger wagged. Mrs. Addison and Mrs. Swarby nodded along with the wagging, while Miss Smith frowned and met Blythe's gaze in a furtive glance, quickly averted.

"Or perhaps, Mr. Stockwell, Mr. Crichton, you ought to go ahead before all the food disappears. Lord Chilcombe will find you later."

Crichton promised to speak to Graeme before departing, and both men walked off.

"I'll go and rescue Chilcombe," Mr. Jarrow said, his face grim, and he stepped away.

Hermione linked arms with Blythe. "Come, we'll go and see who might think to cut us in the supper room. I had a most interesting discussion with Mr. Jarrow's mother." She chuckled. "It seems that all my efforts at maintaining a sterling character have been for naught."

"Oh, I am sorry, Hermione. You are guilty by association."

"Lady Loughton explained your circumstances to me."

Blythe inwardly cringed. Not even Lady Loughton knew all, and if she did, would she still be a friend?

"I am here to be your stalwart companion in battling these old besoms." Hermione laughed again. "Oh dear, I suppose I risk becoming an old besom myself. Tell me, are any of them redeemable? If we begin winning one over, perhaps the rest will follow. Mr. Jarrow—"

"He cannot risk his reputation with two ladies such as us," Blythe said, infusing her voice with a cheer she didn't feel. "Oh, that is not fair. With a lady such as myself. You may wish to travel back to London and join Will at Chilcombe House."

"And abandon my chaperonage?" She tipped her head closer. "Though I confess, I have not always been the most attentive of chaperones. You know the story of my dear Mary Elizabeth and Lord Loughton when I accompanied her to a Michaelmas house party."

Blythe had not heard the story, but she could count. Lord Loughton's heir had arrived a scant six months after their nuptials.

And bless dear Hermione, she was trying to distract her and lift her mood. All around them as they passed through the crowd, ladies and gentlemen were turning their backs.

"That was your lapse then, was it, my lady?" Blythe teased.

"All's well that ends well." Hermione scanned the laden tables. "You must be as parched as I am," she said. "I shall fetch us both lemonades."

Blythe watched the older lady walk away.

"Lady Chilcombe, is it?"

A man had come to stand near her, a young man in a dark frock coat, a garish waistcoat, and gray pantaloons. His hair was brushed forward as if driven by a gale force wind. His gaze fixed on her, brown eyes gleaming with hunger as he licked full lips.

"Do you not remember me?" he asked. "Frederick Falfield."

Ah. Though this fellow was slimmer and his eyes more brown than amber, she saw the resemblance to Lord Vernon. He was related to Diddenton. That's why her skin was crawling.

From the corner of her eye, she saw three young bucks nearby, leering and giggling.

She was tempted to cut him, as the others were cutting her, and she suddenly wished that Graeme had accompanied her. He would set the lad straight.

She gritted her teeth and stood taller. She wouldn't pretend that Frederick Falfield did not exist.

"I do not remember you," she said. "You are related to Diddenton?"

"A nephew, and your neighbor. Staying at Wickworth Hall."

If Graeme wished to question someone about the damage to the drain, this was one man he needed to speak to.

"Lord Vernon admires you greatly." Falfield's gaze swept her from head to foot and up again. "I can certainly see why."

She blinked, speechless, and noticed people nearby watching.

"No lemonade left," Hermione said, handing her a glass, "but I have brought ratafia." She eyed the young man and said, "Good evening. Will you introduce us, Lady Chilcombe?"

"Lady Hermione Gravelston, this impertinent young lad is Frederick Falfield, Diddenton's nephew, currently staying at Wickfield Hall."

"I see."

Hermione *did* see. Blythe had apprised her of the damage done and suspected culpability.

"Lord Chilcombe will certainly want to meet you Mr. Falfield," Blythe said. "Ah, and you're in luck. He approaches now."

ANGER SIMMERED WITHIN GRAEME, HIS THROAT RAW FROM holding it back. The disrespect shown Blythe was worse than he had expected. The disrespect shown to him... that had certainly surprised him.

In particular, the conversation with Mrs. Jarrow.

"I had hoped you might have heeded my advice this morning," Mrs. Jarrow said. "I must go further and suggest to you to be mindful of the standards of our community. This is not London, where men and women may dance—"

He cleared his throat.

She straightened. "It is just that the lady does not have a good reputation. She is known to—"

"Mother." Jarrow's appearance halted that particular slander.

But did not stop her. "You are new to the title, Lord Chilcombe. I would not like to see your reputation tarred with the same brush—"

"Tarred by whom, madam?" Graeme interrupted. "Yes, I certainly would not like to see my reputation, er, *defamed* because of my civility toward my cousin's widow. Or is *slandered* a better word than *defamed*? More actionable, as it were. What do you think, Jarrow? You're the local magistrate now."

Jarrow pressed his lips together.

"Surely civility doesn't include such dancing as we witnessed tonight?" Mrs. Jarrow went on doggedly.

This local biddy had the gall to think she should advise him on his behavior. He supposed the waltz with Blythe hadn't helped matters, but he'd never admit it to her. "The waltz? I've danced it in Paris and Vienna, though having only just arrived tonight, this was my first opportunity in England to waltz with a lady."

"If she is a lady."

"She very much is, Mother," Jarrow said. "If you noticed, I danced with her myself and will do so again tonight if she will grant me another opportunity."

Graeme had taken his leave then, walking away from the circle of women and Jarrow, and found Blythe and Hermione standing with a man.

From a distance, he thought it was Lord Vernon Falfield, but as he approached he realized it was a younger version of the villain.

Blythe made introductions. Frederick Falfield was residing at Wickworth Hall.

"Wickworth Hall?" Graeme asked. "So you are a near neighbor of the property at Bluebelle Lodge."

The fellow's mouth firmed. "I'm a guest. My great uncle allows me to stay there at times."

"Does he indeed?" Graeme gazed into young Falfield's eyes until the lad started to squirm. "I shall certainly call on you, Falfield," he said. "We have matters to discuss."

Falfield blinked. "I can't imagine—"

"Can you not?"

Falfield demurred and slithered away to join the other

young bucks who were ogling Blythe in a most unpleasant way.

Blythe was quiet. Too quiet.

"How are you faring?" he'd asked.

She managed a smile. "I am cast down entirely. The biscuits and lemonade had disappeared by the time Hermione and I reached the tables."

Graeme smiled, touched that she had found a way to defuse some of the evening's tension, and he listened as she told him the names of the villagers and nearby landowners in attendance.

By the time he went to look for Crichton, Stockwell informed him that the fellow, unable to wait, had left.

Unable or unwilling?

Stockwell said Crichton had heard of the problem at Bluebelle Lodge—one of the tenants had told one of Lord Diddenton's tenants. He claimed to know nothing about it and promised to have a look the next day.

When the dancing resumed, Blythe declined to dance with Mr. Jarrow and it appeared no one else asked her. Graeme himself was busy mingling, meeting the town's doctor, the local solicitor, and some of his own tenants. He met a few more of the good ladies of the town. Each time they hinted he should dance with their daughters, he told them he needed to seek out Lady Chilcombe and Lady Gravelston and see how they were faring.

Those ladies had cut Blythe and Lady Hermione, and as far as he was concerned, the sins of the mothers might as well as be visited upon their daughters.

The exception being Miss Jarrow, but he would not dance with her twice because in a village this small and gossipy, he might find the first banns posted next Sunday.

They'd arrived late, and stayed until the music ended,

and he could feel nothing but admiration for Blythe for soldiering on, and gratitude to Lady Hermione for helping her to find the courage.

CHAPTER TEN

"We had some success tonight," Hermione said. She and Blythe stood apart from other attendees, waiting while Graeme went to order their carriage.

He, at least, had not been spurned by the good folk of Risley. Nor had she been entirely rejected. After the closely watched exchange with Frederick Falfield, a few people new to the area, and some of the local tradespeople, had greeted her. Hermione's presence, good humor and obvious good character, had helped to smooth the way. The next test, she supposed, would come when she took Coralie and Nicholas to church.

"My lady," a small voice whispered.

Blythe gasped and smiled. "Mirabelle. How grown up you are. I did not notice you in attendance tonight."

The girl smiled. "Mama allowed me to come but not to dance." She glanced behind her and leaned closer. "How is Coralie? You must give her my greetings. I miss her so much."

Only two years older than Coralie, Mirabelle had been

her great friend. She and her older siblings and other children had played along the stream and in the meadow at Bluebelle Lodge, and on the land that was now Diddenton's.

"She is well," Blythe said, "and she misses you too."

Coralie had mentioned seeing Mirabelle at the village shops and waving, but her friend had been quickly hauled away by her mother or governess.

The girl chewed her lower lip. "Oh, I wish I could—"

"Mirabelle!" Mirabelle's mother appeared out of the shadows. Her eyes widened and then narrowed on Blythe. "Come away from that woman," she said.

The girl ducked her head. "S-sorry," she whispered and allowed herself to be led away.

Stunned, Blythe froze and closed her eyes. When she opened them, she saw Graeme's frown.

He'd seen.

Bluebelle Lodge. She must get to Bluebelle Lodge, and when she did, she would hide there until this misery dissipated.

But even as she thought that, she knew it wasn't possible for her to run and hide. She had to see this through. She might have a battle to fight, and she couldn't do it from Bluebelle Lodge.

GRAEME HAD LEFT THEM FOR ONLY A MOMENT TO ORDER their carriage, returning to hear the girl asking about someone named Coralie, and her mother's words: *Come away from that woman.*

That woman was a *lady*, a *countess*. That woman deserved better.

The shrew of a mother had been one of the women he'd met, one of those who'd tried to push their daughters forward. Anger coursed through him—anger and a desire to wreak vengeance on all the so-called better families of Risley. Surely an earl could find a way.

Blythe saw him and knew that he'd witnessed the slur. Her eyes flashed open and then she drew herself up, nodded at something Lady Hermione said and gazed calmly away at nothing.

She held that pose through the drive home. Lady Hermione was less chatty than usual. She broached a few comments about the flowers decorating the assembly room, speculated about the quality of the inn's ale, wishing she'd had some of it instead of the watery ratafia, and complemented Graeme on his well-sprung coach and the smoothness of the lane leading to Risley Manor, neither of which he'd had anything to do with of course.

By the time they reached Risley Manor, his anger had hardened into determination. By God, Blythe would tell him exactly what had gone on.

When they arrived, her maid, Radley, met them at the door and took her wrap.

"Come and have a cup of tea, ladies," he said. "Or something stronger."

Blythe pleaded fatigue and a headache and let the maid lead her away.

"I shall go up as well," Lady Hermione said, watching them. "She did very well, my lord. I should advise you to bar Mrs. Jarrow from your home. Invite Mr. Jarrow and Miss Jarrow, and perhaps the one friend of Mrs. Jarrow, Miss Smith. She will come out of curiosity, and Mrs. Jarrow will be cast down."

"Lady Hermione, I shall tell the Foreign Office to find you a place."

She chuckled, reached for his hands and squeezed them, and thanked him for an entertaining evening.

Too late, he wondered what Mrs. Jarrow had told Lady Hermione. They'd had a much longer conversation than he'd had with the old besom before her son's interruption.

He would ask her tomorrow. Or...

Who the devil was Coralie? And what the devil had Blythe done to render herself a pariah?

Only Blythe could give him the full story, and he was tired of waiting for answers.

* * *

He knocked and Radley opened the bedchamber door. Blythe's eyes flashed terror, the emotion quickly shuttered.

The maid stood firm, barring his entry.

That look in her eyes had cooled the worst of his anger. "Blythe," he said. "I need to speak with you. May I come in?"

This was, in fact, her bedchamber, not the sitting room of a suite of rooms as a countess might expect as her due, even a widowed countess. The bed was narrower as well. But there was a settee at the end of it and two chairs near the fireplace.

He took all that in from the edge of his vision.

He took a step, and the maid moved closer, a martial glint in her gaze.

Be damned if he would explain himself to a lady's maid.

He glanced at Blythe. She'd frozen in place, with a look of... what? He couldn't put a name to it but he knew fear was in there somewhere in the mix and he tempered his approach.

"I am no seducer. I will not hurt her," he told Radley

before turning to Blythe. "You have my word. Blythe, I want... I need to talk to you."

She swallowed and nodded, and with a long assessing look, the maid stepped aside.

"I'll be nearby, my lady," she said.

Blythe shook her head. "It's all right, Radley. This Lord Chilcombe is a different sort of scoundrel than the last one."

The words sent his back up. He was no scoundrel where ladies were concerned—had never been.

Except... he'd sounded the alarm on her tryst with Archie. Was that what she meant?

"Very well, my lady. I'll fetch you some chocolate when you're ready."

Radley's words rippled over him, his attention filled with the seemingly composed woman before him still garbed in her ball gown.

When the door closed on the maid, Graeme stepped closer. "Blythe," he said, "I have never seen a lady treated so rudely as you were tonight. Why? What happened here at Risley Manor?"

Her mouth firmed even as her eyes grew shiny. Incipient tears?

He hoped not. He had no skills with weeping women. Handing over a handkerchief never seemed to be enough.

"Who is Coralie?" he asked, keeping his tone as gentle as possible.

She dropped her head and then lifted it on a deep inhale, looking to the left and to the right before answering his gaze with her own firm one.

He wouldn't get the truth tonight, at least not the whole truth.

"Coralie," she said, "is my daughter."

Graeme forced his face into a neutral look, while he

mentally sorted through facts, and saw her assessing him. She'd hoped to shock him.

And she had. To his knowledge, there'd been only one child born of Archie and Blythe's marriage. If Blythe had a daughter that was not Archie's, it was no wonder that the neighbors... So, who had fathered this daughter of hers?

"Your daughter," he said matter-of-factly.

He stepped closer, and she straightened her spine and stood taller.

"Yes. My *step*daughter." She let out a long breath. "Archie's *natural* daughter."

Bloody Archie. Of course he would have cheated on her, but how early in the marriage had he begun seeking other women?

And with Blythe as his wife, how could he have done so?

"Which makes Coralie your cousin, Lord Chilcombe."

A cousin. How many other by-blow cousins had Archie produced? And where was this one now?

The answer was obvious. "You have her at Bluebelle Lodge."

Blythe nodded. "She is my goddaughter and ward."

"How old is this child?"

"Fourteen soon. Almost a young lady. And I have raised her as such."

"*Fourteen?*" Blythe and Archie had married fifteen years earlier. Their son had been born almost nine months to the day after the nuptials, a fact that had grated on Graeme's jealous young self like a sharp-edged rock until he'd shaken off the calf love.

Their son had died, and this girl had lived, but Blythe had raised her as her own to be a lady, albeit at Bluebelle Lodge, not Risley Manor. Why there...?

Ah. The girl's mother must be there. "Mrs. Stockwell—"

"Is not Coralie's mother. Her mother was a maid here."

"Does this maid reside also at Bluebelle Lodge?"

"No. When Coralie was about two years of age, her mother left her with me. I kept her here, in the nursery, with my son until…"

Blythe's cool demeanor faltered.

"Until Archie sent her away."

She raised a gaze so troubled that he reached out and took her hand, and when the trembling started, pulled her into his arms.

* * *

THE WARM HAND ENFOLDING HERS SENT A CASCADE OF SHOCK waves. She hadn't meant to be weak, had planned to be cool —cool, calm, composed. But the warmth, the promise of comfort…

It would surely be a false promise, a façade of caring. There was no enduring comfort to be had in Lord Chilcombe's arms—any Lord Chilcombe. Not Archie's, not Graeme's. Certainly not in any of either man's friends. Perhaps not in the arms of any gentleman.

Now, her cheek pressed to the cool wool of his coat, her body betraying her, she held her breath, trying to still her heart and quiet the nerves rattling through her.

He wanted to know why the good people of the village had spurned her. She could tell him that part, the least of the sins.

Anger stirred in her. *Yes, of course, Lord Chilcombe.* She could reveal this, her deepest humiliation, her profoundest grief, so that Graeme would be so appalled he would stay the *bloody hell* away from her.

Fat lot of good it was doing her to sink into the comfort he offered. She untangled herself and pushed away.

"Archie didn't send her away. I took her away."

Frowning, he lifted her chin and searched her face. "For her safety?"

She pressed her lips together. It was a question, but one that he thought he knew the answer to.

"And your son?" he asked.

This was another part of the old wound to rip open. "My Georgie had died a year earlier." She closed her eyes and swallowed moisture. When she opened them, she found him watching her.

"Please, Blythe. Please tell me."

Despite his stoic look, one he must have perfected in the years of his diplomatic career, his voice was gentle. That tone in his voice—the kindness—had her emotions reeling. And his hands still cradled her elbows.

Why?, she wanted to ask. Though in truth, she couldn't bear to hear sympathetic lies. Her neighbors had shared the truth in whispers and didn't believe it. Why should he be any different?

"I will keep your secrets," he said.

"Secrets? The facts are private, not exactly secret." Not that she'd ever wished to have her personal tragedies bandied about among the neighbors. "I will tell *you* the truth, and like the good Mrs. Jarrow who surely has heard the truth whispered in her ear, you may choose not to believe it as well."

"Give me the chance, Blythe."

He handed her a handkerchief, and she quietly cursed before wiping her eyes and gathering herself. There were things she wouldn't ever tell him.

He stood waiting, watching, all his attention focused on

her. It was a heady thing to have someone wanting to listen to *her*.

She would begin at the beginning. "I wanted to marry Archie," she said. "I thought I was in love with him. You know his story: raised as a good Christian by pious grandparents who kept hold of the leading strings until they could no longer do so. He took up residence in Risley Manor and everyone believed him to be upright and good. And then he found me alone in the garden. Like most of the girls in attendance the night of that party, I was starry-eyed about the handsome, rich, eligible earl. That he picked me out to follow into the garden.... I had no idea it had to do with me being an orphan with no dowry and a guardian who was not influential. I was overwhelmed. And a willing participant. And when someone saw us and raised the alarm..."

She leveled a long look at him.

He nodded. "Me."

"Yes. My guardian insisted we marry. Archie had not expected that. Imagine the blow when I discovered that the handsome young earl who'd whispered endearments," and put his hand down her bodice, "had to be shamed into marrying me."

The wave of humiliation and anger was almost as fresh as the day she'd first experienced it.

"I decided to make the best of it. I hoped that my determination to love would... I did my duty as countess, here and in our few stays in town. I tried to... to make a comfortable home, to be a good wife. Archie was satisfied when his son was born. Not so satisfied with my slow recovery from childbirth, and quite dissatisfied at my reaction when I discovered my new husband had been..." Anger flared in her. "*Swiving* the maids."

"More than one." He bit his lower lip. "Of course."

"He spent a great deal of time in London and was more discreet there, careful to choose liaisons with..."

She squeezed her eyes closed again. Archie had been much more discreet, at least during those early years of their marriage.

"At some point he became friends with Lord Vernon while in town, and spent more time at Risley Manor when Diddenton bought Wickworth Hall and Lord Vernon was in residence there. Georgie was six, and learning to ride on his pony when Archie decided to take him up on his horse for a lark. A drunken lark. At the first jump, Georgie flew off and d-died."

An arm came around her shoulder and she turned away from the comfort he offered.

It took more than a few frantic heartbeats and deep breaths to quell the grief and the painful memories.

"Archie was devastated. Repentant. Filled with guilt. It was such a strange condition for him that it couldn't last. During that brief time, we... we reconciled. I found I was with child again, and he went off to London. When he returned home a few months later, he brought along a company of friends for a hunting party. Male friends."

Mostly male friends.

"Lord Vernon?"

"Yes. And Sir Morris Pierpont and others. He ought not to have done it, or I ought not to have been here. Had I known to expect them, I would have gone to stay at Bluebelle Lodge. Archie promised they would not bother me but..."

A memory seized her, along with a wave of the panic she'd fought to master. Her bedchamber, invaded. Archie insanely drunk. Lord Vernon following him, an avid interest in his eyes. And the woman they'd brought with them.

Graeme reached for her again, and she put up a hand to ward him off.

"I lost the child. Mrs. Stockwell was my maid at the time, unmarried then, but her husband was courting her. I was still ill when they moved me and Coralie to Bluebelle Lodge."

"And you stayed there."

"Yes, mostly. Always, when Archie was in residence here."

"He didn't come after you?"

She shook her head. "To put it rather... rather coarsely, he didn't need me in his bed here."

"Mrs. Jarrow—"

"Knows of that?" She shrugged and then pinned him with a hard look. "What sort of wife would allow that in her home? Would *you* seek that lady's company?"

Graeme's lips firmed and his frown deepened, yet she couldn't entirely sense whether he was feeling disgust or sympathy.

For now, let him judge her as weak. She didn't care.

There were other *sins* she was willing to tell him about. Not her own, of course.

"Mrs. Jarrow will allege that my actions are blacker than that. After I moved to Bluebelle Lodge, a maid from Wickworth Hall appeared on our doorstep fair to bursting with child. We took her in—how could we not have taken pity upon her? She gave birth to a son and died shortly after."

"Archie's child."

Graeme's lips had pressed tighter and his hand had somehow captured hers. His anger was palpable, though she was quite sure—and a little surprised—that it wasn't directed at her.

Blythe shook her head. "My Georgie was fair-haired and robust like Archie. So is Coralie. Nicholas, on the other hand, is a slight child with very dark hair and amber eyes. He is, like Coralie, a child of my heart but not my body. It's whispered in the neighborhood that he is my child by Lord Vernon."

Blythe held her breath, watching Graeme's reaction, while his hand tightened around hers. She'd seen in her husband and his friends the nature of many men. Like guttersnipe women, they could disparage a reputation without a second thought. And with no father or brother or son to defend her—what was a woman to do? There *were* better men; she'd known a few. The late Mr. Davies had been one. The Stockwells were also, as far as she knew. The sons of her friend Lady Loughton seemed to be honorable as well.

There were good men in the world and there were scoundrels. Which group did Graeme belong to?

"I see," he said after a long pause.

His calmness annoyed her.

"I suppose you do. Now you may leave."

"Not yet, Blythe."

His heated gaze drilled into her as if he could see into her very heart.

"I will visit Bluebelle Lodge tomorrow. Will you come with me and introduce me to this unexpected cousin of mine and Nicholas too?"

"Certainly."

"I understand now why Bluebelle Lodge is so important to you."

The diffident tone, the stiff manner, sent her heart

sinking and her fears rising. What had she expected from Graeme Blatchford, rigid diplomat? He'd said she had no reason to fear him, but...

"Know this, Lord Chilcombe. Coralie and Nicholas are mine." Angry tears flooded her eyes again and she pulled her hand away.

"I won't take them away," he said, his tone suddenly warm. "Nor will anyone else, Blythe."

He went to the door and opened it. Radley, loyal creature that she was, waited outside. Graeme held a whispered conversation with her and she scurried away.

He returned and took Blythe's hand, leading her to the armchairs near the fireplace. "I want to know why Diddenton thinks he has a claim to Bluebelle Lodge, and what his son's involvement is in this claim. Everything you know, Blythe. We're going to find a way for you to keep your home."

Words failed her and it was just as well because it was some time before she could risk speaking. She perched quietly on the edge of her chair while he made himself useful fetching her a shawl and building a fire to chase the chill from the room until Radley returned with two steaming cups of chocolate.

CHAPTER ELEVEN

*I*n the early hours, Graeme finally snatched a few hours of sleep, after staring at the canopy above his bed, a pale damask of abundant but faded blue flowers.

His conversation with Blythe had kept him awake. Not that he'd learned anything new after the chocolate arrived. That hadn't been his purpose, not truly.

He'd wanted to calm her. He wanted her to trust him, if that could ever be possible.

He'd wanted to know what bloody Archie had bloody done to her in the presence of bloody Lord Vernon to make her lose her child. She'd left out that detail.

Though his own nerves had been stretched thin with anger, he'd watched as the rich, dark sweetness of the chocolate helped sooth hers, using every bit of restraint he'd learned over the years. He'd managed to keep his hands off her.

When all he wanted was to take her into his arms and comfort her.

She hadn't allowed that, of course. He'd never believe she was the jade Mrs. Jarrow was making her out to be.

He rose, washed, and allowed Clive, who'd accompanied him from London, to help him dress. As soon as Blythe was ready, they would take the gig over to Bluebelle Lodge. Or... did Blythe ride? Perhaps he'd need to convince Lady Hermione to stay at Risley Manor. If he and Blythe could cut through the fields, they could reach their destination more quickly and spot any trespassers on the way. And have more time alone.

The children... their existence had been a surprise. He would provide for both of them, without question, whether Blythe wanted his help or not. Coralie, they would find a way to bring out. How one brought an earl's by-blow into society, he had no idea. That required female intervention, which was perhaps part of the reason Blythe was trying to establish herself in town.

The boy posed a more worrisome problem that Blythe perhaps hadn't thought of. If he was Lord Vernon's child—and Diddenton's grandchild—he might prove a valuable pawn to the marquess. Best to keep his existence secret or pass him off as the son of someone else. He wondered if Blythe had chosen that path.

He found her and Lady Hermione in the breakfast room. At his suggestion that he and Blythe ride to Bluebelle Lodge so she could show him the land, Lady Hermione smiled and claimed that she was too tired from the previous evening's adventures to accompany them.

"Were these flowers here yesterday?" Graeme asked.

Seated primly on one of the mounts from the stable at Risley Manor, Blythe was leading them through a wooded area of newly budding trees, the ground rich with bluebells.

She glanced over her shoulder and smiled. "You didn't notice?"

"I fear I didn't take the time to stop and see the beauty around me."

Too busy looking at the beauty in front of me.

He'd always noticed Blythe's beauty, even when her dalliance with Archie had soiled her.

And what a priggish word that was—soiled. What had she done but succumb to Archie's seduction? How many men had he met through the years—of all races and countries, and classes for that matter—who would make an attempt on an innocent girl's virtue? He hadn't—and swore he would never—venture that himself.

But he'd been tempted. How did that make him any better than the others? Or Blythe any worse? She was not a woman of bad character herself but an innocent who had hitched herself to a man of bad character.

"Come and look," she said as they broke through the trees.

He brought his mount up next to hers.

An expanse of blue-carpeted meadow stretched either side of a lane leading up to a small brick and flint manor house with two bay windows and attic dormers above the first floor. In the distance was another cottage and a stable block and farm buildings.

He'd forgotten what it looked like. In fact, when he'd visited Bluebelle Lodge as a young man, he'd thought only of the girl who lived there.

"It's very pretty," he said. "What does Diddenton plan to do with the house?"

"He already has Wickworth Hall, which is larger. He wants to tear down Bluebelle Lodge and turn all of this into an ugly lime pit."

She shook her head and turned a gleaming eye on him, reminding him of the girl she'd once been before Archie. "Shall we race?"

Before he could even agree, she urged her horse into a gallop and flew up the lane.

They were seen before they reached the front door. The same young groom who'd fetched him from Jarrow's appeared around the corner of the house, and Mrs. Stockwell stood on the front step. Behind her was a tall, fair-haired girl. Pink-cheeked and in the first bloom of womanhood, she was destined to be a beauty.

Robust was the word Blythe had used to describe Coralie, but she was feminine as well.

Blythe made introductions, and Coralie sank into an elegant curtsy, her face a careful mask not quite hiding her curiosity.

Mrs. Stockwell directed him to the parlor. He had a better look at her than he'd had the day before when he was preoccupied with the flooded field. She was younger and more attractive than most housekeepers; he could see why Stockwell would not wish her to work at Risley Manor while Archie and his friends were about.

He followed Coralie, who nervously offered him the largest chair in the room, a wing chair upholstered in faded rust-colored damask.

"Why don't we both take a seat on the sofa?" he asked, tipping his head toward it.

She glanced at the door, where Blythe and the housekeeper were conferring in hushed tones.

"Excuse me, my lord," the girl said. "I must just tell—"

"Coralie," Blythe called. "Will you entertain Lord Chilcombe while I go and find Nicholas?"

The girl chewed her lip and said "Of course, Godmama. Please have a seat, my lord," she added.

"Good manners require me to wait until you are seated," he said, softening the words with a smile.

"Oh, of course." But instead of sitting, she moved closer, gnawed her lip a bit more, and then lifted a defiant chin. "I cannot bear it," she said with a quick glance at the door to check that both women had moved on. "Tell me, truly, what do you mean to do? Do you mean to cast Godmama and all of us out of our home?"

Anger flickered in him, quickly quenched by the genuine anguish in her eyes. This was the uncertainty of women and children when the men in their lives, the men tasked with caring for them, failed them. Did Blythe feel the same?

She must, certainly. The thought that Blythe might have said something to Coralie that cast blame on him, irked him.

"No," he said, "did your godmama tell you that I would?"

She rolled her eyes, and he had to stifle a smile. That habit would need to be broken, but perhaps for now, it was a good sign that she didn't fear him.

"Godmama tells me *nothing*. She is forever trying to soothe my worries with… with, um, you might as well know it, platitudes. They are falsehoods. Lies of omission, or *white* lies, well-meant, of course, but I know she worries, and Nicholas…"

Her frown deepened and her blue eyes—the same striking shade of azure blue as Archie's—fixed on him for a long moment before she finally let out a long breath and spoke. "Nicholas is hiding. That is why Godmama has gone off. She's going to search for him."

"Nicholas is… how old?"

"Six."

"Six is a rambunctious age. Is he a bit of a scamp?"

She shook her head.

"Or is he merely shy?"

"He is *not* shy. He is *afraid*."

That brought him up. "He has nothing to fear from me."

"No?" She stared into his face, and he had the impression she was trying to look into his soul.

On the way to becoming a formidable lady was this new cousin.

"He can't help it, my lord. He says that two different men, two different times, have tried to take him. He thought you were here for the same reason."

A frisson of alarm had Graeme standing taller. The taking of boys was the sort of thing that might happen in some of the countries of the subcontinent for a special sort of harem, or in Africa for the slave trade, or in London where chimney sweeps and small thieves were valued. But in the country?

"Does Lady Chilcombe know this?"

She shook her head. "No one knew until this morning when he told me, just before he ran off, and I have not had a chance to tell anyone."

She'd trusted him enough to tell him first. He was touched.

"Come," he said, taking her hand and leading her to the sofa. "Let us sit down. I want to hear this."

Together they cleared some needlework and newssheets out of the way and sat down.

"You won't take us away?" she asked.

"From Lady Chilcombe? No. From Bluebelle Lodge?" There'd be no false promises. "We must see what the court decides about your father's will. Has Lady Chilcombe explained the matter to you?"

She nodded. "I knew something was worrying her even before *he* died. She finally told me."

By *he*, she surely meant Archie.

"Whatever happens, I will provide for Lady Chilcombe, and for you and Nicholas as well. Now, I wonder if Nicholas's problems are related to your godmama's. When did all these worries start for her? I want to hear everything."

"I know the very day they started," she said, hands twisting in her lap. Well, perhaps it truly was earlier, much earlier, when Louisa and Samuel took us away from Risley Manor and brought us here."

"Louisa and Samuel?"

"Mr. and Mrs. Stockwell. I was very little then, but I remember being frightened. I thought Godmama would die. I... I wasn't supposed to see, but I heard all the shouting, and so much was happening no one noticed me coming down from the nursery."

The blue eyes pinned him again, the shock of that long-ago day burning in them. "The baby... there was a baby, a boy, so very tiny, and he died, and there was so much blood. Samuel wrapped Godmama in blankets and carried her away, and Louisa took me, and we all came to Bluebelle Lodge. Then Nicholas's mama came to live with us and he was born, and Godmama promised that I would live here until I grew up and got married and went to my own home." She paused for a long moment.

"Your godmama lived here?" he prompted.

Coralie waved a hand dismissively. "She would go away to see to things at Risley Manor, but not overnight, and she never went up to town, though my papa—Lord Chilcombe as was—went away often."

Her long pause begged the question about whether Archie had come to visit her. He chose to not ask it, waiting.

"I saw him sometimes when he was out riding with his friends. It was better he stayed away."

There was old wisdom in this child.

"It wasn't spoken of here, but I heard things in the village. I have... had... a friend."

"A girl named Mirabelle?"

"Yes. How did you know?"

"I saw her speaking to your godmother at the assembly, asking how you are."

"Godmama won't tell me. She doesn't want me to feel sad." Coralie shook her head and met his gaze. "But you asked when her worrying started? It started the day that man turned over his phaeton in the lane. Godmama had a message summoning her to Risley Manor and she left quite suddenly. And when she came back later, she was flushed, and angry, and agitated too. It wasn't like her, and when I went to see what was wrong. I found her in her study kneeling before the fireplace, burning papers."

Coralie looked away, visibly more troubled by the more recent memory, than by the one from her early childhood.

A cold chill went through him and a memory flashed. Sir Morris had supposedly been carrying the new will.

"She told me to *get out* and close the door behind me. She'd never before sent me away like that. And she was crying."

I am not a murderer, Blythe had said.

But she was surely a thief. That had been the new will she was burning. How had she obtained it from Sir Morris? Was it before or after his death?

Anger flared in him but he was careful to hide it from the girl. It wasn't Coralie's fault. Blythe had lied to the girl as well—lies of omission, Coralie had called them, but lies nevertheless.

She hadn't trusted Graeme with the truth.

"After Lord Chilcombe died, she had to go away," Coralie said. "It was because of Lord Vernon. Do you know him, my lord?"

"I have met him."

Her gaze narrowed. "Is he your friend?"

"Emphatically, no."

She nodded and let out a long breath. "He had taken up residence at Wickworth Hall. He called every day, sometimes twice a day, and he lurked in the fields all around, and... she was afraid." Coralie shuddered. "She would never say it, but I knew it. He wanted her to be his mistress."

The girl's frankness shocked him.

"I should not know about such things, I know, but one can't help but overhear gossip."

"Did he ever bother you or Nicholas?"

"He was never allowed into the house—we were in mourning. Louisa and Samuel barred him from entry. Nicholas and I knew to make ourselves scarce when he came around." Her brows drew together. "And I remembered him, you see. He is not a good man. He was there the night the baby died."

"Did he bother you or Nicholas when you went into the village? Or perhaps at church?"

"After Lord Chilcombe died, Louisa did all our shopping. And we stopped going to church years before that when the vicar asked us to stay away."

The vicar had asked them to stay away? No wonder Blythe had stiffened when they'd discussed the vicar the night before.

No wonder she guarded her secrets so carefully.

"So Lord Vernon had no particular interest in you or in Nicholas?"

She gave him an assessing look. "He is Nicholas's father, isn't he? There is a strong resemblance. The village gossips whisper that he's Lord Vernon's bastard by Godmama, but I know that's not true because I saw him being born." Color rose in her cheeks. "I wasn't supposed to, but I heard all the screaming and sneaked into the birthing room."

He remembered stumbling across a woman giving birth on the outskirts of an army camp years earlier.

"A terrifying experience," he said.

Coralie turned a curious gaze on him and her lips quirked.

"It wasn't so long after Godmama lost her child, and not as scary, because no one had been trying to hurt Nicholas's mother. And when Nicholas came out... well, Godmama feared it would put me off marriage, but..."

She stopped, apparently realizing she'd stumbled into unacceptable territory, and the blush crept up her cheeks again.

She would lead all the young bucks a merry chase if he could give her a season.

"And here we are." Blythe appeared in the doorway, her hand firmly clutching that of a slight little boy in a dusty coat and trousers.

A tousle of curly hair, so dark it was almost black, covered one eye, but Graeme could see that the one visible eye was the same golden hazel as Lord Vernon's and Diddenton's. Like the eyes of a venomous snake ready to strike.

But this was a little boy, and the only emotion Graeme saw in his eyes was fear.

He rose and went to greet the child, going down on his haunches and extending his hand.

"How do you do, Nicholas," he said. "I'm Lord Chilcombe. Coralie and I were just about to call for tea and biscuits. Do you suppose your cook has any available for us?"

The lad leaned into Blythe's skirts and said nothing.

"We have a fresh sponge cake and elderberry jelly," Mrs. Stockwell said. "Will that do, my lord?"

He looked at Nicholas. "What do you think?"

The boy nodded shyly.

* * *

A FEW MOMENTS LATER, BLYTHE WATCHED AS CORALIE AND Nicholas followed Louisa out of the parlor.

A firm hand clasped her own, and Graeme led her to the sofa.

"We must talk." He settled down next to her, a hand's width apart. "Before they return."

His closeness set her nerves to rattling.

"Coralie told me that Nicholas is afraid. He told her this morning that two different men have tried to take him. That's why he hid. He thought I was coming to take him away."

"*What?*" Heart pounding, she tried to stand. He took her arm and stayed her.

"I didn't know, Graeme. They ought to have told me. Louisa—"

"Didn't know either. Nor Coralie, until this morning."

She buried her face in her hands, then thought better of succumbing to emotion. She needed to be stronger than that.

"Lord Vernon has never tried to claim Nicholas. Despite the rumors, which he certainly must have heard." She shuddered, her thoughts trailing off, her anger rising.

Lord Vernon had found a new way to torture her.

"Or it might be Diddenton's doing," Graeme said.

Diddenton, who wanted to take her home and only source of income from her. Would he go after a child nobody else wanted?

She turned her gaze on Graeme and found him watching her. She felt a squeeze and saw that his hand had found hers again.

What would be the price of his help?

"I'd best plan on staying here," she said. "I'll look after him. The Stockwells, and Cook, and Joseph will help me."

"I'll help you, Blythe. I mean to protect him and Coralie."

And me. Will you protect me?

She gritted her teeth and fought her weakness. She'd find a way to protect herself and the children.

He leaned closer, stirring the air with the citrusy scent of his shaving soap. "I propose that we take them to London. I'll hire more servants and others to guard you and the children. The Chilcombe House garden can't compare to a country estate, but we can take them on outings to the park and to see some of the sights."

"They'll be safer here." Even as she said the words, she remembered her own departure from Bluebelle Lodge escaping Lord Vernon's attentions.

"Will they?" Graeme asked. "And will you stay here and guard them while I deal with the Pregorative Court of Canterbury and the resolution of this will? Not, I suppose, that your presence is needed there, but I know the outcome is important to…"

There was another squeeze on her hand.

"To both of us."

Oh, oh, oh. She blinked back a surge of emotion. Graeme was offering comfort, partnership, perhaps friendship. Or hope.

She closed her eyes and tried to think. If he knew the truth, he would shun her. They weren't partners. They'd never be friends. The will stood between them—both wills, the old one and the new one. And Lunetta Casale. Even now, Will was in London looking for the woman.

There was no way to know when any of it would be resolved, or in what manner, and she needed to be in London, not in the country fending off gossips and trespassers.

Coralie would love to visit the lending library, and Nicholas would adore seeing the animals at the Tower. *If* he could stay healthy... and perhaps...

"Lady Loughton gave me the name of a London physician I should like to have examine Nicholas. I haven't yet been able to arrange for—"

"We can see to that. Has Nicholas been ill?"

"He suffers quite frequently from fevers and lung congestion."

"We'll send for the physician when we arrive in town. And we can begin to think about plans for Coralie's future."

We. Nicholas would see a doctor, and bright, beautiful Coralie might have a future—it seemed she would have to trust this new Lord Chilcombe.

She nodded.

"Very well. I propose that we leave early tomorrow morning before anyone has a chance to report it to the residents of Wickworth Hall."

"Another hurried departure," Blythe said. "I shall have to send word to my maid to pack my things. And what of

Hermione? We shall have quite the squeeze in the traveling chaise."

"Leave that to me." He sandwiched her hand between both of his, and she felt herself plummeting into the comfort of his touch and his promises after so many years fending for herself.

A loud knocking brought her to her feet, alarm coursing through her. Bluebelle Lodge did not have regular callers, except for... "We can ignore that caller. Louisa won't hear the knocking in the kitchen, and the maid has gone back to tidying the upstairs bedrooms."

Graeme quirked a grin. "Allow me to play butler and send away any disagreeable visitors."

That grin took her back years, reminding her of the boy he'd once been, and her heart filled with gratitude.

He left, and a few minutes later, returned with Mr. Jarrow.

Graeme had broken his promise to send away a disagreeable visitor. She hid her dismay and managed a courteous greeting.

CHAPTER TWELVE

"I called at Risley Manor," Mr. Jarrow said, "and was told I would find you here today. Lady Chilcombe, I've come to apologize for my mother's rudeness last night."

"Have you indeed? That is getting straight to the point." And she didn't believe him for a second.

There was a ruggedness to this Mr. Jarrow, and a challenging intelligence in his gaze, that must have cowed the men under his command.

She, however, was not one of his men. She held his gaze and waited.

Graeme cleared his throat, and the other man blinked.

"Yes," Mr. Jarrow said, "I will make every effort to curb her gossiping, as will my sister. Though in truth that is not the only reason I've sought you out. I'd like to ask you some questions about your late husband's death."

Tension froze her in place and it was a moment before she could speak. "Are you conducting an official inquiry? Or merely satisfying your curiosity? Or your mother's?" Her voice quivered on the last question and she struggled for composure.

"I do not report to my mother, Lady Chilcombe."

She sensed Graeme's presence next to her. He'd visited Jarrow yesterday. He must have known the man's intentions.

Jarrow glanced at Graeme, all but confirming her suspicions. She sent Graeme a withering look and stood straighter.

"I have nothing to add to what I told your father last year," she said. "Did he not leave a report?"

"He did."

"And he ruled the death due to illness."

"Yes. However, the circumstances of the new will—"

"The purported new will," she interrupted.

"Yes. The purported new will, as well as the dispute over this property, and the alleged disappearance of the, er, copy of the purported new will carried by Sir Morris Pierpont, as well as his untimely death…" He took in a deep breath. "Let me begin again. I've been urged to review all the events anew."

* * *

GRAEME WATCHED AS THE COLOR DRAINED FROM BLYTHE'S face. Whether she was drawing a mask of calm over herself or about to swoon he couldn't determine. He moved closer and felt her stiffen. Whatever bit of trust he'd coaxed from her had just vanished.

"Urged by whom?" she asked in a voice as tight as her clenched hands. She turned her gaze on Graeme, a haunted look in her eyes. "You've discussed this with Mr. Jarrow."

He nodded. "Diddenton."

"Actually, not just the marquess," Jarrow said, "though he has certainly been hounding me. Will you sit, my lady. I am not here to pass on the hounding to you but to help find the truth."

"I did not kill my husband," she said. "I did not wish him dead. I had no influence over his associations with men like Sir Morris or Lord Vernon, or with the women he... he... Many wives do not. Perhaps most. I did not kill wretched Sir Morris either."

She was well and truly rattled, as she'd been the night before. Graeme put his arm around her shoulders.

Jarrow stepped closer. "Won't you be seated, my lady? I can see these are painful memories."

Her back stiffened. "Ask quickly," she said. "You are interrupting Lord Chilcombe's introduction to Bluebelle Lodge." She pressed her lips together and looked up at Graeme. "Or, I'll take Mr. Jarrow into the study, and you may take tea and cakes with the children. I won't have them exposed to..." she flapped a hand toward Jarrow, "to this ugliness."

To his credit, Jarrow's face reflected curiosity rather than offense as he waited in silence.

"Jarrow is the magistrate, Blythe. He saw the damage done yesterday. Given this new threat, would it not be good for him to meet them?"

Panic flared in her eyes, and he hastened to speak again before she could protest.

"Blythe is raising two children at Bluebelle Lodge. Perhaps your mother has spoken of them. They are her wards, and under my protection now as well."

"I have heard, my lady," Jarrow said gently.

"Yes," Graeme said, "and though I cannot stop them from

being shunned by gossips, they will not be barred from the village shops or from the church."

"Of course not. I shall look forward to seeing all of you there on Sunday and lending my support."

Graeme exchanged a look with Blythe.

"You mentioned a new threat," Jarrow said.

Perceptive fellow. And hadn't he said something they'd passed over? That it wasn't just Diddenton urging an inquiry?

The sound of laughter and clumping steps reached them.

"Nicholas has been threatened," Blythe said in a rush. "You must not say anything, Mr. Jarrow. We've just learned of this and we haven't spoken to him yet. You may stay for tea. I'll just go and assist them."

She hurried to the door and stepped out of the room. Graeme hoped she was not running away.

He nodded at Jarrow. "Who else is urging this inquiry?"

"Our old commander," Jarrow said, "and current Lord Lieutenant."

"What possible interest—"

"Is there not something peculiar about this property dispute arising just before Chilcombe's death and the manner of disposition? Perhaps it's that. Or, perhaps it has to do with diplomatic issues. Better to forestall a war with China than to wage one, do you think? Of course I am only speculating."

"I see," Graeme said. Distraught at the rise in addiction, Chinese emperors had banned the importation of opium supplied by the East India Company through middlemen like the sea captains who worked for Lord Diddenton.

The door opened, and Blythe and the housekeeper each carried in trays. Coralie coaxed Nicholas into the room before he spotted Jarrow and halted.

"Zounds," Jarrow muttered. "Your young lady is a beauty."

Coralie took Nicholas' hand and led him directly to Graeme and Jarrow. Lifting her chin, she sent Graeme a look.

"Jarrow, allow me to introduce Miss Coralie and Master Nicholas. Coralie and Nicholas, Mr. Jarrow is a neighbor who lives at Stonebridge Manor."

Jarrow greeted both children, and Mrs. Stockwell, who excused herself to return to her work, and took a seat near the children. Coralie plied both men with questions, and even Nicholas joined in asking about Jarrow's time in the army and Graeme's travels in foreign countries until every teacake and sandwich had disappeared.

"Nicholas and Coralie," Graeme said, "Yesterday, Mr. Jarrow and I helped Mr. Stockwell repair some damage done by someone causing trouble. Have either of you seen any strangers in the garden or in the fields?"

With Coralie's and Blythe's coaxing, they drew out a story of not just two men on two different occasions chasing the boy, but also sightings of other strangers nearby.

"Mr. Jarrow," Coralie said, "you're the magistrate now. If we catch these men, can you not have them put into jail?"

"Perhaps," Jarrow said. "If there is evidence of a crime. Meanwhile, it would be good for you children to stay indoors."

"Your godmama and I have a better idea," Graeme said. "What do you think about a visit to London?"

Coralie's face brightened. "May we go shopping? And..." she glanced at Nicholas, "The circus, Nicholas. The menagerie at the Tower. Yes. We want to go, don't we, Nick?"

Jarrow sent Graeme a skeptical look but kept silent.

Blythe stood. "Help me clear these dishes, Coralie. Nicholas, you too, and we'll all take them back to the kitchen. I'll return in a bit, Mr. Jarrow, for the conversation you requested."

Graeme ushered them out and rejoined Jarrow.

"I'd offer you a brandy but this is not my home," he said.

"No need," he said. "When do you leave for London?"

Graeme pressed his lips together, wondering whether he could trust him not to slip.

"I won't tell my mother. If it's the child they're after, there will be more opportunities for someone to snatch him there."

"And more opportunities to hire protection. We are leaving tomorrow at first light and plan to push through in one day if possible."

"Do you have outriders?"

"I will be the outrider."

"If you'll allow it, I'll share that duty. I have personal affairs to look into there, and," he shook his head, "this matter of trespassers has me concerned. I'll take my leave now. Please give my regards to Lady Chilcombe. I will talk with her more at a later date."

BLYTHE DECIDED TO SPEND THE NIGHT AT BLUEBELLE LODGE. After reading Nicholas to sleep and reminding Coralie to turn down the lamp when she finished her chapter, she retired. After tossing and turning for too long, she made her way to the kitchen.

That morning she'd left the children in Louisa's care and returned to the parlor, steeling herself for the questioning to come, only to find Mr. Jarrow gone and Graeme preparing to return to Risley Manor. Grateful for the reprieve, she dashed off quick notes for him to carry to Hermione and Radley, and breathed a sigh of relief that she wouldn't see him again until the next day. Since he'd decided to ride alongside the traveling chaise, she'd be mostly spared his company until they reached London.

Time spent with him was a trial. His kindness, his concern, tempted her to trust him and enticed her in ways she'd thought she'd grown immune to.

Too much was at stake to wager on Graeme's trustworthiness. Not to mention, it was very hard to place trust in him when she herself was keeping secrets. She might wish for a man to solve her troubles, but marriage and life with Archie had taught her to depend on herself.

Dinner with the children had been early and wonderfully congenial, and if either of them had misgivings about the next day's journey they didn't reveal them. Neither did she reveal hers.

This journey to London was not quite as terrifying as the one she'd made after her stay at Matron Manor. This time, she wasn't facing Chilcombe House and the town alone. The children would be with her, and she would have Will there when she arrived, as well as Hermione, who had sent a servant with a note assuring Blythe she would return with them.

She would have Will and Hermione.

And Graeme. Who she must not expect to rely on. The man he'd become, or, she reminded herself, the man he *appeared* to have become, was not what she'd expected.

That was the problem. She'd expected the indignant young man who'd called her a whore after discovering her with Archie to have grown even more stiff-necked. She'd expected a pompous, impeccable prig, not this seemingly kind man.

One who kept touching her.

With the kitchen to herself, and their departure only a few hours away, she donned an apron over her dressing gown. One couldn't have too much food. The children would need to eat. They might all be cramped and uncomfortable but they didn't have to be hungry.

The men—ugh, Mr. Jarrow was also accompanying them. Graeme wanted to leave early and travel as quickly as possible with stops to change horses. He and Mr. Jarrow might want something they could eat on horseback.

She found flour, the remains of that evening's roast, and some vegetables from the larder, stoked the fire in the Rumsford stove, and settled into the soothing task of making meat pasties.

Her own father had been an only child and a landless gentleman who died when she was still in the nursery. Her mother had remarried a spendthrift, gadabout gentleman estranged from his own family and promptly turned Blythe and her new brother over to the care of servants. Sad though she was at her parents' unexpected deaths, she'd been relieved to find herself living with Mr. and Mrs. Davies. She'd been even happier to learn that such a kind man as Mr. Davies had been named her guardian.

She'd never expected to rise so high as to marry an earl, and Mrs. Davies believed that a lady of the gentry ought to have knowledge of cookery, all the business of preserving food for the larder and making remedies for the still room. Cooking had been one of her favorite pastimes at Bluebelle Lodge.

Some biscuits were needed also, she decided, and

perhaps some hand pies made with the last of the winter apples.

"It smells delightful in here."

Blythe jumped and dropped the spoon she'd been holding. Graeme was not supposed to return until the morning.

She bent to find the spoon in the shadows and saw his buckskin clad legs as he reached for the dropped utensil. He picked it up first, and when she took it from him their hands touched, sending her heart into a gallop.

His gaze swept over her, his eyes widening at her deshabille.

"Apologies for startling you." He glanced at the table where the first batch of pasties were cooling. "Those look delicious. Oughtn't you to be in bed?"

She waved the spoon. "There are dishes in that cabinet over there. Help yourself and then take yourself off to bed. I can sleep in the carriage tomorrow, but you'll need your rest if you're planning to ride all the way to London."

She turned back to her task, picked up an apple and her knife, and heard the clatter of a plate and a bench drawing back.

"May I sit?" he asked. "This reminds me of the time I visited you here. Mrs. Davies insisted we have cakes where she was working and could keep an eye on us."

Graeme had been one of the younger lads coming around every once in a while. She'd had her eye on another lad—until of course, Archie. How different might her life have been if she'd made a life with one of the boys she'd grown up with.

Wiping her hands on her apron, she went to draw a mug of ale and plopped it down in front of him.

"Thank you." His hand shot out and took hers. "A countess who can cook. I had no idea."

She pulled away and went back to her dough, her thoughts all a jumble. In the shadowy kitchen he looked like the young man who'd visited her, so young then, and now, so very virile as he devoured the pasty with gusto.

"It is not a criticism," he said. "I think it is admirable that you can make something so delicious. In point of fact, I'm very hungry. I was too busy at Risley Manor to have much of a dinner. Stockwell and I put our heads together to arrange the post riders and horses. Lady Hermione and your maid and my valet will be here before dawn."

"And Mr. Jarrow?"

"Yes, him as well."

A shiver went down her spine. Graeme had spoken those words directly into her ear, the warmth of his breath tickling her.

"Can I help you?" he whispered.

Her hand slipped, the knife pricked her finger, and she dropped it.

He took her hand and produced a handkerchief, pressing it against the wound and bending to examine the spot of blood.

"It's nothing." She tried to tug her hand away.

"You're right," he said. "It's nothing. But I'll hold this to it a bit longer, and then maybe you'll let me slice the apples. Are we making apple pie? Wasn't it apple pie that Mrs. Davies served us that day?"

"*We* are making nothing. *You* are going to get some rest. And it was rhubarb pie she served."

"Ah," he said on a long sigh. "You remember that day in as much detail as I do." He touched her waist and turned her to face him. "Blythe," he said, leaning closer. "Blythe."

His lips touching hers, he pulled her close until her breasts pressed against his broad chest, their hearts beating together. A soft nibble, a gentle press, and then he angled his head and took the kiss deeper, bending her back against the counter. Heat flared and spread through her, wings of desire fluttering inside her. The kiss was gentle and seductive and then firmly inviting, his mouth opening and coaxing, and she shook off his handkerchief and threaded her fingers through the hair at the back of his head.

She wanted to fly away on that kiss, to submerge herself in sheer pleasure; the sheer pleasure of kissing a man who, if she was honest, she'd been wanting to kiss since he'd walked into the drawing room four days ago. Or had it been five days?

Cool air touched her shoulder and she looked down. He'd loosened her apron and robe and was touching her breast through the cotton of her nightgown, gently, each stroke sparking rivers of molten desire straight to her nether regions.

She leaned back and covered her gasps with one hand and pressed the other flat against his chest. She must stop him.

But maybe not yet. It had been so long, so very, very long since she'd felt anything like desire.

And it wasn't safe. He wasn't safe.

His eyes glowed darkly as he watched her. "I've wanted this for years."

I've wanted this for years.

Another voice rang in her memory. Lips crushing hers, a body pressing against hers.

No, she heard her own voice cry the word inside her head as her body began to tremble.

His hand froze. He stepped back and secured her robe and apron.

"You're not ready," he said.

Summoning her courage, she tried to speak calmly. "This is fraught... fraught, Graeme, with... with the kinds of problems, complications neither of us wants."

"Who will know?"

Her blood turned to ice in her veins. *Who will know.* Lord Vernon's words. Archie's words.

She opened her eyes and saw that he was watching her.

"You're right, of course," he said. "It's complicated and if people don't exactly know, they will speculate. I am not Lord Vernon. Or Archie, or the other fellow who turned over his phaeton. I want you, Blythe. And I care for you."

His intense gaze moved from her eyes to her lips, and her knees went weak.

"People have said, I should take a l-lover..." She cleared her throat. "now that I'm widowed."

And oh, how I want you in this moment.

"But it can't be you, Graeme. If Diddenton prevails, if I lose Bluebelle Lodge, I will have to sue you and how awkward will that be?"

"You won't have to sue me, my love. You will *never* have to sue me." He smoothed a lock of hair behind her ear. "I've wanted to kiss you since I was twelve years old. Yes." He nodded at her skeptical grimace. "At the village fayre when I bumped into you and your lemonade spilled all over your white gown with the blue flowers—"

"I wanted to box your ears."

"But you didn't. You laughed. In that moment, I fell in love with you."

"You had a strange way of showing it."

"I spent my school holidays here in Hampshire with my friend Lionel, do you remember? If we didn't find you in the village, or out walking, we would always come visit you at Bluebelle Lodge. I was always trying to spend time with you."

She shook her head. "I only remember the last time we spoke. You caught me in the lane, and you called me a—"

"I'm sorry." He pressed a finger to her lips. "It was brutal. I was wrong. I made you cry and…"

"A whore, Graeme. And that was after you pulled Archie off of me and started a fight that drew everyone out of the ballroom before I'd put my bodice right. Archie came to our wedding with a black eye that hadn't quite healed."

"I'm not sorry about blackening his eye. I *am* sorry they made you marry him."

"They made me marry him, and I wanted to marry him. More fool I."

"I was crushed, Blythe. I wanted, I hoped, that when I was old enough, you would still be unmarried. I thought, you ought to have waited. I was too proud to say that, so instead…" He took in a breath. "I loved you, and then I hated you, and now—"

"Now you want to swive me."

"*No,*" he said, emphatically. "There's nothing ugly in what I feel, in what I want from you. I tried to put you out of my mind. And I almost succeeded."

"You will try again and this time you will succeed."

"Yes." The heat in his eyes made her toes curl and told her they were talking at cross-purposes. "I won't stop trying." He kissed her again, briefly, tenderly, and stepped back. "I'm very good at peeling apples. How many do you need?"

CHAPTER THIRTEEN

The journey to town was long, the tedium inside the coach broken up by games, naps, food from the basket Blythe had prepared, and Lady Hermione's story telling.

Radley, stout traveler that she was, rode part of the way up on top with Graeme's valet. When it rained, she crammed inside the large vehicle with them. Coralie and Nicholas, who had never traveled farther than the village, enjoyed the new sights and the adventure.

It was well past dark when they crept into London, and the one footman left on duty admitted them. Maids went to hastily make up the nursery and Radley led both children upstairs, while Blythe promised to join them in moments.

"We didn't expect you, my lord." Adwick appeared, pulling on his coat, his tone bordering on peevish.

"Apologies, Adwick," Graeme said. "It couldn't be helped. My wards and Mr. Jarrow will be staying with us. I'll need someone to carry a message tonight, and we'll all need a light meal."

"Not I," Lady Hermione said. "I'm for bed. Good night, my dears."

They wished her a good night too, and Graeme invited Mr. Jarrow and Blythe to join him in the library.

"I'll be along in a moment," she said, and both men left.

"The green room for Mr. Jarrow," she told the butler, "and tell Cook, sandwiches in the library will do. Has my brother gone out?"

"Yes, my lady. He was to attend the theater and a ball afterwards."

"Has he left any messages?"

"In fact, there is a letter he asked me to post to you first thing tomorrow."

Her heart thumped wildly and all her fatigue vanished. "I'd like to see it immediately."

"There are some other letters for you as well."

She'd best look at all of them. Lunetta had promised to write again.

"I'll wait here, while you may bring me those as well."

When Adwick returned, she carried the letters upstairs to her chamber, where one of the footmen was settling her trunk.

Graeme would be sending a message to his friend to secure more men to guard the children, but surely that could not be arranged until the morrow. She hoped he and Jarrow would stay in tonight.

She herself would go to the nursery. Nicholas might be frightened by the new surroundings. Firstly though...

She picked up the unfranked letter and recognized Will's scrawl.

DEAR BLYTHE,

I believe I've found the person you're seeking, though I've not spoken to her in person. The house is in Soho on a not quite respectable street. I've called there and though I duly paid my coin to the landlady, I was told your quarry was out, and it must have been true, as I went around to the back and peeked in the window. I'll try again on the morrow and will conduct this negotiation for you. I have found two jewelers in the East End but otherwise have done nothing with the articles you left with me. I have a fair idea of amounts and will represent you accordingly. You need not return to town, in fact I hope you do not. Leave this to me.

Will

SHE TOSSED THE LETTER ONTO HER WRITING DESK AND glanced through the other correspondence, finding nothing from Lunetta. Well, she had promised to write in a week, and it had only been a few days.

Time was careening though.

A maid appeared to ready her room and help her into a new gown, and then she went to the nursery. Let the men talk among themselves. The children needed her first.

MORLEY HAD NOT BEEN AT WHITE'S, BUT THE FOOTMAN HAD tracked him down at a rout in Mayfair. He'd immediately answered the summons and appeared.

Graeme introduced him to Jarrow.

"Glad you returned so quickly," Morley said, accepting a brandy. "I've discovered the name of the surveyor Diddenton used to draw up the claimed property lines. He's in Hertfordshire, working. I've sent a man to follow him."

"One might infer that Diddenton bribed the surveyor," Jarrow observed.

Morley nodded. "There's a young lord looking into some of the marquess's dodgy practices as well. Heir to Shaftesbury. He's a reformer type—child labor in factories, climbing boys, lunatic asylums, etc.,. The family are Quakers."

Graeme took his seat behind the desk. "Thank you, Morley. I'm not sure how that will help us though. Political sway, maybe?"

He sipped his brandy, fighting the fatigue dogging him. Blythe should be here to hear this.

"It's a matter of the opium," Morley said. "Diddenton's a middleman. Has merchants that buy the opium from the Company's people who grow it, and then Diddenton's ships smuggle it into China in defiance of the Emperor's edict. At great profit, of course."

"And that brings us to that connection I mentioned," Jarrow said. "There are those in the government worried about a war over opium with China."

"And those like Shaftesbury's son worried about opium here, especially in the Fens," Morley said. "I hear tell the stalls sell a thousand vials every market day in Cambridge. I'm an Oxford man myself."

The soggy landscape of the Fens was a breeding ground for damp air and the ague that plagued many of the inhabitants.

"The late earl was a Cambridge man." Graeme drummed his fingers on the desk. "Perhaps he got started on the habit there."

"Diddenton's opium trade won't matter to the consistory court," Jarrow said. "Too many peers are making money from the trade. On the other hand, if the late earl was given too much, perhaps supplied by Diddenton's son, we might be able to reopen the earl's death."

"Or at least stir a scandal that throws doubt on the marquess's property claims," Graeme said. "Perhaps even encourage witnesses to come forward and expose him as a fraud."

"Reputation is important when a man defies decency and makes the sort of claim he's made," Jarrow said.

Blythe had returned to society after her year of mourning for the specific purpose of reestablishing her reputation, her place in the ton, in service of fighting Diddenton's claims. Otherwise, she would have happily stayed at Bluebelle Lodge where he might have visited her, courted her properly, and got to know his new cousin, Coralie, and Nicholas.

Nicholas.

"Morley, I asked you to come tonight because of another matter. There's a child we believe may be in danger."

He told them about the vandalism at Bluebelle Lodge and Nicholas.

"I take it that's the boy at the heart of some of the gossip," Morley said.

Graeme nodded.

"I can send men to Hampshire—"

"The children are here now. I brought him and the girl to London."

"The girl? Ah. Your cousin's, er, illegitimate daughter. Well then, protection will be much easier to arrange."

Morley departed, promising to return with at least one Bow Street man before morning.

"And what is your plan, Jarrow?" Graeme asked. "Lady Chilcombe was inclined to distrust your motives for accompanying us."

"I never did have an opportunity to question her. I note that she didn't join us tonight as promised. Not that I was planning to speak with her now."

"She's probably with the children."

Jarrow frowned down at his glass. "Miss Coralie won't be a child much longer. No matter the manner of her birth, she's an earl's daughter, and she'll make some lucky man an intelligent wife. Beautiful, as well. Make sure he's deserving."

Graeme turned an astonished gaze on him, and Jarrow laughed.

"Miss Coralie is far too young for me... *Now.*"

"And in a few years? This is my young relation you're speaking of."

Jarrow shook his head. "I learned in the army to let the future take care of itself. But if you recall, I have an amiable, intelligent, and dare I say, pretty younger sister, so I'm facing the sort of worries you'll very soon have yourself. And if you launch Miss Coralie into society as my mother is attempting to do with my sister..."

Jarrow grimaced, and Graeme wondered how many sensible suitors Mrs. Jarrow was driving away.

"I take your point," he said. "Do you plan to offer your sister a London season once your father has recovered?"

Or passed away.

"Yes. Though, I'm not sure he'll recover." Jarrow's frown deepened. "From some of his notes, I believe he had suspicions about the earl's death, but what and about whom... well, I wish I could ask him. I truly don't suspect Lady Chilcombe killed her husband. I want to track down that nurse, or forgive me, mistress or whatever she was, if she's still living. I think she'll shed light on the late earl's death as well as this business of the will."

"That blasted will," Graeme said. Blythe might have burned one copy—and he hoped she had, but there was surely another one that had disappeared from the estate's muniment room.

He'd best find the woman before Jarrow did.

"First, though," Jarrow said, "I must attend to personal business. I'm seeking a physician to travel to Hampshire and examine my father."

Graeme sat up. "As it happens, Lady Chilcombe would like Nicholas to be seen by someone in town. The lad has bouts of fever and lung problems, she says. If you hear of a competent man, please let me know."

"Certainly. I'll seek out the woman after that."

That would give him a day's head start.

* * *

AN HOUR PAST JARROW'S DEPARTURE FOR BED, GRAEME HAD been dozing in the chair when Morley returned with a hard-faced man he introduced as Tibbs, a Bow Street Runner who would remain and stand guard that night.

Blythe's brother Will had not arrived home yet. Adwick —who was also still up—said the captain often didn't arrive home until well after dawn. Graeme briefed Tibbs about Will and the servants he might possibly encounter and then left him and a footman on duty.

Still, he couldn't help worrying.

Assuming the nursery might be on the top floor, he made his way there, the urge to check on the children's safety driving him.

He'd never had the care of a child before, not in these circumstances anyway. Oh, now and then, he'd been assigned the duty of escorting an official's wife and children from one post to another, but rarely when there was any real threat of harm, and never when the children were his own family.

As these two were. He supposed they were two more anchors keeping him from leaving England immediately. Despite her resilience and dedication, would Blythe be able to protect them?

He clutched the banister, fatigue dogging his steps. He'd gone twenty-four hours without sleep and needed some rest before the next day's search.

First, though, he'd check on the children.

He saw a light burning under the door of a likely room and silently turned the knob.

A hobby horse stood in one corner near a low table and small chairs and a shelf stacked with books. Two low cots that looked like camp beds stretched from one wall.

Nicholas lay, arms akimbo over his blankets, on one cot; Coralie had curled up on her side on the other bed, her hair in a long blond braid, her breath still and regular. Radley snored in a nearby armchair, and Blythe sat in a wing chair, her feet tucked up under her, her head pillowed against the chair wing.

The dim lamp light cast her in a luminous glow. She'd changed into a night gown and thin dressing gown and taken her hair down.

He went to her and touched her shoulder. When she didn't stir, he slid an arm under her bottom and the other around her shoulder and lifted her.

Radley was there and the house was guarded. Blythe needed to be in her bed.

In her bedchamber, a lamp burned dimly and the covers had been turned back. He lay her down gently.

Even buttoned up to her neck, she was delectable.

Barefoot and with her hair in a long braid for sleep, she looked more like the young girl he'd met so many years ago. On a whim, he toed off his own shoes, cast off his coats, and slid into the bed next to her.

It had been a long while since he'd lain with a woman—too long—but he'd never felt this sort of intimacy. Transitory affection at times, but never this.

She sighed and snuggled closer, and he closed his eyes, inhaling her scent. Despite a whole day of travel, she smelled of clean linens and a delicate perfume.

In contrast to him. He ought to have washed.

It was his last thought before falling asleep.

* * *

BLYTHE STRUGGLED AWAKE FROM A DREAM, FEELING strangely disoriented. Though the room was chilled, she was unaccountably warm.

An arm lay across her waist and slow, steady snoring tickled her ear. The dim lamplight cast enough glow to see the flowers on the bed hangings. Nicholas must have found his way down from the nursery; she hoped the snoring didn't mean he'd caught a cold on the journey.

She patted the arm draping her, froze, and turned her head.

Graeme. Graeme was here, in her bed, holding her close as if… as if…

What had she done?

The snoring paused, one eye cracked open, and his lips curved. He nuzzled her neck, his bristly stubble sending sensation rippling through her middle and lower.

Her heart pounded. She'd just been dreaming of *this*. She'd just been dreaming of *him*.

How...

She'd been in the nursery. Had he carried her down? And then tucked himself into her bed and...

His hand began moving, distracting her.

Closing her eyes, she absorbed the sensation, struggling to think. "Wha-at are you—"

Lips touched hers, gently, and then more forcefully, and as he pressed against her, she felt it—he was fully aroused.

Alarm warred with desire. She opened her eyes and saw that his eyes had drifted closed and his face had taken on the determined set of a man in the throes of passion.

A memory of Archie chilled her. Graeme wasn't properly awake. He didn't even know it was her.

She shoved at him and his eyes flew open.

"Blythe." His hand lifted. "Shhh," he said, "Sorry." He smoothed her hair. "Apologies. So tired."

He shushed and soothed and his strong fingers massaged her shoulder.

"Go back to sleep," he whispered, "you're safe. The children are safe. I... I carried you to your bed and... There's a Bow Street Runner in the house. No one will hurt you."

"I thought..." She closed her eyes. Graeme wasn't Archie. He'd known it was her he was kissing.

She swallowed bile and shook her head. "Will I ever be free of the memories?"

Graeme's hand paused and he drew her closer. "Yes. We'll create new memories, good memories, to wipe out all of the old bad ones. But not tonight. Tonight you sleep."

"Maybe," she mumbled.

Maybe it could be true. She nodded and finally slipped off into slumber.

* * *

Graeme waited until he knew she was sleeping, and then waited a while longer, watching her in the dim light.

He would have made love to her right then and there if there'd been more than the slightest acquiescence. A passionate woman lay underneath all the layers of fears and bad memories.

It had taken a supreme act of will on his part to pause, but it had been anger that drove away the last of his lust.

Not anger at Blythe. Never at Blythe, no matter what document she'd burned or who she'd slept with, willingly, or as he suspected, unwillingly.

He'd forgive her. After all, he was the one who'd got her into that travesty of a marriage.

If Archie wasn't already dead, he'd have him by the throat. He'd beat his peacock of a cousin to a pulp. He could do it, too. He'd learned when to exercise diplomacy and when to apply his fists.

He slipped out of bed, careful not to disturb her, and found his coats and his shoes, guessing that it must be only an hour or so until dawn. Moving quietly to the desk where the lamp stood, he pulled on his garments and noticed a letter lying open.

I believe I've found the person you're seeking though I've not spoken to her in person. As you suspected, her lodgings are in Soho, on a not quite respectable street.

He unfolded the rest of the letter and read on, then returned it carefully to the desk.

Blythe was keeping more secrets.

Anger flickered briefly in him and then died.

Of course she would confide in her brother before confiding in him. He still hadn't earned her trust. But he would. And he'd wait for her to realize that she trusted him. Hadn't he waited fifteen years for her?

That business about the East End—her brother had found names of pawn shops. She was pawning a piece of jewelry to get money, and there was a negotiation to be conducted. Blythe's brother had also found Lunetta Casale, and the woman wanted money in exchange for the will.

Or was there some other reason the woman would blackmail Blythe?

Graeme moved quietly to the bed and watched her. Her breathing was heavy, and regular, convincing him that she was truly asleep and not pretending.

What had her life been like? She was a woman with secrets, and he wanted to uncover them all.

He found his way to the corridor, and none too soon. As he neared his bedchamber, he heard footfalls behind him and turned. Blythe's brother was staggering toward her door.

"Captain Lynford," he said in a whisper.

Lynford paused, one hand braced on the door, the other on the knob. "You're up, Chilcombe?"

"I was checking things. You spoke with the Runner who's here tonight?"

"Cheeky cockney? Yes. Wouldn't tell me squat. Said I must ask you."

Graeme nodded. "Let Blythe be. She's sleeping. Come to the library and I'll fill you in."

Frowning, Lynford approached and staggered again, his hand to his mouth.

"Damn if I'm not going to hurl," he said.

With Graeme's help, Lynford reached his own room just in time.

"Bloody hell," he said, when he'd finished spewing. "I didn't think I drank that much." He fell back on the bed.

"Get out of those coats," Graeme said.

"That blasted Lord Vernon." Lynford wobbled up, groaning and shrugging off his coat. "How'd you know my sister was sleeping?"

"What about Lord Vernon?" Graeme asked.

Lynford's expression grew mulish. "What about my sister?"

It had been a near thing tonight. If Lynford had found him in his sister's bed, it might have meant a demand for pistols at dawn.

"I found her asleep in a chair in the nursery and carried her to her bed."

"The nursery?" Lynford looked confused, and Graeme realized Blythe hadn't mentioned the children to Lynford.

But she'd told Graeme, and the thought gave him hope that just maybe he'd have a chance of earning her trust.

Lynford gagged again and reached for the chamber pot.

He'd get nothing out of Lynford tonight. "We'll talk tomorrow. I'll get you a footman."

Lynford would be too befuddled for an early start escorting Blythe to Lunetta's lodgings. He would bet his last farthing that Blythe, who'd already done so much searching, would be out looking at first light.

CHAPTER FOURTEEN

"*I*'m only going out for an hour or two, my darling." Blythe smoothed a hand over Coralie's hair and whispered, "You'll help Nicholas while I'm gone, won't you? He'll need your steady presence, and I'll tell Cook to let Roddy, the kitchen boy, come up and play with him later." She'd left a note for Lady Hermione as well, though she wouldn't disturb that good lady's slumber.

Coralie yawned. "What time is it?"

Blythe shushed her. Nicholas was still asleep and she didn't want to wake him. Radley had risen to help Blythe dress, and a maid had taken her place in Radley's chair.

The new maid dozed as well. It had been a grueling night for everyone at Chilcombe House.

A morsel of guilt niggled at her. For all that had transpired since Graeme's arrival, she'd slept quite peacefully in her lover's arms until she awakened and found him gone.

Not that Graeme was her lover or ever would be.

Before she could even think about dallying with him, or

any other man, she must get to Lunetta, obtain the copy of the will from the woman, if indeed she had it, and destroy it.

It was shameful, illegal, and absolutely necessary, and she wouldn't involve Graeme. He had an earldom to think of and a future diplomatic career.

Adwick, dear Adwick, who hadn't slept more than a wink, said Will had crept in at the break of dawn. He'd been keeping late hours, both in going to bed and in rising.

She wouldn't disturb him. She didn't need to. Will's mention of Soho had jiggled loose a memory of something Lunetta had once let slip.

She had a good idea where Lunetta Casale had lived before her arrival at Risley Manor, and she needed to go there while the whores and cutpurses were sleeping.

Dressing quickly in her oldest and plainest gown, she went down to the kitchen. Cook was up, beginning the preparations for breakfast. The door to the pantry was open and she spotted the urchin who slept there stretched on a pallet, still asleep. When she returned to London from Matron Manor, she'd found the lad sleeping in the stairwell and taking handouts from Cook.

That good lady looked up from the dough she was kneading. "You're going out, my lady?"

Blythe put a finger to her lips and shook her head. "Let Roddy help take the tray up to the nursery and play for a while," she said. "But only when they call for it. It was a long journey and they're still sleeping. I won't be gone long."

"Here." Cook wrapped two cooling buns in a cloth. "You must eat."

The warmth of the fragrant bundle sent a shiver through her as she accepted it. "Thank you. Come and lock the door behind me."

It was cool for late April, and as she opened the door to

the service stairs at the front of the house, she saw that it was drizzling.

Cook's disapproving silence followed her out of the door.

Drawing her shawl over her head, she made her way up the stairs. A small figure moved into view.

"Anything I can do fer ye today, milady?"

"Bobby, I was hoping I'd see you about." She handed over the warm bundle of bread. "Walk with me to the hackney stand and tell me what you know."

Bobby was another street urchin who lingered about, kin or just friend to Roddy, she wasn't sure, but he'd begun appearing on the street after she'd taken in the smaller child.

"There's been a Runner in your place all night, milady," he said through a mouthful.

"Yes. Finish chewing before you speak. Lord Chilcombe hired him."

"Heard the tall bloke what's been staying here's your brother?"

"Yes. Captain Lynford."

Blythe waved to a passing hackney and the driver pulled up.

"Keep your eyes and ears open for me, will you?" she said, reaching for the carriage's door.

"Where ye going?"

"Never mind, you. It's none of your business."

Opening the door, she paused on the step. A hand reached out and tugged her the rest of the way in.

Graeme's hand.

"Where to?" the driver asked.

"Where to, Blythe?" Graeme still had hold of her.

Too astonished to speak, she spluttered.

"Soho," Graeme called. "We'll give you the street when we get closer."

* * *

BLYTHE STRAIGHTENED IN HER SEAT, HER HEART CLACKING wildly as astonishment and anger flooded her. How... He'd been in her room. He'd gone through her things... or...She cast her mind over her memory of her room. She'd left Will's note on her writing table. Clearly, Graeme had found it and read it.

He didn't know everything though. He didn't know where exactly in Soho she needed to go.

Easing in a breath, she mentally ran through her options. They could turn around and return home and wait for Will to arise.

But of course, then she'd have to argue with her brother about allowing her to pay this call with him. And perhaps by then, other parties would be involved—Graeme's friend, Morley, or even Mr. Jarrow.

Or she could guide them to random addresses in Soho in what would be a futile search for the woman.

"Let me help you," Graeme said.

Or, yes, that was another option. She could take Graeme's assistance. And if they found the new will, then what?

She leaned back into the squab, wishing that she could make herself invisible and slip away without Graeme noticing.

He was a silent presence seated beside her. He'd let go of her hand, and she felt the absence of his touch. It had been reassuring. And friendly. Perhaps almost loving.

Such a small intimacy, a touch on the hand. So much

more stirring than her late husband's aggressive groping. Graeme, so far, had been kind.

How long would that last?

Only until he discovers what you've done and what you intend to do. This dance with him was getting tiring. She might as well meet her fate.

"Very well," she said, her voice more brittle than she would have liked. "Bridie Lane," she called to the driver and then turned to Graeme. "Lunetta Casale claims to have the only copy of the new will," she said softly. "She wants five hundred pounds for it."

Graeme looked away and frowned. "What are her circumstances?"

"She says she contracted an illness from Archie."

"And is unable to work at her trade? What is this place we are visiting?"

"A house where someone she knew had rooms. She had Archie frank correspondence to send to Bridie Lane. She may be living there now."

"Is it a brothel?"

"That is a good guess but I don't know. My emissaries have not had success."

"I'm glad you're not going there alone. Who have you sent to look for her?"

"My brother, of course, and a street urchin, Bobby, who it seems you have befriended already. Did you bribe him to walk me to the hackney you hired?"

* * *

GRAEME HID A SMILE AT HER SHREWDNESS.

"Bobby is as happy as the next urchin to accept a coin,

but in all truth, he was as worried about you going out alone as I am. He regards you fondly, my lady."

"He regards Cook's pies even more fondly."

"What is your plan today? Did you bring the money?"

"If I pawned all my jewelry I could not come up with that amount. And I would not take the Chilcombe jewels, which will rightly belong to the next Lady Chilcombe. I am not a thief. I will simply negotiate with her."

"You are a cool one, Lady Chilcombe."

She turned her gaze on him, and he saw the turmoil in her eyes and felt a twinge of guilt. But he must go on.

"I applaud your… adaptability. Your quick thinking. If I were sitting across the negotiating table from you, I might use the word wiliness. You burned the copy of that new will that Sir Morris was carrying to London, didn't you. How did you obtain it?"

Though her eyes remained open, she'd drawn a shade down on her emotions.

"Let me speculate," he said. "You followed Sir Morris and found him after his crash. You're not a murderer, you said, and I believe you. He was already dead when you arrived. You withdrew the will from his baggage and took it back to Bluebelle Lodge, where Coralie saw you burning it."

That brought the slightest of gasps before her mouth firmed in a mulish line.

"Coralie told me. I don't believe she's told anyone else. And who would think to question a young girl? Was it not a bit cruel for you to leave Sir Morris to the mercy of the elements?"

A long moment ticked by before she spoke.

"As you said, he was already dead when I came across him," she said quietly. "I was going for help at Risley Manor when a coach came along and stopped for him. They did not see me."

"Was the will the same as Diddenton asserts?"

She nodded. "And as Archie described to me that day." She took in a tight breath. "There is more. A letter Sir Morris was carrying to Diddenton. I... I took it also. It was from Lord Vernon to his father, telling him that, as his father had suggested, he'd supplied Archie with the Indian opium and left Sir Morris to persuade Archie to sign the new will. He said that Archie's health and his addiction were such that his death would be imminent, and having performed this task, he expected to take possession of Bluebelle Lodge before summer."

"Astonishing. The letter—"

"Is hidden. I didn't destroy it. But I couldn't see a way to produce it to the court without incurring suspicions of my own."

Graeme sat, thinking.

"If Lunetta has the will, what do you intend to do with it, Lord Chilcombe?"

"I thought we might burn it together," he said.

She shook her head. "I won't have you committing fraud. You're young and ambitious and talented. Once this matter is settled, you might return to your diplomatic career. And with a title, your chance of a plum assignment is greater."

A plum assignment would take him far away from her. Unless she came with him.

"I would think of it as correcting a greater, more egregious fraud. But perhaps we might put our heads together and find a better way."

Before he could explain the carriage drew to a stop at the entrance of a narrow street.

"Which number," the driver asked.

"We'll get out here and walk," Blythe said. "Wait for us, please."

Number thirteen in the line of narrow terraced dwellings had a single front window on each floor of the smoke-blackened brick façade. In an earlier century, it had likely housed a respectable family.

Perhaps there were respectable tenants living here now, but Graeme doubted it. A door knocker hung by one nail. He banged his fist on the door instead. When there was no answer, he tried the latch and the door opened.

"Shall we?" he asked.

She nodded, and he ushered her across the threshold. The age-old scent of mildew and human odors greeted them. A dim light shone through the transom above the door, highlighting scarred flooring, peeling paint, and the worn steps of the staircase. A door led off the interior hall. The house had most likely been divided into separate lodgings, perhaps one per floor in the narrow structure.

"We should start on the top floor," she whispered.

They were half-way up the stairs when the ground floor door opened and a woman of middling years stepped out.

"Here now, where are you going?" she asked.

If this was Lunetta Casale, his cousin Archie's tastes had degenerated. Attired in a threadbare dressing gown that had once been colorful, and with a dingy white cap covering straggling locks that were an improbable shade of yellow, she might be one of London's more disreputable abbesses.

Blythe stepped down and leaned past him. "Lunetta has asked for me to come," she said in a shaky voice.

The woman frowned, her eyebrows drawing together.

Graeme pulled out a coin and tossed it. She caught if deftly.

"Where is her room, madame?" he asked. "Or is she still with a customer?"

"This ain't a bawdy house," the woman said.

Not until evening, he thought.

"You're her friend, are you not?" Blythe asked. "Tell her Lord and Lady Chilcombe are here to see her, as she requested."

"You've brought the money?" the woman asked.

"What money is that?" Graeme asked.

Before the woman could answer, Blythe took another step down. "Wait," she said breathlessly, "I've seen you before, haven't I?"

Without taking a step, the woman shrunk back. "Don't play coy, milord. You know what money. Lunetta's not... not well. She asked me to handle the matter."

"You have what she was offering?" Graeme asked. "Show us, then."

"Show me the money."

* * *

BLYTHE'S CHEST TIGHTENED AS JUMBLED MEMORIES CAREENED about in her head, stirring a panicky anger.

The unnaturally yellow hair, the eyes so dark they were almost black, the jaundiced skin—this woman had been at Risley Manor.

"We are at an impasse, my lady." Graeme's words, spoken softly into her ear, jolted her back to her senses.

"I don't remember your name," Blythe said. "I will call you madame, and I will see Lunetta. Now. If she is ill, I can arrange care for her."

The woman scoffed.

"You appear to be ill as well," Blythe said. "Is that why *you* want money?"

"There's someone else who'll pay more for that will if you don't want to come up with five hundred pounds."

"We'll have to see it first, of course," Graeme said. "Show it to us."

"It's not here. Look now, you're getting a bargain. There's someone else who'll pay more."

The sound of a cat crying drew the woman's attention and had annoyance flashing across her face.

Not a cat, a baby.

Graeme handed the woman another coin. "See to your child," he said. "Tell your friend we'll return this afternoon and expect to see her."

He hurried Blythe out of the door and down the street, his hand clamping hers over his arm. The hackney had waited, and he all but lifted her inside before jumping in after her and shouting directions to the driver.

The truth came to Blythe in a rush. "Lunetta Casale must be dead," she said.

"Perhaps. Or perhaps she sold the will on to that woman."

Blythe shook her head. *"There's someone else who'll pay more.* Those were almost the exact words from the note I received, supposedly from Lunetta."

Graeme was silent a long time and she realized: she hadn't shown him the note.

"She sent me a note. Only one, and I received it the day you arrived."

"Tell me about this woman we met today," he said quietly.

She turned her head to the window, looking out blindly, some of the horror of that night obscuring the passing view.

Madame. That was what Archie had called her. Madame had been painted and primped, and she'd carried a crop in her hand, following a glittery-eyed Archie into Blythe's bedchamber. She'd handed the crop to Archie, and both had approached Blythe.

The sluggish memory was like a poorly remembered nightmare. The cup of cocoa a maid had brought her—not her maid, Louisa, but another maid—had been drugged. She'd not had more than a sip. That had been enough to make her stagger. To turn her limbs to jelly.

Lord Vernon had been the wraith lingering in the doorway, though she'd held off the memories and panic for months before remembering.

A hand touched her shoulder and she reflexively shook it off, clawing at the window, her breath coming in panicked gulps.

"Blythe." The hand touched her again, a gentle pat and she cringed. "Blythe."

Archie calling her. *Come around the bed, Blythe. You will like this.*

"Blythe, my love. You are safe, Blythe."

Blythe. Someone called her name. Graeme. Graeme was here, concern in his voice.

Safe. Her gaze focused on carriages, wagons, houses, sweepers, gentlemen, and maids with children in tow.

They would soon reach Chilcombe House.

He was still here and he'd been trying to comfort her with his touch. What must he think?

Must she care what he thought?

Still… he had the upper hand. There was a political game over the will to be played out, and perhaps he really did mean to help her.

"I am sorry, Graeme." She shook her head. "I assure you, I am not a candidate for Bedlam."

"I know you are not, Blythe."

"What are we to do next?" she asked. "Lure Madame out of the house and search? We ought to do that soon before she offers the will to Diddenton."

"We will keep that in mind as a possibility. First, though, I have another approach in mind. May I see that letter from Lord Vernon to his father?"

"Why not? You know about everything else."

"Blythe," he said, reaching for her.

This time she allowed his touch; allowed him to wrap her in an embrace, allowed him to comfort her.

"I don't quite know everything, do I?" he asked, his voice gentle. "But I can and will wait until you are ready to tell me."

She kept her attention fixed on a spot on the floor where another passenger had brought in mud, fighting the memories. Louisa had come along later to help her. Coralie had only seen the worst of the miscarriage. Only Archie, that woman, Madame, and Lord Vernon had been present, and the thought sent anger surging through her.

She'd wanted Archie dead. She'd be happy to see Madame and Lord Vernon follow him.

But she wasn't a murderer.

* * *

ADWICK GREETED THEM AT THE DOOR WITH A LETTER FOR Graeme, and he recognized the Foreign Office seal.

"They said it was urgent," Adwick said. "Will you take breakfast? Lady Hermione has just arrived in the breakfast room. Captain Lynford has not arisen. The children's food has just gone up to them."

Graeme helped Blythe with her pelisse and handed his hat to Adwick.

"I'd best read this letter first before the other one, Blythe."

"Tell Lady Hermione we will be along directly," Blythe said. "Lord Chilcombe, I can bring that item to the library, if you'll wait for me there."

He shook his head. "My sitting room, I think. Come, I'll escort you."

At the staircase, he paused. "It is in your room, isn't it?"

She nodded. "Well-hidden."

While she went off to retriever her letter, he cracked the seal on the one he'd just received. He'd been called to a meeting in an hour's time. Not at the Foreign Office, but at a private address in Mayfair.

Annoyed at the interruption to his plans, he rubbed his eyes, fatigue gripping him. He would need to change his clothes and he would need coffee.

A knock at the door brought Blythe. She handed him the letter with shaking fingers. Clive, his new valet, appeared behind her.

He sent the lad to fetch him a tray.

"Sit down, Blythe," he said, leading her to a sofa. "Please give my apologies to Lady Hermione. I'm called to an urgent meeting but I'll return here directly afterward."

She moved as if to stand, but he seated himself next to her.

"Stay, please, while I read this. I may have questions."

The letter from Lord Vernon was water-stained in places. Surely not tears—he recalled that it had been snowing that day.

When he finished, he folded the paper. "This will go in the safe. Agreed?"

"Yes."

"And I must ask you where the safe is and who has access to it." He ought to have thought of that before.

Blythe grimaced. "I'm sorry. There are actually two: one in the library that Adwick can open. The Chilcombe jewelry is in there. There also is one in your suite that only you will be able to access." She handed him a key. "I ought to have given you this sooner. You will find this one more convenient. After Archie died, I had a new safe installed here." She stood and drew him up. "It's in your bedchamber. Let me show you."

He would finally have her in his bedchamber. If only the circumstances were different.

He followed her into the inner room, and she led him to the fireplace where the safe had been concealed behind nearby paneling.

"It's a special Chubb lock," she said. "Impossible to pick."

The iron box interior smelled new.

"It's empty."

"Yes. There were some documents in there, stock certificates and such. I've had them moved to the other safe so that Adwick can retrieve them for the broker when he visits."

After the letter was safely stowed in the empty compartment, he handed the key back to her. Color rose in her cheeks as she stood looking at it.

CHAPTER FIFTEEN

Graeme had moved closer, and he hadn't simply handed her the key—he'd pressed it into her palm.

"No." She shook her head. "I ought to have given you this sooner. In all the, er, excitement, I forgot. Nor should I be entering your bedchamber to access the safe."

"My new valet says you were responsible for the elegant refurbishing, the bathing chamber, and the new bed. He said you ordered the old one burned."

He lifted the key from her hand, sweeping his thumb across her palm as he did so, sending a wave of sensation through her.

"Would you consider entering my bedchamber for other reasons?"

Her chest tightened, desire blooming in her. "I would… consider… That is, but I wouldn't do it." At least not until the will was resolved. And that resolution was the important topic. "You said that you have another approach in mind—those were your words. What is it?"

"I would like to involve Morley and Jarrow. Your brother as well. Will you allow it?"

Panic flared in her. "Will you tell them how the letter was obtained?"

"No. Not the truth, anyway. We can imply that we got it from that woman. Jarrow says there is political opposition to Diddenton that may serve our interest, and Morley is looking into fraud with regard to the land claim. Will you allow me to tell them about the letter?"

"Oh. If you must."

"Blythe, love." His arms came around her. "I won't betray you. We'll sort this out. Will you trust me?"

There was a firmness to his lips, and yet, a vulnerability in his eyes.

Hadn't Archie said the same words a few months after their marriage, after her discovery that he'd been seducing the maids? *I won't betray you again, Blythe. Will you trust me?* Hadn't he also looked vulnerable?

No—he'd simply adopted the penitent little boy look he must have used on his grandparents for years.

But this was Graeme, not Archie.

She nodded. "I will trust you. For now."

"That will have to do." He dipped his head and captured her lips in a kiss that filled her with such tenderness and yearning that she wanted to weep.

Desire gripped her and she went up on her toes, angling her head and raking her fingers through his hair, pressing so close she could feel the pounding of his heart against hers.

Yes, she *would* make love to him, here in this new bed, and cleanse the room of the last earl's debauchery. Graeme, who'd been her friend, and then her enemy, and who was now an ally. One who wanted her.

A door clicked shut in the sitting room and they both froze.

"Leave the tray in there," Graeme called through the open door of the bedchamber. "I'll be out in a moment."

He set his forehead against hers and sighed.

"Blythe. You must know, from the first day I met you—"

"Shhh." She set a finger to his lips. It had been just enough of a distraction to bring her to her senses. "I think that you are a good man, Graeme, the sort of man who should christen the earl's new bed with *your* countess, not Archie's, when you choose one." She untangled herself from his embrace. "You must go, and I must go."

"What if the countess I choose was once Archie's countess?"

Marriage? Marriage to a good man where there was respect and tenderness and friendship... She shook her head. The risk was too great. "I'm too old. Too much has happened. You would come to regret it."

"What I regret happened fifteen years ago. I'm not that callous, judgmental boy anymore, and I know what I want."

"No, Graeme. It was *my* fault, *my* vanity, *my* indiscretion. We've already discussed this." She turned to leave.

"I want you, Blythe." His voice stopped her in the doorway, tempting her to turn back to him. "I'll return home as soon as this meeting is completed and we'll have Morley and Jarrow join us. Your brother as well. Will you promise not to go back there? Will you wait for me?"

He knew her well enough to know she was thinking of gathering up Will as soon as he awakened and returning to Soho.

She nodded. "I'll wait for you."

For a while, anyway.

* * *

THE ADDRESS IN MAYFAIR PROVED TO BE A PRIVATE CLUB. A very private one, inasmuch as he'd never heard of it, frequented by the upper echelon of men in trade, as well as titled and untitled gentlemen, most of whom were religious dissenters.

The porter escorted him to a private meeting room where attendees had already assembled.

Jarrow was not at some physician's office, he was here. As was Morley. They stood, heads bent together, talking to a gentleman of middling years, while a younger man hovered nearby—Emory, the Chilcombe solicitor's clerk.

Could the other gentleman be the Chilcombe solicitor, Mr. Fleming?

Graeme had had many surprises in his years of attending gatherings of diplomats and aiding his majesty's representatives on the British side of negotiating tables. Those experiences helped him to hide his shock when a hawk-nosed man with graying hair turned from a conversation with Sir William Taylor and a younger gentleman to glance his way.

The Lord Lieutenant of Hampshire had made a personal appearance.

He stiffened his spine and went to greet the duke and remind him of their previous acquaintance years earlier in Paris when he'd been a lowly aide fetching and carrying.

* * *

HERMIONE PROVED TO BE EXCELLENT AT PLAYING HEARTS, AS well as an excellent teacher to Nicholas and a lady willing to spend hours entertaining both children.

While Blythe paced the drawing room and listened to the friendly chatter of Hermione coaching Nicholas about which card to play, and Coralie about wagering her farthings, out in the hall, Adwick made frequent trips to the front door sending away the nosy visitors wanting to know why she and Graeme had gone to the country and whether they had returned. Adwick assured them that neither she nor Graeme was at home. Since word of their late return to town had apparently already spread, the bolder callers, like Mrs. Netley, scoffed a bit before leaving. Adwick had not needed the help of the hired Runner hovering out of view to assist—so far.

Today, there were three guards on duty, one in the back garden, one at the front of the house, and one roaming the corridors.

She was glad for the Runners. Adwick was no pugilist, and other than Clive, their male servants were older. Nor would her brother Will be any help today.

When a servant reported that Will was still abed, Blythe had visited him. He hadn't got up because he hadn't been able to. After a night spent following Lord Vernon to his various haunts, even drinking with the fellow, he'd been too sick.

She'd wager her next quarter's income that Lord Vernon had tampered with his drink.

Will had patted his bedside and asked her to fill him in on the latest developments. She told him about their hurried trip, the children's presence, and the morning's early unsuccessful attempt to find Lunetta.

"Demme, but I would that you hadn't gone there, Blythe. No place for a lady like you. And you decided to confide in Chilcombe?" Will asked. "Might as well, I suppose. He's promised me on his honor that he'll support your claim to Bluebelle Lodge."

Whether she could truly trust Graeme remained to be seen, but for now, she had no other choice.

She left Will with the footman, who delivered a tray with the housekeeper's concoction for curing a hangover. Will promised to join them in the drawing room as soon as the floor stopped moving, which he hoped would be soon.

The drawing room mantel clock chimed—again—and Blythe rose and paced to the window facing onto the street. The gray day outside mirrored her emotions. How quickly would Jarrow and Morley arrive for this meeting Graeme wanted to hold with them?

Would Graeme keep her secret?

Perhaps she shouldn't have confirmed that she'd burned the copy of the will Sir Morris had been carrying. He'd merely surmised those were the papers she was burning from what Coralie had said; if anyone else heard the story, there was no reason to suspect the papers had been the will.

She had debated talking to Coralie, asking her to keep quiet about what she'd seen, but that would only make Coralie suspicious, and once the dear girl decided to ferret out a secret, she could be relentless. If Coralie should mention to anyone else that she'd seen her burning papers the day Sir Morris died, she could simply say she was upset about the will and was burning something else—love letters from Archie perhaps.

A wretched lie about a wretched husband who'd never written her any such letters.

"Lord Chilcombe will return soon," Hermione called from the card table. "You know how these gentlemen go on when they're together without their ladies to hurry them on."

Blythe sighed and leaned her shoulder against the window and then her pulse quickened. A carriage had passed, obscuring the view of a man near the park and... there. Lord Vernon was crossing the street, dodging a curricle and a town coach, hopping over a pile of horse droppings and advancing on Chilcombe House.

She slid into the window curtain and waited and... there. Another man lounged against the iron fence surrounding the park. Mr. Morley had thought to set a minder to follow Lord Vernon.

The dastard had trotted up the front steps of Chilcombe House and disappeared from view. She quickly moved to the door and slipped through it to stand out of sight on the landing and listen.

"Neither Lady Chilcombe nor Lord Chilcombe are at home," Adwick said.

"Come, come, Adwick. I know that's not true. I know they've just returned from a long journey, and I haven't seen either of them go out."

"They are not at home, my lord," Adwick said firmly.

"Wait."

She imagined Lord Vernon stopping the door with his foot.

"May I come in and write Lady Chilcombe a note?"

"I'm obliged to tell you that—"

"Not even a note?" Lord Vernon exclaimed.

Blythe heard movement behind her and saw Will whizz by and fly down the stairs. He wore trousers and a shirt, but otherwise, he was barefoot and in deshabille.

"Captain Lynford." Lord Vernon laughed. "Done in by your labors last night, I see."

"My labors, my arse," Will said with a laugh that she knew

was forced. "You'll be lucky I don't spew on you, Lord Vernon. Heard you speaking to Adwick and thought I'd come down and let you know I'm alive. No thanks to your company last night. What's your message for my sister? I'll relay it to her."

"Will you, Lynford? Oh, I fear it might be too personal for her brother's eyes."

Blythe held her breath, praying that Will would see that the weasel was baiting him.

"Oh well, that's all right," Will said. "Adwick, fetch a pencil and paper for his lordship and he can write it right here."

"The hall table—"

"Right where you're standing, there's a good lad. I'll turn around and you can use my back for a desk. It's alright, Adwick, he won't stab me with the pencil. You, come here, please," Will said. "This here's Chilcombe's new, er, porter. No livery yet. What's your name, fellow?"

A low voice grumbled out a name.

"Blythe *did* need more servants." She heard the sneer in Lord Vernon's voice and wondered if he had worked out the Runner's true role.

"Here's another new man," Will said cheerfully. "And here's Adwick with paper and pencil. Now go ahead and scribble that note and maybe save the long love verses for later. Oh, I said I'd turn around."

"On second thought," Lord Vernon said, "I'll call again when her ladyship finds herself at home."

"Where are you off to?" Will asked, masking his impertinence with that same cheerful elan. How was he managing it?

She heard the sound of the heavy door closing.

"Bring that chair for the Captain," Adwick said.

Blythe came out onto the landing and watched her brother plop down. Two of the Runners lingered nearby.

"Keep that bastard away from here," Will said. "Keep him away from my sister. If he sends a note, I want to see it."

"Let me see it first, if you please," Blythe called.

"Where is that weasel off to?" Will grunted. "Demme if I could only follow him."

"We've got someone onto him," one of the Runners said.

*   *   *

Mr. Fleming—indeed, the man who'd been talking to Morley and Jarrow was the Chilcombe solicitor—had brought news to the meeting. As soon as Diddenton had filed a challenge to the will, Fleming had begun an investigation into the property dispute. He'd searched the deeds and documents that had been transferred to Risley Manor from Bluebelle Lodge upon Mr. Davies' death, as well as tax records at Somerset House and those kept by county offices and the local land tax collectors. He'd also commissioned another survey of the disputed land.

Diddenton's claims were at best mistaken, and at worst, utterly fraudulent.

"Reckless of him," the Lord Lieutenant said before leaving the meeting early with Sir William. "And a grave injustice to Chilcombe's widow. Can't have peers dispossessing widows. I suppose he thought that you would be off in another country and uninterested in Lady Chilcombe's disinheritance."

"He does not know me," Graeme said. "This is a matter of honor."

Wellington nodded. "You'll have our backing on this, Chilcombe."

The young earl's heir who'd organized the meeting took over when the more senior men left. Lord Ashley was not more than one and twenty but he had a serious mien that brooked no nonsense. It was in the public's interest, and the government's, he said, to take Diddenton down a peg. More than a peg. To Lord Ashley's way of thinking, Diddenton ought to be driven from England. His heir was equally pernicious, as well as son number two. The only son of Diddenton's worth anything had been number three, who'd died at Cambridge many years earlier. And of course, his youngest son, Lord Vernon, everyone knew to be a detestable blot on society.

"Now the question becomes, what step to take next," Ashley said.

Fleming cleared his throat. "With your permission, Lord Chilcombe, we may present the results of our searches to the court. Although, it might complicate matters if it's found that the late Lord Chilcombe did indeed execute a new will."

"If he was in his right mind," Ashley said. "Pardon me, Chilcombe, but was your late cousin not profoundly addicted to opium and subject to coercion?"

"Given the lack of witnesses, coercion will be hard to prove," Jarrow said.

"As is the existence of the new will," Morley said. "Perhaps, Mr. Fleming, Chilcombe, we should wait until we find the nurse who was attending the late earl when he died."

"Surely she won't have the will," Ashley said. "What of Lady Chilcombe? Did she see it?"

Before Graeme could formulate a response that would not be an outright lie, Jarrow spoke up.

"My father was both coroner and magistrate when Sir

Morris Pierpont died on the day the new will was supposedly signed, and then later when Lord Chilcombe died. His illness prevents him from speaking, but his notes make no reference to her being questioned about the existence of the will."

And she would never be questioned if Graeme had any say. It was time to play his last chip. A niggle of guilt told him he should wait until Blythe was present. But on the other hand, as fragile as her emotions had been lately, perhaps he'd best do this without her.

"Gentlemen," he said, "as it happens, I have come into possession of a letter that sheds more light on this matter. The letter is dated one day before the new will was supposedly executed and was addressed to Diddenton and signed by Lord Vernon. In his letter to his father, Lord Vernon writes that he'd supplied the late Lord Chilcombe with a potent Indian opium and had tasked Sir Morris with adding to this persuasion to get Chilcombe to sign the new will. He said he anticipated my cousin's demise soon, after which he, Lord Vernon would take possession of Bluebelle Lodge."

Morley let out a long breath. "He's the youngest son and greatest ne'er do well of the bunch. Diddenton has refused to keep funding him and won't give him a property. Maybe this is his way of accomplishing that. The plan for the lime pit was all a hum."

Jarrow's level frown had Graeme holding his breath, awaiting the question about the provenance of the letter.

"That doesn't stand up," Jarrow said, finally. "At least not entirely. There's got to be another reason for targeting Chilcombe."

"Consolidating his domain?" Morley mused. "The

properties run alongside each other, now that Diddenton's bought Wickworth Hall."

"The late Lord Chilcombe was at Cambridge," Ashley said. "Diddenton's third son died there in an accident. Chilcombe's name came up giving testimony at the inquest. Might that be the connection?"

Graeme searched through his memories. "Our families weren't close," he said. "I recall some whispering about my cousin being sent down for bad behavior. The grandparents were livid."

"I'll look into it," Jarrow said.

Morley cleared his throat. "I'll see what I can learn about that also. However, there may be another motivation. I beg your pardon, Chilcombe, but it always seemed to me that Lord Vernon had an unnatural interest in your cousin's wife. Not speaking ill of the lady, you understand, but of him. There must have been a reason for her to take herself off to Bluebelle Lodge so often."

Graeme thought of the boldness of Lord Vernon's statements the day he met him, first at White's and then at the rout that evening. *She won't be troubling you for support much longer. Suppose I ought to tell you. Archie felt bad about leaving Blythe nothing. He asked me to take care of her. Good friends for years, you know. I promised him I'd marry her.*

"You may have a point," Graeme said. "He told me he promised my cousin he would marry her."

"Thus giving him a backup plan if the new will doesn't hold," Morley said.

"Yes, that was my thought also, though you may be right that there's more to it than merely obtaining the property."

"Is the lady willing?" Ashley asked.

"Not at all." Graeme shook his head. "She loathes him,

and I've assured her that she will always have a home. She is under my protection."

And right now, he needed to see her, needed to know she was still safe and not haring off trying to pursue the copy of that will on her own.

He stood. "Gentlemen, I must return to Chilcombe House. Lord Ashley, I know that Lady Chilcombe will be grateful for your support. Mr. Fleming, Morley's recommendation is a wise one. We will wait a few days before approaching the court again."

He pulled Morley and Jarrow aside as the others were leaving. "Will you ride with me back to Chilcombe House? Lady Chilcombe will want to hear our progress."

When they had settled into the Chilcombe town carriage, Jarrow turned an assessing gaze on him. "I noted that you didn't say where you obtained that letter from Lord Vernon to his father."

"Yes, I did not. I have it in safekeeping."

"I should like to see it," he said.

"As would I," Morley said.

"I also didn't mention that Lady Chilcombe and I paid a visit to an address in Soho this morning. We did not find Lunetta Casale, but we did speak with another woman whom Blythe recognized as someone who'd visited Risley Manor to attend to her husband. Blythe found the encounter quite unsettling."

"Attend to her husband..." Morley shook his head. "What did she say about the woman?"

"I did not press her," Graeme said.

"Well, that will save me some time searching."

"How did it come about that you knew to look there for her?" Jarrow asked. "You have only just arrived in England."

He could outright lie, but he'd just as soon save the

untruths for more damning issues. "In fact, since her return to London, Lady Chilcombe has been looking for the woman."

"Why?"

"You can imagine why. To see if she has the signed copy of the will."

Morley chuckled and shook his head. "No one could blame her if the will—if it exists—disappears."

"Has the woman sent a demand for money?" Jarrow asked.

As the carriage stopped in front of Chilcombe House, Graeme put on his best diplomatic mask. "None that I've seen."

The answering look Jarrow sent was keen, but he said nothing and climbed out.

While a footman took their hats, Graeme asked Morley and Jarrow to wait for him in the library, then he pulled Adwick aside and asked him to have Lady Chilcombe meet him in his private sitting room.

* * *

BLYTHE WATCHED THE ARRIVAL OF GRAEME, THE MAGISTRATE, and the inquiry agent from the drawing room window.

"They're back, finally." Coralie had edged close to her.

She'd remained with Blythe while Lady Hermione and a newly designated nursery maid escorted Nicholas upstairs for tea and some play time with Roddy. Lady Hermione had begged leave to retire to her room and write letters.

"Is that Mr. Morley?" Coralie whispered. "He's rather handsome."

Blythe noticed the sly grin on her ward's face. "What?"

"I do like Mr. Jarrow's looks, but..." She grimaced. "I don't appreciate being talked to as if I am a child."

She gave Coralie a one-armed hug. "You are not a child, and you are not yet a woman. You are a very young lady. And it is one thing for you to think about which gentlemen are handsome, but—"

"But I must behave properly. I know, Godmama. Do not worry, I am not mooning over any gentlemen at present." The sly smile appeared again. "Do you not wonder why I didn't mention whether Lord Chilcombe is handsome?"

"I would assume because you are being the sensible, level-headed girl... that is, young lady, I've always known you to be."

Coralie hugged her back. "Yes. Sensible and very observant. Lord Chilcombe is, in strict terms, the least handsome of the three men. Not as wide-shouldered as Mr. Jarrow, or as square-jawed as Mr. Morley. But aside from that, there would be no sense in me mooning over Lord Chilcombe because he only has eyes for you."

"*Coralie.*"

"He looks at you the way I sometimes catch Samuel looking at Louisa. I noticed it the first day he came to Bluebelle Lodge. That is why I told him about finding you burning those papers. Because I could see that he cares for you."

"My lady." Adwick stood in the doorway. "Lord Chilcombe asked that you join him in his private sitting room."

Too astonished by Coralie to find words, Blythe nodded to her butler and waved him away. Now was the moment to tell her she was merely burning those nonexistent love letters. But she hated to lie.

"It's all right, Godmama. May I stay here and read?"

Coralie asked. "Nicholas and his new friend found some old tin soldiers and will be setting up a battle."

She looked long and hard at this girl she'd loved and raised and decided to take the coward's way out.

Besides, Graeme was waiting for her.

"Of course," she said.

Coralie's patience with Nicholas in the carriage the day before had been heroic. Blythe could trust the girl's common sense.

Mostly, that is. This business of how Graeme looked at her... She would have to, one day, explain to Coralie the difference between admiration and lust.

"Best not to wander around too much just yet. If you need anything, ring for a servant."

She passed Clive in the corridor just outside Graeme's suite.

"His lordship is waiting for you, my lady," the servant said without any sign that he was scandalized by her visit to Graeme's private domain. He turned back and held the door for her.

How quickly would the word of her visits to Graeme's bedchamber spread among their servants and those of their neighbors?

"Blythe." Graeme cast down the letter he was reading and rose from his desk.

The door snicked shut behind her, and he came and took both of her hands. "Morley and Jarrow are in the library. I asked them to come along and meet with you."

"I see. I thought your meeting was with the Foreign Office. Where did you—"

"Let me explain before we go to them."

He told her about the private club, the presence of the Lord Lieutenant and the reformer, Lord Ashley, and his surprise at finding both Jarrow and Morley in attendance, as well as Mr. Fleming and his clerk. He briefly summarized their ensuing discussion.

"We are not alone in this battle," he said. "Diddenton's claim to Bluebelle Lodge is certainly fraudulent and the will, if there is one, was coerced to cover this fraud. I told them about the letter, and they'd like to see it."

"Did you tell them how you obtained it?"

"I told them I could not reveal that information. And I don't intend to."

She looked down at their joined hands. She had managed, so far, to not lie, at least never under oath.

CHAPTER SIXTEEN

"Three other things you need to know," Graeme said. "Later, in the carriage, I mentioned to Morley and Jarrow the call we paid this morning. And I told them you've been searching for Lunetta since you returned to London to see if she had the new will. And when Jarrow asked me if Lunetta had made a demand for money, I told him, none that I've seen."

Anger rose in her and an overwhelming sense of betrayal.

She managed a nod. "I'll go and get that letter."

When she tried to pull away, he gripped her hands more firmly.

"Show me again how to open the panel, please." He freed a hand and stroked her cheek. "Morley will not be a problem, my love. Jarrow, though, is a magistrate and may feel honor-bound. If he asks any difficult questions, I will answer for you, if you will allow it."

Tears pricked her eyes and she squeezed them shut against the unwanted moisture.

"I won't have you lie for me, Graeme. I will answer for

myself. Just promise me..." She struggled for words, choking. "The children."

"Blythe." She found herself pressed against his shoulder, the uncontrollable shaking she'd experienced that morning threatening. "I'll take care of the children. I'll take care of you. No matter if you refuse to marry me. No matter if I never have you in my bed. You have my love and my loyalty. Always. Forever."

As the astonishing words poured over her, she held very still, soaking in the warmth of him, the solidness of him until her heart and body stopped quaking.

Love and loyalty. Love was precious, often short-lived, and easy enough to be counterfeited. But loyalty—oh, that was a priceless treasure. That was something she yearned for.

She stiffened her spine. Graeme barely knew her. Time would tell if he would give her his loyalty, and if love could last.

She pulled away and patted his chest. "I'll only hold you to the promise to take care of the children. Now, let me show you again how to operate the panel, and then I'll go and fetch that other letter."

Graeme insisted on following her to her bedchamber so that he could escort her into the meeting.

Morley and Jarrow rose when she entered and offered her one of the more comfortable overstuffed wing chairs. She declined and took a seat on a straight-backed chair that Graeme brought over for her. He pulled another chair close to hers, offering her a support she dearly appreciated.

She wouldn't lie today, though she firmly intended to dance around the truth until she had to drop from exhaustion. She'd had so much practice at that in her marriage.

Graeme nodded to her and began the meeting. "I told Lady Chilcombe what I learned at our gathering this morning, though it was a mere summary. What I didn't discover was how you, Jarrow and Morley, came to both be in attendance with Mr. Fleming, my solicitor."

"I wasn't being deceptive when I left here this morning," Jarrow said. "I paid an early call at White's to see who might have recommendations for physicians. As it happens, I ran into Ashley and Wellington and Sir William. The meeting this morning was hastily arranged. Morley happened along and joined us. We all agreed it was advisable to move the matter to another locale where Lord Vernon had fewer—or no—acquaintances. Morley also thought to invite Fleming, who he'd spoken with just that morning. And of course you needed to be included, Chilcombe. Sir William knew you would respond to an urgent request on his letterhead."

"Which just proves," Morley said, "that even when it comes to government matters things can be done quickly at times."

"Lord Ashley is keen to go after Diddenton," Jarrow said. "Word is he'll find a pocket borough and take a seat in the Commons at the next election. Woe betide Diddenton and others of his ilk when Ashley inherits the earldom."

The three men recounted the discussion from the meeting while Blythe held her tongue and listened silently.

In truth, she was glad she hadn't been present and subject to their scrutiny. This was bad enough.

When they were finished, she glanced at Graeme and nodded. "You will want to see this letter," she said, handing over the money demand she'd received from Lunetta. Graeme had read it before leaving her bedchamber, a frown on his face.

Now, he adjusted his face to conceal his emotions, but he

watched Mr. Morley and Mr. Jarrow carefully as they took turns reading.

"Who is Maddy?" Mr. Morley asked.

"A maid molested while in service at Wickworth Hall after it was purchased by Diddenton, and cast out after she was found to be increasing."

"Ah."

"She died in childbirth at Bluebelle Lodge. Nicholas is her son."

"Miss Casale knew you were looking for her," Mr. Jarrow observed. "Had you made contact before?"

"No. I had a boy ask around about her at the sort of establishments where one might expect to find her, places that I myself could not risk visiting. He was, of course, unsuccessful. I suppose word was passed on to her."

"When was the last time you saw her?"

"The day my late husband, died. The servants summoned me to Risley Manor because his time was near. Your father, Mr. Jarrow, was in attendance, along with the doctor. They removed Lunetta from the room and allowed me to stay."

She'd been allowed that bit of propriety. Watching him die had been almost as painful as observing the way he'd lived in the years since she'd departed Risley Manor. He'd escaped the wretched mess he'd created, and though she'd felt some relief at his passing, she knew he'd left a bigger wretched mess that she needed to untangle.

"How did you come to find the house in Soho that Lord Chilcombe said you visited this morning?" Jarrow asked, bringing her back to the matter at hand.

"Through my brother. I haven't had a chance to discuss the matter with Will, Captain Lynford. I asked him to make inquiries for me. As a military officer home on leave he would have access to the sort of haunts where one might look for her. He'd prepared a letter to be sent to me in Hampshire which I read when we arrived in London last night, and I have not yet had a chance to speak at length with him. He…" She glanced at Graeme. "He was out and about last night, following Lord Vernon and even drinking with him at one of his hells. Will was deathly ill this morning and unable to join us in the drawing room."

Graeme's mouth tightened. "I helped him into bed last night and he mentioned Vernon's name. Did he tamper with Will's drink?"

"So *I* believe. It would not be out of character." She suppressed a shudder. She'd experienced what Lord Vernon was capable of. "In his letter, my brother referenced a house in Soho, and I remembered the mention some years ago of a Soho address for Lunetta. Number 13, Bridie Lane. The steward had occasion to send correspondence to that address for her."

"You have an excellent memory, Lady Chilcombe," Mr. Jarrow said.

"You are skeptical?" She pushed down a rising panic. Mr. Jarrow might now begin to interrogate her more forcefully. "It was to me a distinctive address."

Graeme stepped in and told them about the woman they'd met and what she'd said, giving her time to calm herself, as if he sensed her disquiet.

"Was it your intention to pay money for the will, Lady Chilcombe, if that is in fact what she had?" Jarrow asked.

Blythe released a slow breath. Time to dance.

"Five hundred pounds is a great deal of money," she said. "I couldn't easily obtain that much. Perhaps not at all. But a smaller amount? Yes, it would be tempting to lay hands on that will."

"And do what?"

She chewed her lip, thinking. *Give them what they would expect.*

"It would be tempting to destroy it, if I am being honest. However, if she sold it to Diddenton and he presented it to the court... well..." She tapped her chin, thinking. "Might such a sale be an illegal act on her part? Might she be questioned, and might her testimony cast scandal on the marquess that would persuade the court to dismiss his claim? Perhaps, in the end, the suit I will have to file against Lord Chilcombe for his predecessor's violation of the marriage contract would not be required."

Graeme reached for her hand and squeezed it. "You know, my dear, whatever happens you will not have to take me to court."

Mr. Morley's lips quirked and Mr. Jarrow studied his cup of tea until the embarrassing moment passed.

Graeme, however, still had hold of her hand. She stopped resisting and left it there.

"I believe Lunetta might be dead," she continued. "The letter might have been written by the other woman at Bridie Lane. Whether she has the will, I don't know."

"Have you read the will, Lady Chilcombe?" Mr. Jarrow asked.

"I have read the copy Lord Diddenton submitted to the court."

That was true.

"And the day your late husband signed it. Did you see it then?"

Ah, now she must dance with a bit more vigor. Though she wasn't such an actress that she could readily call up tears, she was chagrined to sense moisture welling.

She closed her eyes a moment, reliving the horrible

memories of that morning. "I received an urgent summons to Risley Manor and I went. Archie—Lord Chilcombe—announced to me that he had changed his will. He apologized and told me that Bluebelle Lodge would go to Lord Diddenton to settle a land dispute."

She'd been both livid with anger and terrified.

"He was so... so intoxicated or drugged, he rambled. He'd simplified things, I remember him saying that. There'd be no dribs and drabs of money going to various retainers was how he said it. Imagine? Loyal servants who'd been with the family for years, who might expect to be remembered with a few pounds upon the earl's death, and who had been provided for in the will Archie signed at the time of our marriage."

She squeezed her eyes closed on a memory of Archie, half reclining in bed, his blond hair limp and dirty, his skin yellow, his nightshirt open to reveal a haggard, bony chest. He'd been a shockingly handsome young man, an Adonis, but no more.

"By then, he was slurring his words and telling me I would be taken care of. He passed out before he explained more."

A handkerchief appeared in her free hand. She took in a long breath and composed herself before going on.

"Archie did not show me the will. Later, though, after his death, Mr. Stockwell, one of the solicitor's clerks and I made an effort in good faith to find it before Mr. Fleming proceeded with matters. We searched high and low for it. Everywhere, to no avail. That was before Lord Diddenton instructed your father to repeat the search."

Jarrow ignored her insulting tone and went on. "Did you see Lord Vernon or Sir Morris the day of the signing?" He asked, his voice gentle.

Like a gentle hound mouthing his prey before chomping down on it. He would be a far more formidable magistrate than his father had been.

"I was told that Lord Vernon had left the day before, and that Sir Morris had been there and departed before I arrived. So no, I spoke with neither man."

"So, you did not see Sir Morris's accident?"

"No."

She hadn't seen the curricle as it toppled. That was true enough.

"I returned to Bluebelle Lodge. It was snowing quite heavily and I wanted to get home. We received news of the accident later."

* * *

GRAEME HELD TIGHTLY ONTO HER HAND, THOUGH HE ITCHED to set his arm around her shoulders and pull her close. She'd begun, unawares, to tremble under the weight of trying to respond without outright lying. He knew what she was about, and in truth, he was impressed.

"I'll go and visit this woman," Jarrow said. "You are right, Lady Chilcombe, that she'll probably offer it to Diddenton. The gossips might make much of him paying for a stolen will, but it still might hold up in the consistory court."

A knock at the door brought Adwick, before one of the Runners rushed past him and a boy followed behind ; Blythe's errand boy.

"What is it, Burrows?" Morley asked.

"Bobby," Blythe cried.

The Runner had the lad by the collar. "This lad—"

"Lord V," Bobby cried. "Just saw him on Bridie Lane."

Graeme stood, pulling Blythe up beside him. "Adwick, send someone for a hack."

They all moved to the hall while servants brought their hats. Morley told the Runner to remain at Chilcombe House and keep watch on the ladies and children.

"I'm going as well," Blythe said, accepting the bonnet and spencer that Radley had come running with.

Graeme opened his mouth to protest but thought better of it. He ushered her out of the door and they all squeezed into the hired carriage.

They had the driver set them down outside the narrow alley that was Bridie Lane. Blythe stepped out briskly for number thirteen before Graeme pulled her back.

"I should go in first," she said. "I'll be expected."

The thought of her walking in on that cur and the vile woman set his blood boiling. "No, we'll go together."

"I have a better idea," Jarrow said. "Let's see if we can listen to their conversation. He might say or do something incriminating."

"There's a way in through the back," Bobby said. "I can climb up and—"

"I'll go with Bobby," Morley said. "The three of you go in through the front door. Lady Chilcombe is right, she may be allowed in faster than the men. See if you can provoke Lord Vernon, my lady. Chilcombe and Jarrow can both be nearby."

She nodded and set off again.

"Damn you, Morley," Graeme muttered, hurrying after her with Jarrow close behind.

The door creaked as Blythe opened it and advanced

toward the ground floor door off the hall where the yellow haired woman had appeared.

Graeme pulled her back and framed her face with his hands. "Do nothing rash," he said. "I can't lose you again."

Her mouth dropped open and she quickly closed it, nodded, and then reached for the doorknob.

Muffled cries came to them, a woman and a man arguing.

Blythe froze.

"Upstairs," Jarrow said and bounded for the staircase.

"Wait." Blythe tugged Graeme back, her head cocked, listening intently. "It may not be them."

Graeme heard it then—the cockney accent, the deep bellow. Those were not the sneering whiny tones of Lord Vernon. A loud thud and a woman's scream were followed by the sound of splintering wood.

Graeme squeezed her shoulder. "Jarrow might need help. Wait for me here. Don't go in there alone."

He found Jarrow bent over the body of a scrawny fellow in threadbare coats, a thin woman standing over him, weeping.

"Passed out, I'd say," Jarrow said.

"Ye broke me door," the woman said. "How'm I to pay for it? Mrs. Thornsby'll have me out on the street."

"She'll have you out on the street for disturbing the peace fighting with your man," Jarrow said.

The woman scoffed. "She does worse, her and that woman who lives with her and that baby crying night and day."

"Is Thornsby the yellow-haired woman on the ground floor?" Graeme asked.

The woman swept a gaze over him head to foot and then

back up again. He'd worn his best coats for the morning meeting and hadn't had time to change.

He pulled a half crown from his pocket and held it up for her.

"Yes," she said, holding out her hand.

"And the woman who lives with her?"

She scoffed again. "Calls herself Lunetta. Now…" She extended her hand further, and Graeme dropped the coin into her palm.

"That's not enough to fix the door," the woman said.

"Who visits Mrs. Thornsby?" Jarrow asked, holding up another coin.

"No one that I know. Just the two of them and that squalling brat. She goes away, Thornsby does, from time to time. Doesn't have a man if that's what ye're asking."

"What is her business?"

"She's a whore as far as I know. Not one as brings her business here, otherwise we wouldn't be living here. My man has a stall at the fish market."

Downstairs, a door slammed. Graeme stepped around the man on the floor.

"There was a man here this morning. Saw him through the window going in just now."

Graeme hurried past the splintered door and rushed down the stairs.

Blythe was gone.

* * *

As Graeme hurried up the stairs to help Jarrow, Blythe edged closer to the door and bent her ear to the panel.

The thick door obscured words but she heard the unmistakable tenor of a man's voice. A chill went through her, a chill that told her it was Diddenton's vile spawn conversing with Madame. Perhaps they were planning to ruin some other lady's life.

Anger coursed through her and a thirst for revenge.

But she wasn't a fool. Though she'd been weakened by a drug and concern for her babe during her last encounter with the woman, she still might not be a match for the two of them, who were both so skilled at wielding a whip.

Mr. Morley might be close at hand but that was uncertain. She'd wait for Graeme, at least a few more minutes.

She was counting out seconds when the door opened and the clawlike tentacles of Madame closed on her forearm and pulled her in, slamming the door behind her.

CHAPTER SEVENTEEN

"Alone?" Lord Vernon crowed from the chair where he sprawled. "You continue to surprise me, Blythe. Where is Chilcombe, your new protector? Or am I mistaken? Is it young Jarrow who has won your favors?"

His eyes glittered with what she once would have attributed only to the poison. But now she knew it wasn't just the laudanum. There was an evil inside him that made him gloat when he thought he had a weaker creature in his grasp.

She tore her gaze away and surveyed the room. The furnishings, carpets, and curtains were of a quality that might grace a slightly shabby Mayfair drawing room. The chair where he sprawled was upholstered in faded blue damask, matching the curtains and the long sofa where another woman reclined.

Clad in a colorful man's banyan printed with tropical flowers, her head wrapped in a turban, Lunetta Casale offered a weak smile. Jaundiced and drawn, she couldn't be long for this world.

"Thornsby told me you called this morning," she said, her voice raspy, yet her tone was seductive.

"Thornsby?" Blythe asked.

"That would be me," the woman she thought of as Madame said in an unaccountably cheery voice. "And now you're back. And Lord Vernon has deigned to call on us as well."

Ah. The cheery tone was meant to defuse Lord Vernon.

"Alas, I am not here by invitation, sweet Blythe," he said. "I had to inquire here and there to find Thornsby's *pied a terre*, and a charming one it is. Gifted her by one of your former protectors, was it not, Thornsby? So your butler was not lying this morning when he said you weren't at home. Slipped out without Chilcombe noticing, eh? And where was the impeccable new earl this morning?"

She held her breath, fixing her gaze on him so she wouldn't glance at the women and give away the fact that they must have lied to him.

"I shall send a doctor to help you, Lunetta." She reached behind her and opened the door.

Lord Vernon leapt from the chair and braced his hands on either side of her, slamming the door shut in the process. "Not so fast," he growled. "Where is that will?"

"I don't have it."

"No? Lunetta said she gave it to you this morning."

"Did she? Well, I *don't* have it now."

"Bitch." He punched at her, but she ducked, and his fist connected with the high crown of her bonnet. She tore at the tie and spun away, her hair falling loose from its pins.

"Where is it? If you destroyed it..." He turned a glare on Lunetta. "Or, did you lie to me, Lunetta? Yes, I believe you did, or Blythe wouldn't have returned this afternoon."

Lunetta struggled to sit up, too weak to stand. "Go away, Vernon."

"Why you…" He stepped closer and drew a pistol from his pocket. "Give it to me."

"It was wrong what you did."

"I want that will."

"Drugging Archie so he would sign it was wrong. Leaving his lady with one pound was wrong. All so you could get your hands on her."

The villain laughed. "The way she ignored her husband's needs, she deserved it. I cannot wait to, as you say, get my hands on her. Blythe's such a pleasurable handful. When she screams it's real, not an act like you and the other whores put on, Lunetta."

Blythe inhaled sharply and edged close to the door, groping for the knob.

Thornsby reached for a stick near the hearth, and Lord Vernon flashed the pistol her way. "Where is it, Thornsby. You of all people wouldn't let go of something that valuable."

"And that's not all," Lunetta said, drawing his attention away from her friend.

Blythe felt the knob turn under her fingers and moved out of the way as the door opened and Graeme slid silently into the room with Jarrow behind him. Both men had drawn pistols.

"I saw you putting powders into Archie's medicine bottle, making the dose ever stronger each week until—"

"It was you who fed him that medicine, Lunetta. Not me."

"I cut it back," she said. "Gave him less, and then nothing at all."

"Ah. So that's why he lingered. And here was I thinking

he had an iron constitution. You merely killed Archie more slowly."

"'Twas you who killed him. And you'll swing for it."

"Shut up."

"Bragged about the opium your father could get you," Lunetta said. "Bet your pa hoped you'd take too much yourself and he'd be done with you. But you were too smart for that, weren't you Vern. You convinced him there was a way to get vengeance on the man who killed his favorite son. You found a surveyor you could bribe in your pa's name and then you blackmailed the old man into going along with your scheme."

Lord Vernon laughed. "There was no blackmail. He thought it was a grand idea."

Nerves tingling, Blythe held her breath watching Graeme and Jarrow edge closer.

Lord Vernon eased back the hammer on the gun.

"He drugged you too, Lady Chilcombe," Lunetta said. "*That* night. I saw him."

"And I'm sorry for all that happened, my lady," Thornsby said. "I didn't know you were with child."

"I know," Blythe said, hoping to draw his attention her way. "And I knew the drink was drugged after the first sip."

Lord Vernon glanced away from Lunetta, though his gun still pointed at her.

"Don't do it, Falfield," Graeme said.

Lord Vernon whipped around and two sharp cracks resounded. A chunk of plaster whizzed past Blythe's cheek. Lunetta collapsed back on the sofa while a pistol skidded across the floor. Blythe looked up to see Lord Vernon clawing at the leather cords curling around his wrist and arm from the whip held by Thornsby.

Lord Vernon lunged for the woman and Graeme and

Jarrow hurled themselves at him, knocking him to the carpet and pinning him there.

The sound of glass breaking in the room beyond stirred a baby's cries, and then Morley and Bobby ran through the door from the back room.

Hands shaking, Blythe picked up Lord Vernon's discarded pistol, wincing at the heat of the barrel and almost dropping it.

She silently handed it to Graeme, who'd yielded his part in restraining Lord Vernon to Morley.

"Pistols," she said. "I never thought…" She shook her head to clear it. She was babbling.

Graeme pulled her close in a hug. "Let's get you out of here."

She pushed him away and went to Lunetta. "Were you hit?" she asked.

"No," she said breathlessly. The baby continued to squall and the look of distress on Lunetta's face told Blythe it was her child.

Thornsby was busy untangling the fronds of her whip.

Blythe hurried through the connecting door into an inner room that was a kitchen with a table. A black pot dangled from a jack on the old-fashioned hearth and a kettle stood on a trivet. She passed them and went to the large basket where the baby lay crying.

"At least you are warm in here, little one," she said, lifting the downy-haired bundle out carefully. The crying stopped and blue eyes gazed up at her, eyes the same pure cerulean blue as Coralie's.

She shoved down a too familiar anger and held the precious bundle close. The child needed comfort, and probably feeding, and definitely a change of clouts. The pouty lips smacked together a few times, and Blythe looked around.

"There's gruel here." Graeme had followed her in and was checking the pot over the hearth. "Still warm." He scooped up a bit with his finger, tasted it, and then went to retrieve a dish and spoon.

She settled on a chair by the plain deal table and began feeding the babe, who smacked its lips some more and grumbled hungrily.

Graeme circled the room and then disappeared through another doorway, returning in minutes. "That's the bedroom," he said. "One large lavishly appointed bed and a small one tucked into the corner. No desk or papers that I could see. I suppose they'd have those hidden." He came to stand near her. "About what—six months, eight months?" he asked. "It's the image of Coralie."

"Yes."

"Archie's?"

She nodded, tightly. "Probably. I cannot hold it against the babe."

"I know you cannot, my love."

He squeezed her shoulder, and she shuddered. *My love,* he'd said. Had he not heard the conversation between Lunetta and Lord Vernon about that night?

She shook off the unsettling emotions the memory inspired and put her attention to her task. One spoonful and then another, and then another.

She had almost reached the bottom of the bowl when the baby scrunched up its face and turned away. She set the spoon aside and wiped its mouth with a corner of the swaddling.

He chuckled. "Full now. He—or she—was hungry."

"And wet." She lifted the child. "And now I am as well.

Fetch me some of those cloths from over there and I'll change him. Or her. We shall know soon which it is."

As she unwrapped the swaddling, Graeme stood so close she could feel his breath on her cheek, followed by his lips as he dove in for a quick kiss. "A girl," he said. "Coralie has a baby sister. Don't bring her into the sitting room until Morley and his men have hauled Lord Vernon off to Bow Street."

And then he was gone, and she felt... a trifle bereft. The genuine affection in that quick kiss and been worth a trunkful of letters from a dutiful lover.

* * *

One week later

A hack arrived at Grosvenor Square and Morley stepped out carrying a small valise with an even smaller one tucked under his arm. Then he helped Radley juggle the baby she was holding and climb down. Blythe, Coralie, and Nicholas stood at the drawing room window watching.

Graeme came to join them, setting one hand on Coralie's shoulder and the other on Nicholas'. "You'll have no peace in the nursery now," he teased.

"A nursery is not a spot for tranquility, Lord Chilcombe," Lady Hermione called from her place on the sofa where she sat knitting a shawl for the baby. Only Will was missing. He'd needed to make an appearance at Horse Guards that day.

Blythe smiled back at Graeme, thinking about the meeting they'd had with the children only a short while earlier, telling them the news.

Coralie had been filled with questions, which Blythe answered as truthfully as possible. This child was Coralie's half-sister, and as it turned out, a distant cousin to Nicholas, whose mother had been related to Lunetta. Nicholas had caught some of Coralie's contagious exuberance but he was generally more subdued.

"We don't care if she's noisy," Coralie said. "Well, not much," she added, grinning. "We helped with the Stockwell babies, remember? In any case, I've told Nick about how annoying he was when he came to *my* nursery. Come, Nick, let's go and escort Maddy upstairs."

Maddy's greeting, a shrill, indignant wail, reached them before Radley stepped into the room holding her charge, with Morley close behind.

Coralie scooped up the baby and bounced her, shocking her into wide-eyed, curious silence as Nicholas tickled her cheeks and made faces at her. Lady Hermione put aside her knitting to join the chorus of Maddy's admirers.

Radley approached Blythe and Graeme and took two bags from Morley. "This larger one is what swaddling and clouts she has. I'll take that up to the nursery and go through it. This other…" she handed the smaller bag to Blythe, "is special things for the babe for you to hold for her."

Moisture clogged Blythe's throat as she remembered the cache of special things she'd saved from her firstborn, as well as the garments she'd been working on for the baby she lost.

"How was she?" Blythe asked, finally.

Radley knew who she meant and shook her head. "It won't be much longer."

Graeme had brought a doctor to examine Lunetta the day they'd captured Lord Vernon, and the very same day he'd somehow arranged for a nurse for the baby. After hauling Lord Vernon to Newgate, Morley and Jarrow had returned and taken detailed statements from both Lunetta and Thornsby. Thornsby would not be charged with any crimes, nor, given the state of her health, would Lunetta.

As for the marquess, Graeme had been very busy. Since the events of that day, Blythe had barely seen him, a fact that had her emotions alternating between apprehension and anger. *Trust me*, he'd said. With no news on the matter at hand, she was feeling desperate.

With her brother escorting her, she'd returned to Bridie Lane the day after Lord Vernon's arrest to discuss little Maddy's future and offer her help. Though her own income was shaky, Blythe could somehow continue to pay the nursemaid, or she could provide a stipend to help a relative with the child's care. Or, if Lunetta wished it, she could take Maddy in and raise her with her sister, Coralie.

She hadn't asked Graeme's permission—he'd been off elsewhere in meetings. And whatever happened, if he truly wanted to help Blythe, he would have to help everyone who was under her protection.

Lunetta had listened stonily, and at the end, she'd summoned her strength and rudely told Blythe to leave and never come back.

Proof, Blythe supposed, that no good deed goes unpunished.

A note from Lunetta arrived a few days later. It was a stilted apology and an acceptance of Blythe's offer to take Maddy into her home as her ward. Only impending death had broken her pride. That and perhaps Thornsby's unwillingness to take on the child's care.

"She told me a bit about herself today," Radley said. "About her people and how she came to be doing that work. The usual sad story."

"You must write it down," Blythe said. "When Maddy is older, she may want to know."

There was another rap at the hall door, and a few minutes later, Mr. Jarrow came bounding into the room. He called a greeting to them and went over to meet the new member of the household and pat Nicholas on the head, and then he said something to a blushing Coralie in a teasing tone.

"Ye gods," Graeme muttered.

"Don't worry," Blythe whispered. "Coralie and I have discussed this."

He sent her an astonished look and smiled. "She must have a season before—"

"Yes, yes." She extended her hand to Jarrow, who was in fact crossing the room to join them.

"I'll take them all to the nursery," Radley said, and ushered the children and the baby upstairs where two new nursery maids were waiting. Lady Hermione excused herself and went with them.

"Well, Mr. Jarrow," Blythe said, "what will your mother say about the new member of my household?"

His smile was rueful. "She will no doubt relish the gossip, but now that matters are settled, I am sure you will see to it that you have the upper hand in our local society."

Matters were settled? She'd been at home to callers the past two days, hoping to glean some gossip. Unfortunately, though she discovered Diddenton seemed to have more enemies than she'd previously known, no one had any rumors to impart. There'd been a hint in the morning's newssheets about the Chilcombe matter, but she'd hardly dared to hope, assuming it might just be a story planted by one of Diddenton's enemies.

"As long as Mrs. Jarrow doesn't suffer an apoplexy," Graeme said. "One parent in poor health is enough."

"What news do you have, sir?" Blythe asked. "You seem rather cheerful."

He smiled. "Yes, well, I have found a physician—which truly was the primary reason I came to London—and will escort him home with me. We leave in the morning."

Blythe smiled tightly. "I hope he is able to help your father. Now, Mr. Jarrow. Mr. Morley. Lord Chilcombe." She fixed each of them in turn with a frown. "I've been promised a briefing. Lord Chilcombe has been gone every day before breakfast and hasn't returned home until long after I've retired. All I know of my fate is the precious little that appeared in the newssheets today. And we all know how scurrilous that can be."

"There'll be more in tomorrow's paper," Graeme said. "Diddenton has, today, formally accepted that a new will could not be found and has withdrawn his challenge to the one executed at the time of your marriage. Not quite without prejudice as he insists that a new one existed."

"But the old one will stand?"

"Yes."

She squeezed her eyes shut a moment and let out a long breath. And then remembered. "But his claim to Bluebelle Lodge…"

"He won't be pursuing it," Graeme said. "That is a longer story. I wonder… I'm famished. May we tell you over a tray of sandwiches?"

Blythe glanced at the clock. "Shall we call it an early dinner? Since you've been gone every night, we've resorted to simple fare, but if you gentlemen are willing—"

"Yes of course," Graeme said. "You must join us, Jarrow, Morley. Ah, and here is Captain Lynford."

Blythe greeted her brother and then went to arrange matters with the servants and fetch Hermione from the nursery, stopping only in her bedchamber to drop off the valise with Lunetta's treasures for Maddy.

Dinner was a less formal affair in the breakfast room. Graeme sent the servants away and he, Morley, and Jarrow, told the tale of the last few days.

Blythe found herself too excited to touch the tender piece of roast that Graeme sliced and put on her plate, until his urgings turned to teasing threats that they would tell her no more unless she took a few mouthfuls. Too exhausted to fight, she chewed woodenly.

The story that unfolded began with events that occurred before she'd ever met Archie or Lord Vernon. The Marquess of Diddenton bore a particular grudge against Archie's grandfather dating back to the abolishment of the slave trade, which had interfered with Diddenton's profits from his plantations in the West Indies.

Then, at Cambridge, Archie had befriended the marquess's third son, who'd died in an accident that the marquess blamed on Archie.

So Diddenton's antipathy toward the Earl of Chilcombe was firmly established, and he was particularly incensed when his youngest son, Lord Vernon, became fast friends with Archie.

Lord Vernon, however, had seen Archie's weaknesses, and he knew his father's. He conceived a plan and convinced his father that Bluebelle Lodge would be prime land for a lime pit. He convinced Diddenton to buy Wickworth Hall, found a surveyor to adjust the property lines and, since a survey was so mind-numbingly easy to contest, he falsified the land descriptions in title documents stored at Wickworth Hall. Then persuaded his good friend Chilcombe to avoid an expensive land dispute.

Diddenton could hardly claim to be innocent. He had now, however, besides his foreign trading interests, a railway bill he was trying to push through parliament. Thus, he yielded quite readily.

"He is taking himself off to the Continent for a time until the scandal dies down," Morley said.

"And what of his son?" Lady Hermione asked. "Will he hang?"

Graeme exchanged a look with Jarrow and frowned. "No. Lord Diddenton has worked out an arrangement. Lord Vernon will be placed in a private lunatic asylum."

Blythe gripped the edge of the table while panic coursed through her. "Then we are still in danger."

"He is being taken to Charenton in France," Jarrow said. "Former home of the Marquis de Sade. It is a secure facility. Though I perfectly understand your concern."

"The king was reluctant to allow a trial to proceed," Graeme said, gently. "We cannot prove he murdered Archie. We have Lunetta's statement, but we won't be able to call her to testify in a trial. His attack on her…" Graeme groped for words.

"A prostitute's life has less value," Blythe said, bitterly.

Lord Vernon was wily. He would find his way out of any asylum. And when he came to Bluebelle Lodge, she would… Would what? Kill him? Could she possibly bring herself to take a life?

"Blythe." Graeme's gentle tone called her back to the present.

They had reached the end of the story and the end of the meal.

She stood. "Do stay and enjoy your port, gentlemen.

Hermione, will you excuse me as well? Safe travels, Mr. Jarrow."

She hurried out of the room and went to the nursery where she found a maid watching over the sleeping baby while Coralie and Nicholas curled up with books.

She managed a cheerful good night and kisses and then went to her bedchamber, her mind in a turmoil.

What was she to do? Memories flooded her of the night she'd miscarried. Lord Vernon hadn't put the drugs in her tisane; he hadn't cornered her and ripped the nightgown from her body; he hadn't held the whip that struck her back; or...

She dropped her head onto her hands and tried to breathe. Her husband's clumsy assault that night had not been love making. Lord Vernon had done no more than watch, but he'd been the puppet master and Archie the puppet.

And yet Graeme thought the punishment proposed for Lord Vernon was fair. Because it was politically advisable. Because *he* wanted to force *her* to accept his protection.

She stood and paced the room, grasping for calm. She would stay the course. She would see through the Season, socialize, find her place in society so that Coralie might have a chance at a season in a few years. Then she and the children would return to Bluebelle Lodge and begin again mingling with local society. Perhaps Diddenton could be pressured to sell Wickworth Hall. She must ask Graeme if that was possible. He said he would help her.

She plopped down on the bed and saw the valise lying there.

She would not cry over Lunetta Casale, no matter how sad her life had been. But her child... what special items would Lunetta have saved for her?

Giving in to curiosity, she opened the case. An embroidered baby's christening cap, aging and yellowing, fell out. There was a handkerchief under that, also embroidered with golden daffodils, and this one newer, bearing the initial M. An unadorned handkerchief twisted around coins. She set all of that aside and reached for a large envelope that had been secured with a twist of string.

Heart racing and fingers shaking, she opened it and unfolded the papers inside.

The Last Will and Testament of Archibald Townsend Stafford Blatchford, Baron Chilcombe, Viscount Stafford, Earl of Chilcombe. Flipping to the last page, she read the signatures and date.

She fell back on the bed, clutching the papers to her heart, her body beginning to tremble.

CHAPTER EIGHTEEN

This late in the spring, the fair days gave way to chilly nights, but not so chilly as to require a fire in the grate in her bedchamber. There would be one in the kitchen, banked, but easy enough to stir.

Downstairs in the hall, a footman greeted her, and lamps still burned. Her pulse quickened.

"Have the dinner guests left?" she asked.

"A little while ago, my lady. Captain Lynford went out also. Lady Hermione has retired, but his lordship is in the library."

Footsteps on the stairs startled a squeak out of her. Clive bowed and held up a pair of spectacles.

"Pardon, my lady. His lordship asked me to fetch his reading glasses from his room and bring them to him in the library."

"A letter arrived a short time ago for him," the footman assigned as porter said.

"My lady," Clive said, "are you... pardon me, is there some way I may help you?"

In the few seconds during which the two servants stood

trying to hide their curiosity about the trembling that gripped her, Blythe shook her head and squashed the hysterical urge to laugh. Tonight, her future had been settled by the court's decision, then unsettled by Lord Vernon's lack of punishment, and now unsettled even more.

Graeme had promised to help her. She'd carried the dishonorable burden of destroying one copy of the will. Once was enough.

Clive bowed again, preparing to pass.

"Wait, Clive," she said. "I'll bring those to his lordship."

Concern creased his brow but he handed the spectacles over, and she made her way to the ground floor room with a strange sensation sweeping through her.

Relief. Though why she should feel that now she had no idea.

She found Graeme standing by the hearth where a low fire eked out warmth, one hand braced against the mantel.

He hadn't heard her enter, and she stood for a moment watching him. The young boy he'd been had grown into a powerful man, considerate, determined, perhaps even wise. The impeccable manners came from those qualities. Even as a younger man, he'd thought before indulging in carelessness and yet he wasn't a moralizing pedant.

He must have sensed her presence because he looked up and his face cleared. "Blythe," he said.

"I've brought your spectacles." She held the item up and moved closer. "You will want to put them on. I've been going through the things Lunetta sent."

He accepted the glasses from her and then captured her shaking hand.

"You're cold," he said. "And shaking like a leaf. And so pale. Come closer to the fire."

She shook her head. The fire was too tempting. "There's a shawl on the chair by the window."

He went to retrieve it and tenderly draped it around her shoulders.

"What have you brought?"

She huffed out a breath and shook her head. "I suppose... I suppose one might consider this Maddy's dowry. Here." She shoved the papers at him and, relieved of temptation, went to take one of the chairs by the hearth and stare into the smoldering coal.

Silence followed. Not even the paper rustled. Certainly, Graeme was too much of a diplomat to offer a surprised gasp.

Long minutes passed and when she looked up, she saw that he had seated himself in the chair across from her, his head bent, reading every line carefully, his frown set in stone.

The droop of his loosened neckcloth clashed with the tautness of his demeanor, and a frisson of desire shot through her.

She pushed it down. Even in spectacles, he was appealing; he would make for the sort of challenging lover ladies whispered about.

But he wasn't for her. She'd had a challenging husband, one who'd made her feel desire—for a brief time anyway—until she'd seen what a fool he truly was.

When he reached the last page, he set the paper aside and walked away, returning with two glasses of brandy. He set one by the document on the table next to him.

"A message came saying that Lunetta has died," he said. "She sent along Maddy's other dowry, some stocks and notes, as well as the child's birth certificate. Thornsby has sailed for Italy. Not a good enough friend to stay to the end. The flat was, after all, Lunetta's, not Thornsby's."

Unable to find words for the unbearable sadness, she nodded.

He lifted her hand and closed her fingers around the glass. "Just take a sip," he said. "Please."

The warmth of the spirits seeped into her and through her, and then she set the drink aside. When he touched his lips to her forehead, she shut her eyes tight on incipient tears.

When she opened them, he was standing before the hearth, the document in one hand, his brandy in the other. He shrugged, tossed the will onto the coals, and then splashed the remains of his brandy upon it.

She jumped to her feet, more speechless than ever.

* * *

GRAEME WATCHED THE FLAMES LEAPING, SHRIVELING, turning the noxious document to embers as black as the souls of the men who'd created it and signed it. Lord Vernon, Diddenton, Sir Morris, and worst of all his cousin, Archie.

What sort of man took a woman to wife and treated her like the doxies he hired to whip?

In all the excitement of the day, Blythe might not remember the conversation that took place in Lunetta's parlor, but *he* did. That conversation and the few facts parsed together from Blythe's reaction to their morning visit to Soho, and Coralie's story days earlier, told him everything.

Could he help her heal? Would she let him?

He looked up to find her standing next to him, hands twisted at her waist.

"I'm sorry," she said. "I would never have thought..." She took a deep breath. "I would not have this on your conscience."

"My conscience?" he said.

"Yes. You are a good man, Graeme. Your honor—"

"Is perfectly in order. What is dishonorable is those pieces of parchment shriveling there." He took her hands. "I told you I would share this burden. You did the right thing to bring that to me. It gives me hope."

Her mouth dropped open, but no words came out, so he went on.

"Hope. Yes. Hope that despite my mistakes, despite everything that has gone before, that you might—"

She set a finger over his lips, and desire stirred in him. He ought to take her finger into his mouth, to suck on it in hopes of stirring similar feelings in her.

Instead, he took her hand away. "I am going to court you," he said, "properly. Whether you want me to or not."

She stood just watching him.

"Not seduce you. Not force you. Court you. I hope that you will remain here in London. With Lady Hermione as our chaperone, we'll attend social events. We'll go to the theater. We'll host guests. During the day, I'll see to business —the business of Chilcombe as well as government business —while you correspond with young Mr. Stockwell regarding matters at Bluebelle Lodge. When the season ends, I'll escort you and the children to Bluebelle Lodge, and I'll go on to Risley Manor. I'll invite neighbors there and would very much like you to serve as my hostess. Together, and with the support of Mr. Jarrow, we'll tackle the local society. You'll have time, Blythe. Time to get to know me, to decide what you want, and I hope, to grow to love me as much as I love you."

More moisture pooled in her eyes and she swallowed, but still remained silent.

"What say you?" he asked gently.

She nodded and expelled a breath. "All right."

"We'll be family, Blythe, as well as neighbors. We won't be lovers until we marry." He bit his lip. "Much as I desire you now."

Color flooded her cheeks. "I would not spoil things, Graeme, for some young lady who—"

"No young ladies for me." He managed a smile. "I want the ancient Blythe Blatchford."

"Ancient?" She pulled her shoulders back and blinked, and then a smile bloomed.

"An October wedding?" he asked, "Or ought we to wait until Christmas?"

"Graeme."

"Surely your hair will not be gray by then?"

She scoffed and swatted him. And then she let him kiss her quite thoroughly.

EPILOGUE

OCTOBER 1824

BLUEBELLE LODGE

It was growing dark when Graeme handled the reins of the phaeton for the short trip from Risley Manor to Bluebelle Lodge. A lad came around to take charge of the horse, and Graeme helped Blythe down, her smile as wide as his must be.

A spring and summer courtship had just led naturally to a decision to call banns and marry at the parish church, with the wedding breakfast to follow at Risley Manor. The wedding night, however, would be spent at Bluebelle Lodge, where they'd first become friends so many years earlier.

Louisa and Samuel Stockwell had left the wedding breakfast early and were there to greet them on the doorstep.

"All is ready for you," Louisa said, hugging Blythe, and

smiling at Graeme, while a beaming Samuel offered his hand.

"There's a tray in your bedchamber and a bottle of wine." Louisa said. "If there's aught else—"

"Lady Chilcombe will know where to look." Samuel tugged at his wife. "We shall be off my lord, my lady," he added with a grin.

"Well," Blythe said. She smiled up shyly at Graeme, looking quite unlike the bold young woman he'd first met so many years ago. Her marriage had made her more prudent. Her trust now was a precious gift he intended to treasure.

He pulled her close and dropped a kiss on her nose. "I'm famished. Despite all the food at the wedding breakfast, I've barely had a mouthful. Let's see what they have for us." And then he picked her up and carried her across the threshold.

The house was quiet. The servants had left them to fend for themselves, and the children were safely ensconced at Risley Manor. Lady Hermione had returned to her own home at the end of the Season, but she'd come for the wedding, along with a few members of Lord Loughton's family. She'd be staying on at Risley Manor for a few days to supervise the nursery staff. As if Coralie couldn't manage things herself.

The church had been jammed to the rafters for the wedding of the new Lord Chilcombe and the scandalous Lady Chilcombe. Blythe had made inroads among many of the local families, who'd thawed because of his efforts at hospitality and good manners, as well as to Blythe's determined cordiality and kindness. It didn't hurt that aside from a few items of clothing, everything needed for the wedding and breakfast was purchased locally.

He followed Blythe to the bedchamber that had been

hers alone for several years. The servants had turned down the bedcover and laid out a negligee and dressing gown, both of fine red silk trimmed with black lace.

Graeme watched as she focused her gaze on the small table laden with food and wondered if she was purposely avoiding looking at the bed and dreading what was to come.

He went to help her with her pelisse, noticed her shiver, and pulled a shawl from a chair while she tossed away the skimpy bonnet she'd worn for the wedding. Then he went to stir the coals in the hearth and poke the fire to life.

When he turned, he caught her staring at the bed.

"That is one of my wedding gifts. Do you like it?"

She took in a deep breath and went to lift the negligee, putting the silk to her cheek and closing her eyes a moment.

"Yes," she said. "I'll change into it later."

"Phew."

Blythe laughed. "Did you think I'd wear flannel?"

He opened his arms and she came and settled against him. "Light the candles and lamps and I'll prepare a plate for you," she said.

"And one for yourself. You had no chance to eat. Why, even Mrs. Jarrow deigned to speak with you."

Mr. Jarrow senior had died in early summer, and despite still being in mourning, all of the Jarrows had appeared for the wedding, young Mr. Jarrow serving as Graeme's best man, and his sister as a bridesmaid alongside a very grown-up looking Coralie.

"I suppose I'll need sustenance for the night to come," she said, biting her lip and looking up at him through her lashes. Then she laughed. "Look at you, Lord Chilcombe. The look of shock. I'm not afraid of you, you know."

"Well, I'm very glad to hear that."

"Since the will was settled, you've barely touched me,

Graeme, even though we've had plenty of opportunities alone. Instead of a tryst, you've discussed drainage and planting rotations. Or the roofs on your tenants' homes. Or what sort of lessons Nicholas ought to have to prepare for school."

"Ah." His heart lifted and desire stirred a bit more insistently. "You would rather I had talked about your beauty, which grows more enticing every day. And about the fascinating color of your eyes, which one moment seem blue, and in another, gray. And then there's your hair."

He leaned close and inhaled. "Lilacs and oranges." One pin slid out, and then another, until her chignon loosened and he was able to rake the other pins out and send her hair cascading down her back.

"And then," he said, "there's the shape of a goddess hidden, always hidden under too much muslin and wool."

He caressed her neck and then kissed it, lingering there for long moments until she was breathing hard, and he was close to bursting.

He tamped down his lust and hugged her, reminding himself not to undo six months of patience in one hasty coupling.

While he was getting his private parts into check, she was shrugging off the shawl, letting it slide to the floor and kicking it aside.

"I'm feeling rather warm," she said. "My dress hooks are at the back."

Thank heavens. He smiled into her hair, slid his hands under the thick mane, and began working his way down.

In moments, she kicked the gown aside also, and standing in her chemise and stays, pushed off first his coat and then his waistcoat.

And then she stepped back looking shy again. "You

wanted to eat first." And then she blushed a deep rosy pink. "I mean, you want to have supper before…"

"My darling girl." She thought he was too stuffy for that sort of dining. "Whatever pleases you is what will please me. Come here and let's make you more comfortable."

The stays came off, and he seated her on the bed and removed each shoe, garter, and stocking.

Praise heaven, she was not wearing the long drawers women had started adopting.

He helped her to her feet. "Shall I assist you with the chemise?"

"Perhaps, just this time, so I can put on this scandalous wedding gift, you would turn around?"

Chuckling, he did. He had the rest of their lives to see her naked.

He kicked off his shoes and tore his shirt over his head. His banyan was draped over a chair, so he fetched it and was shoving one arm through when a hand yanked it back.

"No." Blythe pulled the garment away and tossed it back on the chair. "I want to see all of you."

It was his turn to blush. *All of him.* The silky nightgown outlined her curves, especially her decolletage. *All of him* came alive. One part in particular.

He didn't want to frighten her… but of course, she'd been married.

She dropped to her knees, reached under the trouser legs and rolled down first one stocking and then the other, all the while giving him a view of her magnificent bosom.

When she stood and reached for the trouser button, he clamped his hand over hers.

"Oh," she said, stepping back. "To be fair…" She slipped a strap of the gown over one shoulder revealing all but the tip of one luscious breast.

"Now your buttons," she said. "I must insist."

"Must you?" He opened the fly and pushed the trousers around his hips.

She slipped the other strap and the gown pooled at her waist.

"I'm being brave, you see," she said, voice shaking.

"My darling girl," he said, holding his control by a thread.

He wanted to ravish her.

"Let us do this together," he said as pedantically as possible, and his tone stirred a faint smile. "On the count of three?"

She nodded. Her gown slid all the way to the floor, and he shoved his trousers all the way off. And then she was in his arms, and he was carrying her to the bed.

* * *

GRAEME HAD MADE LOVE TO HER MORE PATIENTLY A SECOND time before the loud growling of both their stomachs led them to the table and the food and wine set out for them. After filling their stomachs, they moved to the warmth of the hearth, and he took her onto his lap.

"I saw Sir William speaking with you," she said. "What's afoot?"

She held her breath waiting. Graeme wasn't one to tell State secrets, but she knew that, besides agricultural matters, he was avidly interested in the affairs of government. Those, truly, were his first interest. He was young and capable, and she'd worried she might harm his career prospects. But Sir William Taylor and his wife had been kind and welcoming, and she'd had a chance to mingle with diplomatic staff during their time in London.

"He'd like me to participate in a mission. I told him no, of course."

"Where?"

"St. Petersburg. A treaty is being negotiated over the territories on the northwest coast of America. It would mean being gone several months. Perhaps a year. I won't leave you."

"We could go with you."

"We?"

"Yes. Me, you, the children. We could leave Maddy with Louisa and Samuel. I know they'd look after her. I worried, you know, that I would hold you back in your career. You must go, with or without us."

"My dear Lady Chilcombe, I've waited fifteen years for you. I only just convinced you to marry me. Do you think I'd want to be apart from you for even a few days?"

"Well then," she said and kissed him.

The End

A NOTE FROM THE AUTHOR

The research for Her Impeccable Scoundrel took me on a deep dive into laws of dower and jointure, as well as property disputes. Considering the difficulties a woman might have when widowed, it was a caring parent or guardian who made sure to negotiate a prudent prenuptial agreement for a young lady. The marriage contracts of the period could be quite complicated, detailing what sort of support a widow would receive and what provisions would be made for children of the marriage. Not romantic maybe, but practical, even in an era when divorce was nigh impossible.

In researching opium use in the era, I was surprised to learn it was commonly used, especially in the Fens, the low-lying marshy area of eastern England, to treat the malarial agues afflicting the people who lived there.

While most of my characters are fictional, Lord Ashley, later Lord Shaftesbury upon the death of his father, was a real person. He was an avid social reformer, though my fictional villain, Lord Diddenton would not have been one of his real-life political opponents. And of course,

Wellington was real, though I've taken liberties by having him also oppose Diddenton.

Many thanks go to my author friends at the Bluestocking Belles, for their encouragement, and to my editor, Tessa Shapcott, who corralled all my Americanisms and etymological lapses. As usual, any historical errors you spot are entirely my own.

I hope you've enjoyed Blythe and Graeme's story. If you have time and are willing, please share an honest review at the book seller of your choice.

BOOKS BY ALINA K. FIELD

Sons of the Spy Lord Series

Marrying Mr. Gibson

Previously titled *The Bastard's Iberian Bride*

Paulette Heardwyn rushes to visit her dying guardian, set on learning the truth about her father. But the only man with answers takes his secrets to the grave, leaving her penniless—unless she marries his illegitimate son.

https://alinakfield.com/book/marrying-mr-gibson/

The Viscount's Seduction

Lady Sirena Hollister has lost everything, even her fey abilities. But when the fairies hand her a chance at a London Season, her schemes for revenge stir up an unknown enemy, and spark danger of a different sort, in the person of a handsome Viscount.

https://alinakfield.com/book/the-viscounts-seduction/

The Rogue's Last Scandal

Falling—literally—into the arms of the *ton*'s most outrageous rogue seems a risky path of escape, but Maria Graciela Kingsley y Romero has no other choice. Only England's greatest spy lord can help her, and he is not to be found—so his son will have to do!

https://alinakfield.com/book/rogues-last-scandal/

The Counterfeit Lady

Vowing she'll never submit to an arranged marriage, an earl's daughter bolts for the seaside cottage that will someday be hers. But she finds her quiet refuge occupied by the last man she ever wants to see—an American artist, who's also a thief. And quite possibly one of her father's spies.

https://alinakfield.com/book/the-counterfeit-lady/

Avenging the Earl's Lady

The long war is over, but honor requires vanquishing one last enemy, and the Earl of Shaldon has no time for romance. But when the lady he longs for interferes in his plot, and his enemy strikes at her, nothing else matters but avenging his lady.

https://alinakfield.com/book/avenging-the-earls-lady/

Novellas and Holiday Stories

The Marquess and the Midwife

Finalist, 2016 National Reader's Choice Award

Uncovering a lie drives a new marquess back from a self-imposed exile at Christmas to find the only woman he's ever loved. Finding her turns out to be easy, uncovering her stunning secrets, a bit harder. But winning her back will be the greatest challenge of all.

https://alinakfield.com/book/the-marquess-and-the-midwife/

A Leap Into Love

Can a gentleman be too charming?

The ladies of Upper Upton think so.

When the single ladies of the village conspire to teach their charmer a lesson that might bankrupt him, the town's loveliest young widow—who's sworn off marriage forever—steps up to warn him.

https://alinakfield.com/book/a-leap-into-love/

Liliana's Letter

The Matchmaker Meets the Matchbreaker

Liliana Ashford's future as a professional chaperone depends on her wealthy charge's successful marriage, but her own close encounter with a scoundrel years ago makes her determined to save the girl from the same kind of rogue.

https://alinakfield.com/book/lilianas-letter/

The Ghost of Deplored Hall

A sweet Halloween short story

It's her mother's last All Hallows' Eve.

When family, friends, and tenants gather, goblins, ghouls, and ghosts are banned from this All Hallows' Eve party.

Only, no one told the Ghost of Depford Hall!

https://alinakfield.com/book/ghost-depford-hall/

Courted by the Earl

previously titled *Bella's Band*

A 2015 RONE Award Finalist

Saddled with his brother's title and debts, nothing about this new life makes the Earl of Hackwell want to stay—until he meets a lady with a secret that can change everything.

https://alinakfield.com/book/courted-by-the-earl/

Rosalyn's Ring

2014 Book Buyer's Best Winner, Novella Category

Done with grieving her losses, a late nobleman's daughter has fallen into a tidy spinster's life in London. But when one snowy Christmas Eve, a young woman needs rescue, she seizes the chance to do good—and to recover a family heirloom that ought to be hers.

https://alinakfield.com/book/rosalyns-ring/

Haunting Miss Fenwick

Thrilled to finally have a permanent home, a Squire's daughter won't let a supernatural creature scare her away. While hunting the ghost she doesn't believe in, she stumbles upon a mysterious flesh and blood man who might be the key to all of her problems.

https://alinakfield.com/book/haunting-miss-fenwick/

Lady Twisden's Picture Perfect Match

Promised York's marriage mart and the hospitality of his cousin's doddering stepmother, Major August Kellborn is shocked to find that his fetching hostess is the one woman who stirs his heart.

https://alinakfield.com/book/lady-twisdens-picture-perfect-match/

Flowers for His Lady

Eleanor Gurnwood has only one goal in sight: to make this year's Christmas service beautiful for the parishioners of St. Tancred's—until the Christmas eve when a man from her past rides in on a white horse. https://alinakfield.com/book/flowers-for-his-lady/

Under the Champagne Moon

Homeless and living on the charity of her former guardian, Fleur Hardouin's heart longs for Captain Gareth Ardleigh, whose kindness to her as a child she's never forgotten, but she needs an advantageous marriage.

Gareth has promised to find Fleur—on behalf of another man. Now he must choose between honoring a promise and trying to win the hand of the woman he loves.

https://alinakfield.com/book/under-the-champagne-moon/

The Upstart Christmas Brides Series

The Duke She Despised

Hiding her true identity, a young vicar's widow takes a position as housekeeper in a remote Scottish castle at Christmas for a new duke who years ago sabotaged her chance for happiness. She quickly falls for the duke's charming but not very competent factor, not knowing that he's hiding something also—he's the duke she despised!

https://alinakfield.com/book/the-duke-she-despised/

Convincing the Countess

A penniless widowed countess with trade in her blood descends upon the country manor of her sons' negligent guardian, intent on confronting him about her boys' futures. Instead, she finds his younger brother, a business-minded aristocrat with a penchant for widows and a distaste for emotional entanglements. A man who once witnessed her greatest humiliation. A man offering enticing distractions that threaten to derail all her plans.

https://alinakfield.com/book/convincing-the-countess/

The Impetuous Heiress

Before dashing Lord Loughton can make amends with his neglected fiancée, the lady's meddling cousin delivers her to his doorstep. He soon realizes more is amiss than his carelessness. Can he uncover her secrets and win her back before he loses her altogether?

https://alinakfield.com/book/the-impetuous-heiress/

The Nabob's Designing Daughter

Ripped from his prestigious London practice to deliver a Highland duke's heir, a young doctor finds there are more snares awaiting than a risky birth, including a surprise—and worthless—bequest. There's also his best friend's cousin, who's blossomed from mousey to heart-stirringly beautiful, with enough wiles to convince an ambitious man that his heart belongs in the Highlands.

https://alinakfield.com/book/the-nabobs-designing-daughter/

The Earl's Scottish Hoyden

Coerced by her brother to spend an English Christmas at the country estate of the handsome but cold earl who all but jilted her a year earlier, Edme Beecham is determined to do no more than assist her brother in his business negotiations with the earl, and by all means, to protect her heart.

https://alinakfield.com/book/the-earls-scottish-hoyden/

The Macbeth Series

Fated Hearts

A Love After All Retelling of the Scottish Play

A Scottish Baron returning from two decades at war meets the wife he divorced and the daughter he disavowed before she was born, only to learn that everything he'd believed was a lie. Determined to win back the only woman he's ever loved he must first face the viper who drove them apart.

https://alinakfield.com/book/fated-hearts/

The Comtesse of Midnight

A Scottish Earl on a quest for the elusive Comtesse de Fontenay, rescues a French lady smuggler during a devastating storm, taking shelter with her. As the stormy night drags on, he suspects she knows the lady he's seeking, the lady who holds the secret to his identity.

https://alinakfield.com/book/the-comtesse-of-midnight/

Claims of the Heart

Since a perilous fall, Lucie Macbeth has been seeing more than a settled future as the heiress to a Scottish barony. The visions plaguing her include a man—one far above her class and breeding, and English to boot. He's engaged to a duke's granddaughter as well, and thus wholly inappropriate. Though she can't marry him, and she won't become any man's leman, when the Sight warns her of danger to him, her conscience, and her heart tell her she can't walk away.

https://alinakfield.com/book/claims-of-the-heart/

A Wallflower's Midsummer Night's Caper

Book 15 in The Revenge of the Wallflowers multi-author series

A Midsummer Night's masquerade at her family's country home presents the Honorable Nancy Lovelace with the perfect opportunity for revenge against the man who ruined her first London season—a man she's known since childhood, a man she'd once thought she loved.

Available for pre-order

https://alinakfield.com/book/a-wallflowers-midsummer-nights-caper/

Sir Westcott Steals a Heart

in Love's Perilous Road, a Bluestocking Belles Collection with Friends

Sir Westcott Twisden didn't know he wanted to marry until the tallest lady he'd ever met crossed his path. Sybil Dunsford is too busy managing her farm and brothers to contemplate romance. Then she's threatened by smugglers. Wes's rescue attempt fails, but when they're locked in together, will romance follow?

Find out more at https://alinakfield.com/book/loves-perilous-road/